I0637692

IN THE DOORYARD BLOOM'D

a novel

B. Robert Sharry

Author of
For Renata

Praise for *For Renata*

"Moving at a fast clip...the narrative explores many weighty issues...which Sharry covers with insight and finesse. ...the tale becomes quite gripping as... past mysteries unfold. A nostalgic romance, rich with Portuguese culture and ... surprising twists at the end." *KIRKUS REVIEWS*

© 2015 by B. Robert Sharry

All rights reserved.

ISBN: 9780692403143

BRobertSharry@gmail.com

For family and friends

Chapter 1

Mansonville, Quebec, Canada
May 6, 1970

ELAINE BELLEFONTAINE HEARD the tractor approaching and peered through the window above her kitchen sink. Last night's rainstorm had cleared out, and now early morning sun shone on acres of bright, white-blossomed apple trees framed by lush green grass beneath and deep blue sky above. Her husband, Gil, sat at the wheel, steering the green and yellow John Deere tractor toward the farmhouse. Elaine's brow furrowed at a sight that seemed out of place. Gil had started his morning, barely an hour ago, wearing a flannel shirt over long johns against the chill. Now he was naked from the waist up. Elaine hurried out the back door and shouted over the growl of the engine.

"Es-ce que tout est okay?" *Is everything okay?*

Gil Bellefontaine cut the engine. "Regarde ce que j'ai trouvé: Un jeune Américain. Y'a été tiré." *Look what I've found: An American boy. He's been shot.*

Elaine saw the body in the cart behind the tractor. "Mon Dieu."

Gil slid from the tractor seat to the ground. "He's alive, but who knows for how long. I used my shirts to bind his wound.

"Stay with him while I call an ambulance and the police."

Elaine walked around the cart and tried to assess the young man's condition. Gil's bloody shirts were wrapped around the young man's left shoulder. His shivering body was clad in a white undershirt, fatigue pants, and combat boots. A long, tan, bloodstained raincoat lay next to him. Elaine ran to the house and burst into the kitchen just as her husband was dialing the harvest green wall phone. "Gil! Gil, stop! He's military!"

"So? I saw that."

"You can't call the police. He's probably trying to escape the war. Calling the police will make big trouble for him."

Gil looked annoyed. "How is that my concern?"

"It's not, I know, but he's just a boy."

"What do you want to do, Elaine? Keep him?"

"Just for a little while."

"I was *joking*. You can't keep him, not even for a little while. That's crazy. We know nothing about him. Maybe he's dangerous!"

"He's unconscious. How dangerous can he be?"

"That's another thing. You don't know how badly wounded he is."

"I'll call Serge and have him come here."

Gil sighed and hung up the phone. "I can't win, can I?"

§

Less than a mile away, Dr. Serge Robert was awakened by the shrill ring of his bedside phone just ten minutes before his alarm clock was scheduled to buzz. Minutes later, his car screeched to a halt close to the farmhouse. Still in his pajamas, the young doctor leapt from his car, black bag in hand, and sprinted to the open front door, where Elaine was waiting.

"Qu'est ce qui ce passe?" he cried. "Why didn't you tell me what's wrong on the phone? You sounded so frantic. Has Gil been hurt? Are the girls okay?"

"I'm sorry, Serge. We are all fine. It is someone else, a young American. He's been shot. He's in the back bedroom, unconscious and delirious. He rambles in English."

Serge hurried to the bedroom with Elaine close on his heels. Elaine and Gil had stripped the boy down to his boxer shorts and laid him on the antique oak double bed. He was covered in sweat, his long, blond hair matted to his face.

"Oh, Serge, a moment ago he was shivering, so I put a lot of blankets on him. Now he sweats so much."

Dr. Robert worked quickly, starting with the gunshot wound. "He was shot from behind. The bullet went through and exited here at the front of his shoulder. He was lucky."

He treated and dressed the shoulder wound, administered a dose of antibiotic, and then turned his attention to a laceration on the boy's forehead. It didn't look too bad, a small bump. "This probably happened when he fell."

He checked for signs of internal bleeding and found none. With his stethoscope he listened to the heart and lungs. He checked for broken bones but found only a sprained ankle. He felt the glands in his neck, looked at his throat using a tongue depressor, took his temperature, and finally drew a small blood sample.

When he finished his examination, Dr. Robert turned to Elaine. "I think he'll be all right, but we'll need to watch his fever. I'll call for an ambulance to take him to the hospital…"

"No! He must stay here," Elaine said, "and no one must know. He is military. The police will send him back, and he will be in big trouble. His life will be ruined."

"*His* life? What about yours? If the police find out that you harbored him, it will be big trouble for you!"

"That's why no one can know." Elaine then tightened her lips in the same determined fashion that Serge had witnessed a thousand times when they were growing up.

Stunned, the doctor stared at his sister, and then looked to Gil for support. Gil shook his head and shrugged.

"What can they do for him at the hospital that you can't do here?" Elaine demanded.

Serge thought for a moment. "Nothing, really, I suppose. It's just that the nurses there could monitor his temperature and watch for signs of worsening infection."

"I can do that, Serge, with your help."

Serge hesitated again, then shook his head and sighed. "All right, Elaine. But if his condition does not improve soon, I'll insist on moving him to the hospital."

IN THE DOORYARD BLOOM'D

Elaine smiled. "Have I told you that you are the best little brother in the world?"

"Not often enough. You know, I charge double for house calls."

"Then tell me, Monsieur Le Docteur, what is two times nothing? I will write you a check."

"You were always too smart for me, Elaine. Do you know what it does to your self-esteem when you have a big sister who is always two steps ahead of you? The least you can do is make me breakfast."

Chapter 2

THE WEDNESDAY, MAY 6, 1970, headline in the Springfield, Massachusetts, *Daily News* read: *Guardsman Goes Berserk at UMass Amherst.* The accompanying article stated that

> ... although eyewitness accounts vary, this much is certain: In the wake of the Kent State tragedy, Pfc. Robert Michael Coyle, a member of the Massachusetts Army National Guard, was called to active duty on the morning of May 5th to protect the UMass campus from potential violence caused by student demonstrations. Coyle is also a full-time student at the university.

From that point on, the eyewitness accounts diverged. A few student demonstrators insisted that a female student had been the victim of military brutality and that Coyle had interceded on her behalf.

The military version of events differed substantially. A statement issued by the National Guard's public affairs officer said that although their investigation was ongoing, it appeared that Private Coyle had become violent and irrational, that he had beaten a superior unconscious and then assisted a group of student protestors in burning an American flag. Private Coyle had been charged with assault and desertion, and was being sought by military police. The soldier who was beaten suffered broken bones and teeth as well as a concussion, but was expected to make a full recovery.

IN THE DOORYARD BLOOM'D

The article went on to say that, in a possibly related incident, a female student was found dead on the sidewalk in front of Herter Hall. Sources said that state police were investigating the death and a possible link between the deceased and Private Coyle. Her identity was being withheld pending notification of next of kin.

A photo that accompanied the article had been taken by a UMass *Daily Collegian* photographer who snapped it from a distance, using a telescopic lens. The image captured Private Coyle with a young woman protester who clutched the charred remnants of an American flag.

The last line of the article identified Private Coyle as "the son of prominent Mount Plain insurance executive Eugene Coyle."

Chapter 3

Mount Plain, Massachusetts

DESPITE VISITS THE NIGHT before from military and state police, Gene and Mickey Coyle were stunned when they read their own copy of the *Daily News* article. Mickey had read the headline article completely, stopping several times to wipe the tears from her eyes. Now, she watched her husband's face as he read the story.

They sat in silence for a time. Mickey began to weep again. "Oh, Gene, where is he? Where would he go?"

"I don't know, Mickey. I just don't know."

It wasn't quite 7:00 a.m. when the anonymous phone calls started.

"*Is the murderer home?*" the first caller asked, and then hung up.

Others came is quick succession.

"*Maybe your house should be burned, instead of the flag.*"

"*Why don't you move to Russia?*"

Gene wanted to leave it off the hook, but Mickey insisted they answer every call. "What if it's Bobby? I'm not going to miss his call just because these crackpots are calling."

At eight o'clock the Coyles heard a knock at the front door. "Vultures," Gene said. "Stay in the kitchen. I'll handle this."

"Be careful, Gene." Mickey was shaking.

IN THE DOORYARD BLOOM'D

Gene stopped at the front hall closet and grabbed his nine iron. He took a deep breath and flung the front door open, his arm cocked with the golf club. On the front stoop stood Dan and Miriam Lewis. Gene's face was red and contorted.

Looking at the nine iron still poised in Gene's hand, Dan smiled and said, "Do you mind if we play through?"

Miriam flew past Gene. "Mickey!"

"Is that you, Miriam?" Mickey called.

Miriam ran to the kitchen with her arms outstretched. "Oh, you poor darling!" she cried, embracing Mickey.

Dan stepped into the living room. "We've been trying to call you all morning, but your line's been tied up. We read this morning's paper. What can we do to help?"

Gene said, "I'm sorry. We've been getting crank phone calls all morning, some of them threatening. I was afraid some nutcase would try and make good on his threat."

Dan gave a sympathetic nod. "It'll probably get worse before it gets better. Have you heard from Bobby?"

"No. We have no idea where he is or exactly what happened. The state police and MPs were here last night, asking questions. A girl is dead, Dan, and Bobby apparently knew her. They didn't come right out and say it, but it's pretty obvious they think Bobby had something to do with her death."

Dan nodded. "I know it can be intimidating. They'll probably be back—the staties, anyway.

Don't volunteer anything. If you hear from Bobby, get him to call me. I'd like to hear his side of the story and arrange for an orderly surrender. The longer he stays out there, the worse it will be for him."

"I really appreciate this, Dan."

"I wouldn't worry too much about the phone calls. They'll taper off in a few days and before long, they'll stop altogether."

The Lewises spent the rest of that day with the Coyles. In the late afternoon Miriam scoured the kitchen for supper ingredients and asked Mickey to help her make dinner.

After the Lewises had gone home, sometime after midnight, Mickey remembered Bobby's laundry. The load left in the washer was still damp; the one left in the dryer, too wrinkled. She decided to start all over again. She found some small comfort in the smell of clean laundry and the hum and warmth of the clothes dryer. At 3:00 a.m., she'd finished ironing and folding the last of Bobby's laundry. She wanted the clothes ready for him when he came home.

Chapter 4

BOBBY COYLE THOUGHT he had died. *How else could I see an angel?*

The vision lasted scarcely a moment. The angel had walnut-colored eyes and a flawless face bordered by straight, shoulder-length, jet black hair with Dutch-boy bangs. Dressed in white, she had a serene smile and a halo. *She has a halo!*

"*LEE-lah*" was the whispered sound he thought must be the tongue of heaven before drifting once more into oblivion.

§

"Lilas," Elaine repeated in French, "you must let him rest."

Lilas Bellefontaine moved from the sun-drenched, sheer-curtained window behind her, which had given the halo effect from Bobby's viewpoint. She wore the white shirt and plaid skirt of her tenth-grade parochial school uniform.

On the day she was born, purple lilac bushes near the house were in bloom. The alluring fragrance of Elaine Bellefontaine's favorite flower had wafted in to her. At that moment, Elaine rejected the other names she and Gil were considering and decided to name her baby *Lilas*, the French word for "lilac."

Lilas whispered in French, "I'm sorry, Moman. I didn't mean to upset him. He opened his eyes for a moment, though. That's a good thing, no?"

She glanced back at Bobby. A determined look came to her face. "I wish I could help him."

"I know, ma Pêche, but Uncle Serge says we must just let him rest."

Lilas sighed. "Okay, Moman, I won't bother him. Where did Popa find him?"

"In the lower orchard, near the stream. The poor boy was unconscious and lying half in the water."

"Why would someone do this to him?"

Elaine reached out and touched her daughter's cheek. "We don't know, ma Pêche. No one has been able to talk to him yet. We must wait and pray."

For three days, Bobby slipped in and out of consciousness. When he screamed from his nightmares, Elaine rushed to him, soothing his brow and speaking to him in soft, comforting tones.

Lilas sneaked in occasionally, though she knew she shouldn't. Once, she leaned in close and whispered in French, "Don't worry. I will watch over you."

§

Late on the fourth night, he suffered delirium again. Elaine fidgeted with her apron as she paced the kitchen linoleum floor, stopping at the wall phone several times and half reaching for it. She had picked up the receiver and started dialing when something startled her. Bobby stood unsteadily in the archway, Gil's pajamas drooping from his scrawny frame.

"Water?" he requested in a raspy voice.

Elaine breathed a sigh of relief and hung up the phone. She hastened to draw a glassful of water from the tap as she spoke in French. "You must get back to bed. It's important that you rest."

IN THE DOORYARD BLOOM'D

She led Bobby back to the bedroom. He sat on the edge of the bed, sipping weakly from the glass. "Canada?" he asked.

"Oui. You are safe here."

A few more sips and he fell back into bed.

Elaine covered him. "Sleep now. We will talk tomorrow."

§

Bobby didn't understand her words, but her voice and tone reminded him of his mother.

Chapter 5

University of Massachusetts Amherst

ON THE DAY MARY CHAPMAN died, Adam Payne was hastily interviewed by a Massachusetts State Police trooper who'd been called to the scene.

Had he seen Mary Chapman? No, he hadn't.

Had he noticed anything out of the ordinary? Well, he had seen Bobby Coyle acting strangely, even agitated. "He said he was afraid he'd killed somebody and was asking what he should do. Of course, I told him to turn himself in."

"Thank you, Professor—you've been a big help. One of our detectives will be in touch. Just routine."

The next day Detective Sergeant David Long of the Massachusetts State Police called ahead and asked if he could stop by Payne's office.

"Of course," Adam said on the phone, "but I don't know how much help I can be."

"Not to worry," Long had told him. "Just routine."

When Long arrived, Payne masked his surprise at the detective's young age. He judged Long to be less than thirty years old, although he had sounded much older on the phone.

Within a minute of Long's arrival, an army officer appeared. "I'm Captain John McTeague from Military Police Investigations." The captain directed his announcement more to Detective Long than to Adam Payne. Turning to Payne, McTeague said, "I can come back later if this is a bad time."

Long looked perturbed. "We're not gonna have a pissing contest, are we?"

"No, no. I'm just here about the assault and desertion. The stiff's all yours."

It dawned on Payne that the separate crimes had separate jurisdictions.

"If it's all the same to you, Detective, I'd just as soon have Captain McTeague stay. After all, he may get some of his questions answered from yours. It seems to me it might save us all some time."

"I have no problem with that," said Long.

"Great," said McTeague, as he settled in a chair at the back corner of the office. "You won't even know I'm here."

The initial perfunctory inquiry had been handled by a captain at the command level, but he had no investigative experience, and given the seriousness of the assault injury and the link to a possible civilian homicide, command decided to kick it up to MPI. John "Jack" McTeague's weekend rank was captain, but during the week, he had another—that of detective lieutenant with the Boston Police Homicide Department.

Detective Long sat in a guest chair facing the professor's desk. Jack had positioned himself diagonally behind the state police detective, and he half-listened to the standard questions Long asked of Payne, starting with full name, contact info, etc., which Long dutifully recorded in his notebook.

"Did you know the deceased, Dr. Payne?" Detective Long used the anglicized pronunciation of his name, as Adam, himself, did now, and had for years. Growing up, he had watched as his father endlessly corrected people. "It's not pronounced like it's spelled. Not *Pain: Pah-een*", his father would say, pleadingly, and then go on to explain to hapless new acquaintances about how the name meant "pine, you see? Like the tree" in Russian but that the Cyrillic spelling, *п-а-ū-н,* translated to *p-a-i-n* in English. Adam could still remember the disapproving glare his father shot at him when it became clear that his only son had taken the easy way out and was mispronouncing his own name. But his father had looked wounded and defeated when he learned that Adam had changed the spelling from P-a-i-n to P-a-y-n-e.

"You mean 'the stiff,' as Captain McTeague so eloquently referred to her?"

Jack McTeague became rigid. "I apologize, Professor. That was very insensitive of me."

Detective Long smirked. "Dr. Payne?"

"A qualified yes," said Payne. "She was a student in one of my classes, but I have hundreds of students at any given time."

"You were here in the building at the time of her death?"

"Apparently so, but I didn't know it at the time, of course."

"Of course." Long continued, "Do you know of any reason why anyone would want to harm her, or that she would want to harm herself?"

"Absolutely not. It's hard for me to even imagine anyone hurting a sweet young girl like that."

For some reason this statement prompted McTeague to lean forward in his chair. Payne caught the reaction in his peripheral vision and wondered what he'd said to attract the captain's attention.

"Dr. Payne, did Mr. Coyle tell you why he left his equipment on the roof?" Detective Long asked.

"No, he did not," Payne replied. "Perhaps it was to facilitate his getaway."

McTeague glanced at Long, then back at Payne.

After half an hour of questions from Long, it was McTeague's turn. "Thanks for letting me sit in, Detective Long. You're welcome to stick around for my questions."

In a condescending tone, Long said, "No, thanks. I think I have everything I need." He thanked Adam Payne again and left.

§

McTeague started with several innocuous questions about Private Coyle's demeanor and asked if the professor could shed any light on Bobby's state of mind at the time. McTeague asked for specifics of what Bobby had told Payne about the assault on his sergeant and whether Payne had any idea where he had fled to.

Then he asked the questions he really wanted to ask, the ones he wished Long had asked.

McTeague kept his eyes on his notebook. "Professor, why would Private Coyle murder someone and then come to *you*?"

Payne hesitated. "I don't know that he did murder anyone, and, as to why he would come to

B. ROBERT SHARRY

see me, I can only speculate. Often a student will form an attachment to a favorite teacher, seeing him or her as a mentor or even a big brother or sister. He was obviously upset and wanted someone to talk to."

McTeague nodded. Then he raised his eyes from his notebook and looked directly into Payne's. "How did you know that Private Coyle had left things on the roof?"

Again, the briefest of hesitations before Payne replied. "I didn't... until Detective Long said it." Payne kept his eyes focused on McTeague's.

"Oh, right... right. Well, thank you, Professor. You've been a great help."

Chapter 6

BOBBY COYLE SLEPT ANOTHER sixteen hours after Elaine put him back to bed. When he awoke again on the fifth evening, the angel reappeared. Although the halo was gone, the angelic face and sweet smile were intact.

Lilas spoke in English. "Hello."

"Hi," Bobby rasped.

She turned and called, "Moman! Popa!" Then she turned back to Bobby and said, "I am Lilas. I am sorry my English is not good. I study English at school."

"Your English is great," said Bobby.

Lilas blushed with obvious pleasure. "Merci. Thank you."

In a moment, the entire Bellefontaine family surrounded the bed—Gil, Elaine, Lilas, and the youngest, Giselle, age eleven.

Gil was the only one not wearing a smile. "What happened to you? How did you get here?" he asked in French.

"Gil, take it easy. He's been through a lot," Elaine said.

The language and the tone of the exchange perplexed Bobby. "Ah, I'm sorry... no comprendo?"

A look of disdain crossed Gil's face. "He thinks he is in Mexico."

Elaine shook her head as if to say to Gil, *You're not helping*. "Lilas, ask him if he has come here to get away from the war."

"I will try, Moman." Switching to English, Lilas asked, "Are you come here to be from the war?"

Caught off guard by such a direct question, which had the feel of an interrogation, Bobby hesitated.

Elaine turned to Lilas. "Tell him it is okay; he is safe here."

"Moman says is okay. Do not have fear."

"Thank you. Thank you for everything," Bobby said.

Gil kept the harsh stare. "I don't like this," he said to Elaine. "I have questions."

"Not now, Gil. He is tired and afraid."

As an exasperated Gil left the room, he called over his shoulder, "I want him out of here as soon as he can walk."

Elaine rolled her eyes and then smiled at Bobby. A loud growl sprang from his stomach.

"I'm going to make some clear broth for you," Elaine said.

"Moman makes soup for you," Lilas interpreted.

"Thank you. Merci," he said.

Chapter 7

BOBBY STOOD IN THE orchard, shut his eyes and raised his face to the noontime sun. Most of the apple blossoms had fallen to make way for budding fruit. "That feels so good."

Lilas hand was in his. "I am happy that you are getting better."

Bobby gave her hand a little squeeze. "Thanks to you."

In the early days of his recuperation, when Bobby was still bedridden, Lilas would bring his breakfast and speak to him in English before heading off to school. After school she would rush home to check on him. Later she would bring his dinner, and talk with him some more. Bobby helped her improve her English, and Lilas, in turn, taught him some rudimentary French.

As Bobby's health improved, Lilas took him for short walks about the farm. On their very first walk, Lilas had taken his hand in hers. Surprised at first, he soon realized there was nothing flirtatious in the gesture; it was as natural a thing for Lilas to do as take her next breath, just Lilas being Lilas.

Each day their walks got a little longer. And each day, heart racing, he could hardly wait for Lilas to take his hand again. At the end of their walks the two would sit and rest beneath aromatic lilacs.

§

The idea of his daughter spending time with a fugitive did not sit well with Gil Bellefontaine, who expressed his feelings to Elaine in no uncertain terms. "This is not good for her. I don't like him. I don't trust him. I want him gone."

Elaine put him off for as long as she dared. She liked Bobby and saw herself as a surrogate for his mother, whom she knew must be somewhere, heartsick with worry.

But when Elaine overheard an argument between her daughters, she developed reservations of her own. Younger Giselle had screamed, "You never spend time with me anymore. You are always with *him*. I wish he never came here."

"No, Giselle," Lilas pleaded. "Don't talk like that." Then she blurted, "I love him."

§

At the end of the third week, Elaine began to drop subtle hints to Lilas.

He's put some meat on his bones.

He's walking much steadier now.

It won't be long before he's completely recovered.

So it was, after almost a month, that Elaine finally said, "Ma Pêche, it is time. Bobby must leave us."

Chapter 8

WITHIN A FEW DAYS of the initial newspaper article, the anonymous phone calls tapered off, just as Dan Lewis had predicted. Gene Coyle resumed going to his office. He went nowhere else, though. He brown-bagged his lunch and went straight home after work.

He and Mickey didn't talk much. Gene saw no point in talking about a problem he couldn't fix and avoided the subject of Bobby altogether.

The fourth week, Dan convinced Gene to go back to Rotary with him. Silence fell over the room when they walked in, followed by stares, and then low murmurings.

The Pledge of Allegiance, given at the beginning of each meeting, was a time-honored and proud tradition for the Rotarians. But this time Karl Schmidt, president of both the club and the local savings bank, made a grandiose show of it, eyeing Gene as he did so.

Gene flew out the door as soon as the meeting ended, made a beeline for Dan's car, and asked to be taken straight home. Dan obliged, and then watched his old friend trudge from the car to the breezeway, looking stooped and defeated.

§

Dan was in private practice now, but he still had contacts from his previous career as a prosecutor. After learning everything the state police knew about the case, he met with Gene and Mickey at their home.

"Apparently, Bobby was dating this Chapman girl. Did he ever mention her to either one of you?"

"No, never a word," said Mickey. "But Bobby's at that age where he doesn't talk about things like that with us. Actually, there's been a lot of tension around here lately and not a lot of communication. He never mentioned the poor girl, but Bobby would never have hurt her."

Dan swallowed. "It gets worse. The autopsy shows she was pregnant."

"Oh, God!" Mickey gasped and covered her mouth with cupped hands.

Gene sat stunned for a moment. Then he stood up and slowly walked from the room.

"Gene?" Mickey called. "Gene, where are you going? We have to talk about this." Turning back to Dan, she said, "Dan, tell us what to do."

Gene Coyle was already out the door.

"Dan, I don't know what to do. Tell me what to do."

"I'm sorry, Mickey. I wish I could tell you, but until we hear from Bobby, or the police find him, there's nothing we really can do."

"Our son did not hurt this girl." Mickey was emphatic. "You believe that, don't you, Dan?"

Dan Lewis gave a slight smile of reassurance and said, "Of course, Mickey."

"Does *he* believe it?" She nodded toward the door Gene had passed through.

"He's under a lot of stress, Mickey."

"Talk to him, Dan. He'll listen to you. God knows he won't listen to me."

"I know this has been rough on both of you," Dan said. "Gene has lost some business over this, and suffered some shunning by some who have made a rush to judgment."

"Then he'd better get over it, and quickly. Our son needs us, both of us."

"I'll do what I can, Mickey."

"I know you will, Dan." Mickey paused for a moment. "Gene's a good man. He always does the right thing... eventually. But sometimes he needs help to see what the right thing is."

§

When Gene returned two hours later, Mickey was waiting at the kitchen table, with supper keeping warm in the oven.

"I'm not hungry," he said.

"Gene, we have to talk about this."

"Why? What is there to talk about?"

"We have to talk about Bobby."

"There's nothing to be said."

"I know what they did to you at the Rotary Club, and I know what's happening with the business, but don't let them make you turn your back on your own son."

Gene's lips tightened and face grew red. "They didn't cause this; Bobby's done this to us. Don't you understand? He's killed a girl!"

"I don't believe that. *You* don't believe that."

"Don't tell me what I believe."

"He's our son!"

Gene looked into Mickey's eyes for the first time since he'd walked in, and gritted his teeth. "I *have* no son. *We* have no son."

"You have no son?" Mickey's eyes began to tear and her voice shook. "You have no *son*?" She shook her head slowly from side to side. "Shame on you, Gene Coyle. Shame on you, and God forgive you."

r

Chapter 9

LILAS HAD FASHIONED a remembrance—a thick, cream-colored parchment slightly smaller than a playing card. With ink and watercolor, she had drawn a dark purple lilac blossom. She scented the miniature with lilac perfume and signed it *Lilas*.

Fighting back tears, she placed it in Bobby's hand, stood on tiptoes and whispered, "So that you will not forget me."

"Never," Bobby replied with a sad smile.

"Does your heart hurt?"

He felt the pain in his chest and his throat caught. "Yes."

He placed the picture in his shirt pocket, turned from Lilas, and boarded Gil's truck.

Not a word was spoken during the forty-five minute drive north to Eastman. Gil brought his pickup truck to a halt, and said in French, "We are here. I don't want to know where you are going. Goodbye."

Bobby hopped out of the truck. He began to close the door, then swung it back open and said, "Thank you for saving my life." Then, trying his best from what little French Lilas had taught him, he added, "Merci pour mon vie. Merci beaucoup."

Gil scowled. Bobby hung his head and closed the door. The truck sped away.

§

Within half an hour Bobby had hitched a ride on Route 10 West with an elderly Frenchman in a beat-up 1960 Chevrolet station wagon. The driver spoke in French nonstop for an hour and a half. His soliloquy seemed to run the entire range of emotion from anger at other drivers to robust laughter at his own jokes. They entered Montreal, and the old man stopped the car at the foot of University Street, the city's southern gateway.

Wearing ill-fitting dungarees and a cotton shirt of Gil's, Bobby stood and stared at the island city. Elaine had tucked a Canadian twenty-dollar bill into his shirt pocket when she hugged him goodbye. After asking a passerby for directions, he swung a raincoat with mended bullet holes, front and back, over his shoulder and walked uphill toward McGill University.

How had it come to this? A month ago he had been just another college student slogging his way through turbulent times to an uncertain future.

§

Tin soldiers and Nixon coming

On the warm, sunny afternoon of May 4, 1970, Bobby Coyle had brought his dirty laundry home from his UMass dorm room in the JFK high-rise. The warm smell of his mother's pot roast permeated the house.

That evening, after dinner, with one load in the washer and one in the dryer, the Coyle family had settled in the living room and watched Walter Cronkite deliver the shocking news: Ohio National Guardsmen had fired into a crowd of student protestors at Kent State University, killing four and wounding nine.

IN THE DOORYARD BLOOM'D

Gene in his easy chair and Mickey and Bobby on the sofa sat stunned as Cronkite detailed the facts of the shooting as best they were known to CBS News.

"My God, they shot them," said Mickey. "They killed students. What is this country coming to?"

"Goddam hippies, Mickey," Gene said. "These aren't students. They're animals! Didn't you see that they buried the Constitution? They burned the flag, and then they tried to burn down the campus! What are we supposed to do, just let them take over and burn down the whole damn country?"

"These are *children*, Gene."

"They're not *my* children." Gene shot a derisive look at Bobby. "At least, not yet..."

"Right on, Dad. Hey, you're a big war hero; why don't you dig out your old rifle and kill a few yourself?"

Gene's face grew scarlet. He sprang from his easy chair. Bobby nervously did the same from the sofa. Gene slapped his son's face as hard as he could and sent him reeling back down to the couch.

"I'll kill you!" Bobby screamed. But by the time he got back up, Mickey had stood and placed herself between them.

"Stop it! Stop it!" she cried.

Father and son stared at her. Shaking and sobbing, she looked from one to the other. "Please stop, both of you. You're breaking my heart."

Bobby's eyes sought the floor. "Who cares what *he* thinks, anyway?" He stormed away, passing through the kitchen and slamming the back door with such force that the living room windows rattled.

§

Bobby reached the corner of Rue University and Rue Sherbrooke Ouest, and asked a passerby for directions to Lorne Avenue. The address was very near McGill, just as Adam Payne had said it would be. He walked slowly, afraid to arrive at his destination, afraid of the unknown.

Bobby stood before the three-story grey stone row house for a long while. He stared at the steps leading up to the front door on the second level and debated his alternatives until the rain made his mind up for him. His long hair already matted to his face and neck, he climbed the staircase.

The college-aged girl who answered his knock told him that Barber lived in the basement apartment.

Zombielike, he descended the stairs and knocked on the basement door. At intervals, he knocked harder until he was tired of knocking, tired of waiting, and tired of thinking. He had just turned back into the rain when the door opened behind him.

"Yeah?" came a voice at his back.

He turned to face a young man whose appearance was eerily Christlike. "Are you Chuck Barber?"

"Who're you? Wait a minute—are you Coyle?"

Bobby nodded.

IN THE DOORYARD BLOOM'D

"Oh, man, I was expecting you like a month ago. Where ya been?" Barber looked up and down the street. "Come on in."

Bobby entered the dark, dingy flat. Barber continued, "You been out here long, man? Sorry, I was in the can."

"No problem. It wasn't that long."

"So where you been, man? Our friend's worried about you. He keeps callin' me to see if you got here."

"Dr. Payne?"

"Yeah, man. So, where were ya?"

"I kinda got sick on the way up here. So I had to rest for a while. I'm fine now."

The greasy smile had left Barber's face. "Well, that's good, man, but where *were* you?"

"A little town near the border. A French family took care of me for a while."

"Yeah? Hey, don't get me wrong, man... but did you tell them about me or where you were going? 'Cause I'm trying to do you a favor here, man, and I don't want any trouble."

It occurred to Bobby that he'd better be conciliatory, or he just might end up sleeping on a park bench. "Don't worry, man, they have no idea who you are or where I was going."

"So nobody in the whole world knows you're here or who I am, right? You didn't call Mommy and Daddy? You didn't call any chicks back home to let 'em know you're okay? No friends? Nobody?"

"No. Payne told me that would be dangerous."

Barber nodded his head as he sized up Bobby. "That's right. That's right. That would be dangerous. You're in some heavy shit, man."

"Do you know if he's okay?" Bobby asked. Sergeant Visky's condition still played on his mind more than anything else.

"Who?"

"My sergeant. I hit him pretty hard. Do you know if he's okay? Did Dr. Payne say anything?"

"He's fine; just a concussion."

Bobby's cheeks bellowed out a huge breath. His body relaxed noticeably.

But Barber wasn't finished. "It's that dead chick you should be worried about."

"What? What are you talking about?"

"The chick that took a flying leap off Herter Hall."

Bobby remembered the driver of a Volkswagen Beetle who had picked him up when he hitchhiked during his escape. He had told Bobby about a girl who had jumped from the top of Herter Hall.

§

The morning of May 5, after donning his fatigue uniform, Bobby had tucked his long hair under a regulation-length wig and reported for duty at the Springfield Armory. The Massachusetts National Guard's mission was to quell violence that might erupt at UMass in the wake of the Kent State tragedy. Rennie Davis of the Students for a Democratic Society (SDS) had called for a general strike to shut down the university.

IN THE DOORYARD BLOOM'D

In fact, students had already voted on May 3 to strike. The next day, support intensified with an endorsement by the UMass student newspaper, *The Massachusetts Daily Collegian*. Tensions escalated further when news of the Kent State killings spread through the nation. Several students threw rocks at the windows of UMass buildings, but no one had been hurt.

The Massachusetts citizen-soldiers, armed with M1 rifles and riot gear with gas masks, were herded into a convoy of transport trucks, jeeps, and armored and support vehicles that slowly motored north on Interstate Route 91 from Springfield to Northampton, then followed the smaller Route 9 to the UMass Amherst campus.

They arrived at eight o'clock in the morning with orders to surround the Whitmore administration building, next to Herter Hall. Dickinson Hall, the home of ROTC activity, was occupied by student strikers, but the munitions had already been removed to Fort Devens. The guardsmen established checkpoints at strategic locations on the university grounds.

The first few hours were quiet. By eleven, however, small groups of students began to gather in front of the Whitmore administration building. One group set up a makeshift platform, and, using a megaphone, one student began delivering antiwar rhetoric interspersed with references to the Kent State massacre. From a third-floor window, students unfurled a bedsheet on which they had written in large, black letters *THEY CAN'T KILL US ALL*.

B. ROBERT SHARRY

The army did not want a repeat of Kent State, so the unambiguous order had come down: *Do NOT fire unless fired upon.*

By noon, counting the ideologically committed and the merely curious, the crowd of student-strikers had swelled to more than a thousand. The numbers of megaphones and antimilitary taunts grew exponentially. The soldiers, who just a few hours earlier had been relaxed and even joking, found themselves increasingly outnumbered and on edge.

Private Robert M. Coyle, posted outside the administration building, faced students with whom he would ordinarily be mingling. He hoped that his uniform, complete with helmet and wig, would allow him to go unrecognized by classmates. He hoped that the whole thing would blow over quickly and that he could go home and change to his civilian clothes. He felt the heft of his rifle. The smooth, dark wood of its stock and forestock, warmed by the sun, made his palms sweat.

Bobby stood his post, flanked on his right by Sergeant Andrew "Chip" Visky, Jr.

Visky's crowning achievement, thus far, had been as a tackle on his high school football team, class of 1964. With more testosterone than grey matter, and not enough athletic ability to get into a college through the locker-room door, the beefy young man spent his days on an assembly line at the Chicopee Wire Company and dreamed of someday becoming a police officer. Visky had developed a disdain for everything collegiate, nonwhite, or counterculture.

Driven to verbalize almost every thought, Visky talked incessantly. His thoughts this day centered on all of the things he hated about college students and hippies, and his hope for the opportunity to "kick some hippie-freak ass."

As Visky watched the movements of students in the crowd, his soliloquy resembled a half-whispered play-by-play of an athletic event. "Here comes Joe College. Probbly goin' to the library to look up somethin' stupid.

"Chiquita Banana, where's your spic boyfriend? Probbly gettin' his fuzzy dice dry-cleaned."

As he listened to Sergeant Visky's diatribe, Bobby muttered to himself, "Where do they find these gung-ho assholes?" and was grateful that, as far as he could tell, only he and the snickering private stationed on the other side of Visky could actually hear Visky's remarks.

When Visky heard the other soldier snicker, he knew he'd found an audience. After choosing the object of his scorn from the crowd, Visky would deliver his gag, and then look toward the other soldier to share the laugh.

"What do we got here? A hippie chick with hairy legs and armpits. Just what every guy's lookin' for—a gorilla to fuck."

But then the "hippie chick with hairy legs and armpits" approached, and Visky's grin vanished. A few other strikers joined her, one of whom held a poster that read *Drop Acid, Not Bombs*.

Her eyes locked with Visky's. He had just completed his joke about her and was surprised to see her making a beeline for his position. "She couldn't have heard me. She must be stoned," he mumbled.

When she was four feet away, Visky spoke. "That's far enough, Miss." His voice had a slight tremble.

She took another step forward. Three more strikers, two males and a female, followed her.

"Please step back, Miss," Visky ordered.

She came closer still.

"Step back!" Visky shouted, as the other soldiers looked on.

Ignoring his order, the young woman reached around to the back pocket of her hip-hugger jeans with her left hand, quickly pulled something out, and thrust it in front of her. Visky's heart skipped a beat. He instinctively ducked and held his rifle above his head for protection.

A small American flag fluttered in the young woman's left hand. The sergeant breathed a momentary sigh of relief, but relief soon turned to anger. She wore a shit-eating grin on her face. Visky could hear other soldiers laughing now, laughing at him.

"All right, you had your fun. Now, about-face and get outta here before I arrest your ass."

The young striker didn't budge.

"Go on!" Visky's face reddened.

She reached into her front pocket and pulled out a brass Zippo lighter, opened it, and struck the spark wheel. Still smirking, her eyes locked on Visky's, she held the flame to the flag until it began to burn. Then she spoke. "Kill any babies today?" Her voice was rhythmic and taunting.

"You commie bitch!" Visky screamed. He broke ranks and charged at her, heaving the butt of his M1 rifle into her stomach. By the time she had settled on the ground, Visky had flipped his rifle around and pointed the barrel at her head. Her friends took a step forward.

"Come on!" Visky cried. "You want some of this? Come on, you hippie pussies! Come on!"

Her friends shrank back.

Bobby Coyle had stepped out of formation right after Visky's charge. He tried a soft, reassuring tone. "C'mon, Sarge, it's not worth it."

"Get back in formation, Coyle."

"Sarge, please."

"Get back to your post!"

Bobby hesitated.

"Coyle, that is an order!"

Bobby turned to head back to his position.

The girl had gotten her wind back. "Pig." She spat.

Then Bobby heard the distinctive click of the safety on Visky's rifle.

Bobby turned back around quickly, lifted the butt of his rifle and smashed it into the left side of Visky's face. A terrible crunching sound of fracturing teeth and bone preceded Visky's collapse.

Bobby ran to the girl. His left hand holding his rifle, he reached down with his right, grabbed her bicep and pulled her upright. "Get her out of here," he said to her stunned friends. "Now!"

The two males each took an underarm and dragged the injured girl back into the crowd.

Bobby turned back to Visky, who lay motionless. Then he spotted a jeep speeding toward him. He dropped his rifle and ran.

§

Bobby stared blankly at Chuck Barber. "I didn't have anything to do with that girl's death. She jumped. I didn't even hear about it till later, when I was off campus.

"I have to call Dr. Payne right away!"

"No, man, that's the last thing you wanna do. Remember what he said about you calling anyone? It's dangerous, man."

"But…"

"Just take it easy. I can't call him, but he'll be calling me. Shit, he calls just about every day."

Bobby looked skeptical.

"Be cool, man, be cool. I'm the only one you can trust. Listen, I'm gonna go to the store and get some munchies. You stay right here, understand? You can't go nowhere. You can't talk to nobody, understand?"

Bobby nodded.

"Good. I'll be right back. You can crash in here. I got the new Zeppelin. You can listen to it and mellow out for a while, okay?"

§

IN THE DOORYARD BLOOM'D

When Barber arrived at the store, he got plenty of change for the pay phone and called for Payne through the UMass switchboard. "He's here, Prick."

Adam Payne ignored the jab. Keeping his voice low, he said, "Where has he been?"

"It's a long story, but nobody knows he's here, and he said he hasn't said nothin' to nobody."

"You believe him?" asked Payne.

"Yeah, he's scared shitless, man. He says he didn't know anything about that girl. He's freakin' out about it. So, if he didn't do it, who helped that chick down from the roof, Prick?"

"Shut up."

Barber chuckled. "If you still wanna do this, we better do it fast. So, you still wanna do this?"

"I gave you five thousand dollars, didn't I?"

"Yeah, and another five when it's done, which you're gonna bring up here... right away, Prick."

"Don't worry. You'll have it by the weekend."

"No, you get your skinny ass up here tomorrow, 'cause I'm gonna do this tonight."

"I can't just leave work. Don't be stupid. I'll leave early Friday afternoon, after my last class. I'll be there Friday night. And another day or two isn't going to make a difference, so make sure you do this right, not fast. And make sure he doesn't talk to anyone."

An automated female voice broke into their conversation. "Please deposit another... dollar-fifty... for the next... three minutes."

B. ROBERT SHARRY

Barber ended with "Friday night, Prick" and hung up. He bought some food and hurried back to Lorne Avenue.

§

Payne hung up the receiver, stared out from his desk, and stroked his chin. He thought it ironic that Barber would be less of a threat to him once he had killed Bobby Coyle. What could Barber do, go to the police and tell them that he killed somebody because Payne had asked him to? Barber wouldn't be in a position to squeeze him for money anymore, either. He doubted whether Barber had thought that far ahead.

Adam Payne picked up the phone again and called Judy Rosen. "It's time we talked about setting a date," he said cheerily.

"You really mean it?"

"Hey, guys don't joke about things like that."

§

When Adam decided he should marry, he had considered the paltry pool of young Jewish women. He settled on Judy Rosen, a psychology professor. Judy's bland appearance and insipid personality were mitigated by the fact that her father, a wealthy attorney, sat on the university's board of trustees. Adam concentrated his charisma like a laser beam on Judy until she fell hopelessly in love with him.

He gave plausible reasons for a long engagement, such as tradition and respect for her and her family. But the truth was he didn't want to be burdened with her full-time until absolutely necessary.

IN THE DOORYARD BLOOM'D

His risky penchant for seducing students was out of character for him. In every other part of his life, he calculated every move, assessed every risk, and developed a plan and then a contingency plan. But his libido, like his intellect, was off the charts, and, after all, this was the era of free love. Adam Payne was entitled to a much larger share than most.

Chapter 10

CHUCK BARBER'S LIVING room owed its décor to the staple of student interior design—the cinder block. The stereo, complete with smoked-plastic cover, sat in the living room on a three-tiered bookcase made of pine boards sandwiched between cinder blocks. A loose cinder block on either end supported each of the speakers. Four more cinder blocks acted as legs for the thick-glass coffee table. Other loose blocks placed near musty chairs and a sofa functioned as end tables and held ashtrays or candles.

The Led Zeppelin album was on the turntable. Bobby turned the volume low and pushed the power button. He lay down on the sofa and, still feeling the effects of his wound, soon fell asleep. He awoke to find a large black man standing over him.

"Who're you?" the man said in a deep voice.

"I... I'm a friend of Chuck's. He said I could stay here. He just went to the store. He'll be right back."

"Hmm," said the black man, which Bobby interpreted to mean *We'll see about that.*

The man backed up and sank into an opposing chair. He took a pack of Marlboros from his army jacket pocket, lit one, and took a long drag. All this he accomplished without ever diverting his eyes from Bobby.

Bobby felt vulnerable lying down. He slowly rose to a sitting position and tried to make small talk with the man, but the only response he got was a cold stare.

IN THE DOORYARD BLOOM'D

A few uncomfortable minutes later, Chuck Barber returned, carrying a brown paper sack. "I see you met Willy Maze."

"Yeah," Bobby said nervously. "I was just telling him that you said it was okay for me to be here."

"Damn straight. Okay with you, big guy?" Barber asked Willy.

Willy's eyes left Bobby for the first time as he nodded to Barber's satchel. "You got somethin' to eat in there?"

"Yeah, man." Barber dropped the sack in Willy's lap. "Knock yourself out. Don't eat too much, though. I wanna take Bobby out tonight to the Old Munich. You're comin', too."

"I got no bread, man."

"You don't need any. You're with me."

"How'd you get so rich all of a sudden?"

"None of your damn business. You just get your black ass in gear when I tell you to."

Bobby watched the exchange with apprehension. The big, black basso profundo smiled at Barber and said, "You best watch what you say, boy, or I'll be up one side an' down t'other of your skinny white ass. Now get that white-boy shit off the stereo and put on some *music*."

Barber grinned. "Sure, man. How about I sing some Steppenwolf for ya? '*God damn the Pusher man,*'" he sang. He laughed and turned to Bobby. "You're gonna love this place, the Old Munich. It's really cool. They got really good food, lotsa different beers. Even got one of those oompah bands, and everybody sings, like in a beer garden. The waitresses all wear those old-fashioned costumes that are so low-cut their titties practically slap you in the face, man."

Bobby said, "I don't know. I don't want to miss it if Dr. Payne calls."

"Don't worry about it. He'll call back. Besides, I'm responsible for you, and you gotta eat, right?"

"I guess."

"Good. Why don't you go crash in the front bedroom? We'll get you up when it's time to go, man."

"Okay, thanks. Thanks for everything."

"No problemo."

§

When Barber woke Bobby at 8:30 p.m., the sun had just set. He showed Bobby to the bathroom, and while Bobby showered, Barber laid out some clothes for him to choose from.

After his shower, Bobby stood before the foggy medicine-cabinet mirror and stared at the purplish, angry-looking scar where the bullet had exited the front of his left shoulder. He poked at it with the fingers of his right hand.

He dressed and went to the living room. Barber and Willy Maze had just finished helping each other shoot up and were reclining on the couch with their eyes closed.

Hypodermics, alcohol swabs, and long shoelaces sat in their laps. The cut-off bottom of a beer can held part of a cigarette filter, and sat next to a lit candle. Barber and Maze opened their eyes, their lips spreading into identical euphoric smiles.

IN THE DOORYARD BLOOM'D

By 9:30, the three men had left the house. Barber lit a joint and the trio passed it back and forth as they wound through back streets. Supper smells enhanced the feel of a warm, late-spring evening in the city. When they reached Rue Saint-Urbain, they turned right and walked a few blocks to Rue Sherbrooke, then headed east until they reached Rue Saint-Denis.

As they meandered downhill, the smells and sounds of several ethnic restaurants filled the air. First, fragrant paella accented by the stomp of flamenco and strum of Spanish guitar. A few more steps and Spain receded, giving way to the aroma of the Orient and the plucking of a zheng and mournful strains of an erhu. Farther still, the smell of roasted lamb mixed with the music and gyrations of a belly dancer.

Before long they reached the Old Munich. The crowd was near-capacity. An oompah band played on an elevated circular stage in the center of the large hall. The room resounded with beer toasts, boisterous laughter, and screams of delight.

As the band played, hundreds of seated patrons swayed in unison to the oompah rhythms. Beer sloshed over the rims as mugs were clunked together. The smells of spiced sausages and sauerkraut permeated the room.

The trio drank and swayed and laughed for hours. For Bobby, the past month had been a series of tragedies and traumas. Now he felt the accumulation of stress being exorcised from his body, little by little, with each convulsive laugh.

Chuck, Willy, and Bobby were among the last out the door at closing time. They stumbled up Rue Saint-Denis, at times marching and accompanying each other with off-key oompah harmony.

As they turned the corner from Rue Sherbrooke to Saint-Urbain, Chuck turned to Willy and said, "We gotta show this boy some French pooh-say. Whadda ya say? Maybe Chez Paris tomorrow night?"

Willy grinned. "I don't know. You think he's ready?"

Chuck smiled at Bobby. "Well, man, are you ready?"

"Right now, I'm just ready for some shut-eye. Can I tell you tomorrow?"

"Sure, man. No hurry. We got plenty of time."

The rest of the walk passed in silence. When they reached the apartment, Barber directed Bobby to sleep on the couch.

Willy took the front bedroom where Bobby had napped earlier, while Barber headed to the back bedroom. Bobby and Willy fell to sleep almost immediately, but not Chuck. He lay awake for a long time thinking about the task before him. He wouldn't do it tonight. He was just too tired. Besides, The Prick was right: Barber needed to do it smart, not fast. He needed a plan.

Chapter 11

ON THURSDAY ADAM Payne went to his bank and withdrew five thousand dollars in cash. He took the money home and placed it at the bottom of the suitcase he packed for the next evening's drive to Montreal. Then he drove to pick up Judy Rosen for dinner.

Judy was bubbly and talkative on the drive to the Lord Jeffery Inn.

She's absolutely giddy.

Adam ordered champagne. The waiter poured it, and Payne lifted his glass to Judy. The words "Here's to the most beautiful bride-to-be in the world" almost caught in his throat.

Judy's champagne flute clinked with Adam's. "Oh, Adam, I'm so happy. Although, for the life of me, I still can't fathom what you see in plain little old me."

Miss Low-Self-Esteem is fishing for compliments.

"What are you talking about? It seems to me I'm the lucky one, here." He reached across the table and took her hand in his.

Judy looked deep into his eyes and blushed. "Adam, darling, have you given any thought to what kind of reception you'd like, whom you'd like to invite, or where you'd like to honeymoon?"

"I just want you to be happy."

Judy said she planned to be at least one dress size smaller by her wedding day, and hardly touched her dinner. Suddenly, a look of concern came to her round face. "You know, we never really talked about it, but... you do want children, don't you, Adam?"

I have to help you spawn, too?

"Of course I do, darling. I love children. I'll especially love ours, as long as they look like you."

Judy looked as though she were living a dream. She gazed into Adam's eyes again. "I want to give myself to you completely, Adam. I'm going to try so hard to be the wife you deserve. I'll spend the rest of our lives trying to make you happy."

"You already have, darling—just by saying *yes*."

§

Even though they'd been engaged for some time, it hadn't seemed real to Judy until now. Adam was acting more romantic than ever. Before, the relationship had felt one-sided to her. Even his marriage proposal struck her as matter-of-fact, almost businesslike. She didn't know the reason for his about-face, but it didn't matter. She'd chalk it up to male jitters. The important thing was that he had changed, and they had the rest of their blissful lives to look forward to.

§

At nine thirty, Adam called for the check. He drove Judy back to her apartment, and performed the obligatory sex quickly. He couldn't wait to get back to his own place. He explained to her that he had to leave for Montreal the next afternoon to visit a colleague at McGill for the weekend, a history professor- —male, of course- —whom he'd known for years.

IN THE DOORYARD BLOOM'D

"Say *hi* for me," Judy said. "Don't forget to get his home information so we can send him a wedding invitation."

"Hmm? Oh, right, will do. I'll call you when I get back."

"I love you, Adam, and I miss you already."

"Me, too."

By 10:45, Adam Payne lay on his waterbed, thinking about Montreal. He fell asleep quickly. He always did.

Chapter 12

ON THURSDAY MORNING, Chuck Barber took Willy aside. "I got some things to do. Show Bobby around town a little. Keep an eye on him, and don't lose him."

Barber traveled by bus to Marché Jean-Talon, a farmers' market in the Little Italy section of Montreal. He stopped at the market just long enough to have an espresso, and then walked to a friend's home on Avenue Mozart to borrow a car. He had decided on how to kill Bobby with a minimum of struggle and mess, and he now concentrated on planning the disposal of the body. Fortunately, his friend's car contained a roadmap of Montreal and a large trunk.

Consulting the map, he drove to within a block or so of his home. Then he plotted a route from the apartment to Rue Notre-Dame in the Old City and drove north along the waterfront, scouting for an isolated spot on the west bank of the St. Lawrence River.

Barber considered recruiting Willy to help, but he just couldn't bring himself to trust Willy that far. Maybe he should start an argument with Willy as a pretext for throwing him out of the apartment for a couple of days. After all, Willy had been living on the streets before Barber had taken him in.

No, Willy could stay. He slept like the dead. And, besides, if something did go wrong, Barber would convince Willy that he was already an accessory. He could control Willy.

He'd make sure they stayed home that evening. Drink some beers, eat Chinese takeout, and watch *The Dean Martin Show*.

It was a good plan: No blood, no noise, and when it was over, no body.

Chapter 13

WILLY MAZE DIDN'T like the idea of babysitting. He was tired and hungover. He wanted a fix and some solitude, but he did things for Barber because he didn't want to sleep on the street.

"Try to keep up," Willy said, snarling at Bobby as they went out the front door.

Bobby sensed Willy's irritable mood. "I could just stay here…"

"Do not make me drag you, boy."

Bobby followed a few steps behind, like a puppy.

Willy stopped in front of a small boulangerie. "Give me some money."

Bobby rummaged through his pockets and gave Willy all the money he had. They entered the bakery, and Willy bought a large baguette and some pâté and cheese. At a small market nearby, he bought a cheap bottle of red wine and gave everything to Bobby to carry.

They crossed Pine Avenue and entered Parc du Mont-Royal. With Bobby struggling to keep pace, Willy hiked uphill to Beaver Lake. He picked a spot with a downward incline toward the lake, and sat beneath a leafy maple tree. Bobby sat nearby.

"Now, I'm gonna take a nap. You best be here when I wake up," Willy warned.

"Okay."

Willy lay down with his head resting on the higher end of the slope. Abruptly, he raised his head and half-turned it in Bobby's direction. "My food better be here, too."

§

Bobby brought his knees up almost to his chest and, interlacing his fingers, rested his forearms on his knees. He sat and watched Montrealers enjoying a flawless June day.

Young couples reclined on blankets, some reading, others embracing face-to-face. Children sailed toy boats near the water's edge. Older couples strolled along the lake's perimeter path. The occasional bicyclist whizzed by.

Although barely a breeze blew at ground level, small white clouds swept quickly by, high above. Somewhere nearby, a transistor radio played a static-filled Mungo Jerry.

In the summertime, when the weather is high,
You can stretch right up and touch the sky

Bobby didn't know the French language, but he could guess what people were saying. Here, three couples laughed at the story one of the men told. There, a young couple, lying face-to-face, murmured endearments accented by tender kisses. A young mother warned her toddler not to go too close to the water. A pair of college-aged girls spoke animatedly, using their hands almost as much as their tongues. Bobby remembered mistaking Lilas Bellefontaine for an angel and thinking her French was the tongue of heaven. He wished she were here now. He wished he could hold her hand and hear her voice again.

More than two hours had passed since they first sat down in the shade of the maple. Bobby stared into space. Loneliness, loss, and regret washed over him in waves.

He hadn't noticed that Willy's snoring had stopped.

"Why you here?" Willy's voice boomed.

Bobby wiped his teary eyes with his fists. "You told me to stay here."

"No, I mean why'd you come here to Montreal? What you runnin' from?"

"What do you mean?"

"You American, ain't you?"

"So?"

"So, ain't no Americans here who ain't runnin' from somethin'."

Bobby looked away. He shouldn't talk about it, but he was bursting to.

Willy must have sensed it. His voice was softer now. "C'mon, man, lay it on me."

Bobby hesitated a moment longer but then took a deep breath and began to spill everything, starting with his guard unit being called up. When Bobby described the gung-ho Sergeant Visky, Willy nodded his head. "Uh-huh. I knowed guys like that in Vietnam. They just mean to the bone."

§

After striking Chip Visky, Bobby had bolted from his post and gone in search of the one person he felt he could trust. He had slipped through the back door of Herter Hall and dashed up the stairs, praying that Professor Payne would be in his office.

IN THE DOORYARD BLOOM'D

Bobby burst in from the other end of the hallway and spotted him. "Dr. Payne! Dr. Payne, I think he might be dead!" he cried breathlessly.

"Who is *she*?" Payne had asked.

"Not *she*. *He*! Him! Sergeant Visky. I hit him really hard. I don't know…"

Payne hustled Bobby down the hall and into his office and shut the door. "Calm down and tell me what's going on."

"Sergeant Visky. He's another guardsman, my boss. We were posted outside Whitmore, and this girl came up and started to burn a flag, and Visky went nuts! I thought he was going to kill her! I had to do something.

"Oh God, I hit him pretty hard, and he wasn't moving! What if he's dead? What should I do? They're looking for me now."

Payne looked thoughtful. "Bobby, we need time to sort this out. You need to lie low for a while."

"Maybe I should just turn myself in."

"No, no. You know how they can be: shoot first and ask questions later. You can't trust the military. I can help you, but right now you have to get out of here and go someplace safe."

Payne appeared to be considering options. "They're looking for you, I know. The uniform doesn't help. You can wear my raincoat over it." Then, as if in revelation: "You need to get to Canada. They can't touch you there. Yes, I know someone in Montreal who can put you up until we sort this whole thing out and you can safely come home."

Payne hastily scribbled and handed the paper to Bobby.

"Yes, get yourself to this address. Ask for Chuck Barber. He'll take care of you. Stay off the main highways. Don't contact anyone, even family. You could be putting them in danger if you do. Canada has no problem with draft evaders, but technically you'll be a deserter, so you'll need to sneak across the border. Now, go and wait to hear from me."

"But…"

"No *buts*! There isn't time. Take my raincoat."

Bobby quickly removed his helmet and equipment belt with gas mask, and donned Payne's long raincoat. He removed his wig, freeing his wavy, shoulder-length locks, and tossed it in the wastebasket.

"Thanks."

"No time. Go. You can thank me later."

Bobby left the office. Quickly retracing his steps, he exited Herter Hall the same way he had come in. As he rounded the building to the opposite side, he noticed a small crowd gathered in a circle for what he assumed must be the start of another antiwar demonstration.

Head hung, and with collar raised to hide his features, he scampered across the UMass campus, taking care to avoid other soldiers. The raincoat and his longish, wavy hair gave good cover from the knees up. Untucking his uniform pant-legs from his boots was the best he could do to complete the disguise.

IN THE DOORYARD BLOOM'D

He made his way off campus to Route 116. Within a few minutes, he had hitched his first ride. A dark green Volkswagen Beetle screeched to a halt. The driver, a college student like himself, yelled from the car, "Hey, man, how far ya goin'?"

Bobby leaned into the passenger window and said, "Vermont."

"I'm just goin' to Conway, but I can get you to Route 91."

Bobby looked around, then hopped in the passenger seat. "That'll be good. Thanks, man."

"Did you just come from the Zoo?" the young driver inquired, referring to the university's "ZooMass" nickname.

"No," Bobby lied.

"Oh, man. I couldn't believe it. Some chick just took a header off the top of one of the buildings. Splat! She musta been high, man, musta thought she was Supergirl or something."

Strangely, Bobby felt thankful for a tragedy that might draw attention away from him.

He remembered Payne's admonition to stay off the main highways, so, when he saw the intersection with Route 47 approaching, he told the driver to drop him off. He knew 47 led to Turners Falls, and from there he could walk, if necessary, to pick up Route 5 near Greenfield.

It took two hitched rides to get him to Turners Falls. He ducked into an alley off Main Street and took stock of his belongings-—wallet with twenty-two dollars, driver's license, UMass student ID, mimeograph of his course schedule, loose change, four Old Gold filter cigarettes, a book of matches, a Timex watch, and dog tags.

Wearing his uniform worried him. He spied a secondhand clothing store and considered buying pants and a shirt, but feared an observant clerk might remember that a young man in fatigues had bought civilian clothes. He decided not to risk it. Better to wait until dark and start hitching again. He found a dumpster in the alley and stuffed his fatigue shirt, sewn with name and chevrons, into a paper bag with other trash. Then he pushed the bag as far down into the dumpster as he could. Now he wore only a white undershirt beneath Payne's raincoat.

The large, round analog clock on the exterior of the Turners Falls Bank and Trust read six o'clock. It wouldn't be dark for almost two hours. He began to walk, staying on back streets, until he crossed the river into Greenfield on the bridge near Canal Street. From there he made his way to Route 2, the Mohawk Trail, and hiked through the woods just off the road to Route 5. When he felt it was dark enough, he put out his thumb.

Just past nine, a Mack truck hauling a trailer stopped for him. The teamster didn't ask where Bobby was headed, but rather volunteered that he was driving to St. Johnsbury, Vermont. Bobby hopped into the cab and smelled chocolate bars. In the few hours that elapsed, barely two dozen words were exchanged. The white noise of the motor coupled with the occasional soft muttering of the CB radio allowed Bobby to doze a little. Once, when the trucker stopped to urinate, Bobby pilfered a Vermont road map from the cab, slipping it into the inside pocket of Payne's raincoat.

When Bobby fled UMass, it was seventy-two degrees and sunny. Now, close to midnight at St. Johnsbury, it was raining hard and close to freezing. The trucker dropped him off near the bus station. He stood outside and watched the warm, yellow glow of the interior for a long time. Tired, cold, wet, and hungry, he came close to chancing it, especially when he saw a Trailways bus with the destination *Montreal* faintly lighted above the windshield. But no—if they were looking for him, they would be watching public transportation in particular.

He consulted the road map and then stuck his thumb out on Route 5 North. Given the weather and lateness of the hour, traffic was sparse. Twenty minutes later a beat-up pickup truck pulled to the side of the road, and a young female voice came from the passenger side of the darkened cab. "Where you headed?"

"North." He knew his answer sounded dumb the moment it left his lips, but the elements were affecting his ability to think clearly.

"Like, to the North Pole?"

Bobby could hear the male driver's laughter along with the young female passenger's giggle.

"Well, get in," she said, as she flung the door open and scooted to the middle of the bench seat.

"Thanks," Bobby muttered. The truck cab smelled faintly of hay and manure, but it was warm. He could feel heat from the young woman sitting next to him, but it wasn't enough to stop his shivering.

"No, thank *you*," the teenage girl said. "I won the bet. My brother saw you outside the bus station while he was waiting for me. He said you didn't have sense enough to get in out of the rain. I bet you weren't that stupid." Again brother laughed and sister giggled.

"Just kidding, man," the brother said, surveying Bobby.

"I'm Beth. I just got in from Boston. I was visiting my friend who's at school down there. And this is my brother, Tom."

"I'm Bill," said Bobby. "So how far north are you going?"

"We live in Coventry. That's about forty miles," Tom answered.

"Oh, that's great. I really appreciate it."

Bobby spent the next hour listening to the brother and sister's chitchat. They tried to include him in the conversation, but his clipped responses soon made it clear that he didn't want to talk. On the verge of tears, he was thankful for the darkness of the cab and the fact that the siblings didn't press him for explanations.

When they reached Coventry, Tom stopped in front of the Congregational Church. "You need a place to stay, man?"

Near exhaustion, Bobby was tempted to accept but decided that he should cross into Canada as soon as possible. "No, no, thanks. I'll be fine."

IN THE DOORYARD BLOOM'D

Tom glanced at Bobby's spit-shined combat boots. "You know, if I was going north, like all the way to the border, I think I'd take Route 105. Probably be less than fifteen miles from here. That's what I'd do."

Bobby's eyes locked with Tom's. "Thanks."

"Bye, Bill," said Beth.

"Bye, Beth. I'm glad I could win your bet for you." Bobby got out of the truck and started walking through the rain.

Fifteen miles. With a ride he could reach Canada in half an hour, but it was one o'clock in the morning now. Fearful that the only cars to come by at that time of night might well be police cars, he decided to keep walking, half-jogging while he could. Whenever he saw headlights, he got off the road and hid until the vehicle passed.

Bobby rewound and replayed the day's events countless times as he traipsed through the rain. Although a multitude of questions scurried through his mind, he primarily wondered about Visky's condition. If Visky was dead, Bobby's life was over too.

He wished none of this had ever happened and wanted nothing more than to be home in his own bed, safe and warm. God, he was cold. Soaked now from head to foot, he hadn't eaten for eighteen hours, and, except for a catnap in the Mack truck, he hadn't slept for twenty.

Keep going.

Thoughts of being in his own bed led to thoughts of his parents. He wished the relationship hadn't been so strained, especially with his father. They seemed to fight over everything, with his poor mother acting as referee. In his mind he replayed the story his mother had told him about what happened to his father on a French battlefield. He knew his father was a war hero, but in spite of many inquiries made as a boy, Bobby never learned the truth until his mother revealed it to him. His father's answer had always been *There I was: just me and the whole damn German army*. And then he had laughed and tickled Bobby.

Reflecting on happier times, he could see his father's smiling face at Little League games, hear his hearty laugh at their fishing spot on the river, feel how it was to sit in his lap and "drive" the station wagon in the driveway. He and his father had been best friends, doing everything together and talking about everything under the sun. But somehow, over time, they had disappointed each other. Tears mixed with the rain on his face as he trudged northward.

At 4:30 a.m. he staggered into North Troy, Vermont. Hours in the elements and travel on foot had taken their toll. He felt fevered and disoriented but knew he must press on. Figuring that the main road would lead to an official border crossing, he took to a side street after noticing the timeworn sign that read *Railroad Depot*. He did not notice the vehicle parked alongside one of the downtown buildings. Even if he had, only a small portion of the black-and-white sedan would have been visible to him.

IN THE DOORYARD BLOOM'D

He knew from his map that the train tracks ran east to west. After crossing the tracks, he judged that he must be less than a quarter mile from the border. But how would he know for certain when he was on Canadian soil? He would have to push forward until he found evidence that he had crossed the border——a road sign, a Canadian license plate on a parked vehicle, something. He would stay on his feet till there was no doubt.

There was no road to follow now. He could make out the edge of a wood a few yards distant.

"Police! Stop right there!" came the deep, megaphoned voice in synchrony with the strong flashlight beam that hit Bobby's back and made his shadow as tall as the surrounding trees.

Startled, his body tensed. He was so close. He knew he was. And now he'd come all this way for nothing.

"On your knees, put your hands in the air, and don't move!" was the second amplified command.

Bobby slowly raised his hands above his head and sunk to his knees. He was so close.

The beam of light went out, leaving everything in darkness. From behind, he heard a muttered "goddammit" and recognized the sound of the cop slapping the deadened flashlight, trying to resuscitate it.

Bobby ran for the trees.

"Stop!" he heard, no megaphone this time. "Stop or I'll shoot!"

Bobby could tell from the sound of the voice that he had put more distance between him and the cop.

B. ROBERT SHARRY

The beam of light flashed back on and began to search. When the light found Bobby again, the policeman called "Stop!" and shot at the sky.

But that didn't stop Bobby. The thick woods renewed his confidence. He ran as fast as he dared in the darkness. Then a second shot rang out, and he felt a burning jolt to his left shoulder.

He shot me! His eyes grew wide with terror. The impact threw him off balance for a moment, and he went down. Adrenalized, he recovered quickly and ran deeper into the trees. He ran for as long as he could; then he staggered.

Twenty minutes had passed since he'd heard any sound of pursuit. *I must have crossed the border by now.* Bleeding and exhausted but afraid to rest, he plodded along. With each faltering step, he became more weary and disoriented. He stumbled on the uneven terrain. Finally, a trip over a tree root sent him tumbling downhill. He landed in a shallow brook, hitting his head on a rock. He couldn't find the strength to stand, but the icy water revived him enough that he dragged himself across the stream, clawing his way to the opposite bank. Then everything went dark.

Later, something stirred him to brief awareness. Bobby feebly raised his head and focused on a pair of muddy, black Wellington boots.

They caught me, he thought. Then blackness returned.

§

Bobby finished his story by telling Willy that he realized he'd been wrong to think he'd been caught.

IN THE DOORYARD BLOOM'D

The Wellington boots had belonged to Gil Bellefontaine, the head of the French farm family who had saved his life and nursed him back to health.

Willy nodded his head. "Uh-huh, the French is good people. They're the niggers up here. You know that?"

Bobby furrowed his brow.

"Oh, yeah, man. They're the niggers up here. You don't know that? Shit, man, they know what it's all about. They been there. They're the ones gets treated like shit up here, man. I read a book about it called *White Niggers of America*.

"They got their own revolution going on here. The FLQ, the Front de libération du Québec, they're into some heavy shit, man. Bombs and shit. They don't screw around. They'd blow your ass up just as soon as look at you."

Willy shook his head. "But, you know somethin'? Here, I can walk down St. Catherine Street any time of day or night with a pretty white girl on my arm, and don't nobody give a shit. You think I could do that in Jackson, Mississippi? No, sir, I could not." Willy paused and then asked, "So what happened next?"

"Nothing, really. When I left the Bellefontaines', I hitchhiked to Montreal, and you know the rest."

"You didn't kill no girl?"

"No! I don't know anything about that. That's why I gotta talk to Dr. Payne, so he can tell me what happened, and why anybody would think I had anything to do with it."

Willy studied Bobby's face for a moment. "I believe you."

Bobby's body relaxed. "Thanks, man. I'm glad somebody does."

"Wait a minute. What you say that professor's name is?"

"Payne. Adam Payne."

"I know that name, man. He been up here to see Barber. He ain't good people, man. I wouldn't trust him for nothin'."

"You know him?"

"Skinny guy? Kinda young for a professor?"

"Yeah."

"That's the one. Don't be calling him, man. I wouldn't be surprised if he had somethin' to do with this shit. Barber has a lotta bread, man. He don't know I know it, but it was Payne that give it to him."

"Payne gave him money?"

"Hell yeah, man. Cash money, and lots of it. And I know from the way he talk after Payne's gone that Barber don't trust him none, and you shouldn't neither."

"I don't know who to trust right now."

Willy Maze grinned. "You can trust me, man!"

Bobby said, "Now it's your turn. What's your story? I can't picture you running from much."

Willy Maze started with his birth, how he came into the world as Wilson Johns in Jackson, Mississippi. He told Bobby about his family. He spoke of them with obvious affection, saying he missed them "somethin' fierce."

Then he told Bobby about his tour in Vietnam, how he'd seen and done things that no man should. He told him about his comrades and the guilt he felt over deserting them. He felt no remorse about leaving the army, or even his country, for that matter. But he felt tremendous shame about abandoning his friends.

"What it came down to is what The Man was tellin' me and what was goin' down was two different things. There's right and there's wrong, and there ain't no twixt in between. Soldierin's one thing, but my mama didn't raise no murderers. When women and children gets in the way, you got to get *out* the way.

"So that's what I did. I got out the way. I got me some R 'n' R, and I just kept on keepin' on."

Willy studied the needle tracks on his arm. "Along the way, I got hooked on this shit that controls my life now. Don't let Chuck hook you up, man. Don't let nobody hook you up, you hear?"

"Okay."

Willy insisted on sharing his food. He divvied up the bread and cheese, and opened the pâté. He pulled a pocketknife from his pants and gouged the wine cork from its bottleneck. They tore off hunks of the crusty baguette, dipped them into the pâté, tossed them into their mouths, and then took a bite of cheese. They swigged the warm red wine and chewed it all together.

B. ROBERT SHARRY

When food and wine were finished, they sat in silence for a long while before they headed back to Barber's apartment. In the living room, Bobby watched as Willy shot up. Later, Willy had the idea to head down to St. Catherine Street. "You're gonna see some fine-lookin' women now, man," he said with a knowing smile.

"I'm ready."

Chapter 14

IT WAS PAST NINE that evening, and Barber paced the apartment. "Where are they? Goddammit, do I have to do everything myself?" he muttered.

A few minutes later, Willy and Bobby stepped through the front door together, arms around each other, sharing a drunken laugh.

Barber was not amused. "You girls have a good time?"

"Come on, man," Willy said. "You told me to show him the town." Turning to Bobby, he added, with a big grin, "And I showed him some, didn't I, man?"

"Yeah, you did." Bobby laughed.

"Didn't I tell you you'd see some fine-lookin' women?"

"Yeah, you did."

Willy turned back to Barber. "Come on, man. Be cool."

Barber smiled. "You're right. I'm cool. But it looks like you got a head start on me. Got some beers here, some Chinese, and Dean Martin's on. Let's mellow out."

"All right, man. Now you talkin'."

At 1:00 a.m. a Bowery Boys movie ended. Barber shut off the television.

"Okay, girls, you need your beauty sleep, especially Bobby-boy, here. Tomorrow night we should take him to Chez Paris. Then he'll really see some fine-lookin' women. Right, Willy?"

"Fuckin'-A, man," Willy called over his shoulder as he padded down the hall.

Bobby, lying on the couch, looked up at Barber. "Thanks again, man—thanks for everything. I don't know where I'd be without you. Probably lying in a ditch somewhere."

"No problem. I'll see you in the morning."

Once Barber was out of sight, Bobby reached for his wallet and drew something out of it. In the dim light, he stared at the miniature watercolor of a lilac blossom on thick, cream-colored parchment. He held it to his nose, took in the lilac scent, and thought of Lilas Bellefontaine. Carefully, he slid it back into his wallet and went to sleep.

§

Barber went to his bedroom, shot up, and waited. He had difficulty staying awake. He felt tired, clammy, and queasy, but he forced himself to focus. He had a job to do.

At 2:30 a.m. Barber retrieved a five-foot cord from the bottom of his sock drawer and put on his gloves. Then he cracked the bedroom door and listened. He wondered whether it would be quieter if he swung the door open quickly, or if he opened it half an inch at a time. He opted for the latter. Moving down the hall in his stocking feet, the scant illumination coming from a bathroom night-light, Barber stopped at Willy's bedroom. As he had with his own door, he turned the knob slowly to the left and prodded the door open just a crack.

IN THE DOORYARD BLOOM'D

He heard soft snoring. After a few moments, he cautiously reversed his motions, pulling the door shut and slowly releasing the doorknob.

He dropped to his hands and knees and crawled into the living room. He kept his line of sight level with the sofa arm that separated him from Bobby's head. Bobby lay on his back with his palms crossed on his chest, as if he were already dead. He snored louder than Willy.

Barber moved toward the front of the couch. He could see the silhouette of Bobby's open-mouthed face. Raising his hands from the floor, he wrapped the cord around his gloved hands and came to a crouch, like a coiled snake. His heart pounded. He made a practice start, then another. Now!

With speed, he slung the cord over the back of Bobby's head. Bobby stirred. Barber pulled the cord tight, completing the noose. He straddled his left knee over Bobby's chest, pinning his arms down.

For an instant, Bobby's senses teetered between a dream state and sleepy reality. Then he realized what was happening was real.

Someone's choking me!

He couldn't breathe, couldn't move his arms. He tried desperately to buck the attacker off his chest, but he hadn't the strength or the leverage.

Why?!

He tried to cry out, but couldn't. A soft, guttural sound escaped, taking precious air with it.

I'm gonna die! Oh God, I'm gonna die!

Bobby saw another figure standing behind the strangler.

B. ROBERT SHARRY

There are two!

He recognized the features in silhouette. *Willy!* He knew now it must be Chuck Barber astride him, choking the life from him.

Chuck and Willy. *Why?!*

Willy disappeared from view. Bobby's legs flailed frantically for another minute, and then he stopped struggling. He was exhausted and defeated. He was losing consciousness and was powerless to stop his own murder. He closed his eyes and pictured his mother and father.

§

Willy brought the cinder block down on Barber's head. Barber's eyes rolled back, and he keeled to his right. His body hit the floor, hands still entwined in the cord around Bobby's throat.

With the speed of a cow roper, Willy unwrapped the cord from Barber's left hand and yanked his right hand back, pulling the rope away from Bobby's neck. Barber's limp body rolled after Willy flung him out of the way.

Bobby didn't move.

Willy shook him.

Nothing.

He pinched Bobby's nose with his right thumb and forefinger, clamped Bobby's chin with his left hand. He blew air into Bobby's mouth. He repeated the breath every few seconds.

Nothing.

Try again.

Nothing.

Again!

IN THE DOORYARD BLOOM'D

Bobby sucked in a huge breath on his own. After several desperate gasps he began to breathe heavily. When he regained consciousness, he saw Willy kneeling beside him and began to thrash at him in terror. Willy used his weight to subdue the young man while he explained what had happened and reassured him that he was safe. When Bobby had calmed down, they both looked down at Barber.

"I never liked that jive turkey no how," Willy said.

"Is he dead?"

"Yeah."

"Why? Why would he want to kill me? What did I do?"

"I dunno, man. I don't think you did nothin', but I dunno."

Bobby continued to stare at Barber's corpse. "What're we gonna do now?"

"You let me worry about that. I'm hatchin' a plan."

Willy cooked a massive dose of heroin—enough, he knew, to kill two men.

He shot the overdose into Barber's neck, saying, "Cinder block, sidewalk, same damn thing. Who gonna think twice about a junkie ODs and then falls and cracks his head open like a eggshell?" In a whisper, he added, "Lord, forgive me."

Willy looked around the room. "We has to clean up, get what things we want. The last thing we does is move the body outside. Then we can't never come back here again."

Willy opened the front door and scanned the street. "We don't have to go too far," Willy whispered, "just far enough."

Keeping to the night shadows, they dragged the limp body fifty feet. "This is good," Willy said, laying Barber face-up on the sidewalk. He posed the body as he imagined it would look if a junkie overdosed, and then fell backwards and hit his head on the sidewalk.

Willy led Bobby to Parc du Mont-Royal. In the woods Willy buried a pillowcase containing the bloody cinder block. Bobby Coyle and Willy Maze spent the rest of the night in the same park where, just hours earlier, they'd had such a peaceful day.

§

By the following afternoon, Bobby felt so confused and despondent that, against Adam Payne's advice, he decided to call home.

His hand trembled as he fed Canadian coins to the pay phone. The home phone in Mount Plain rang so many times that he was about to hang up. Then the ringing stopped. After a moment he heard "Hello?"

Bobby's throat caught.

Again, "Hello?"

"Dad?"

There was a long silence.

"What have you done?"

"It's a long story, Dad."

"A girl is dead."

"Dad, you don't think I..."

"I don't know what to think anymore. Where are you?"

"It's best if you don't know."

Gene felt his face grow hot. "What do you want?"

"I... I just wanted to talk to you... and Mom."

"Your mother's not here, and after what you've done, we have nothing to say to you. My advice to you is to turn yourself in and face the music."

"But, Dad, you can't think..."

"What I think is: You've shamed your family, you've broken your mother's heart, and you've made your bed."

"Dad, please..."

"Don't call here again." Gene returned the handset to its cradle, knowing that he would not tell Mickey about the call. She would only coddle the boy and make excuses for him, as she'd done the last time they'd seen him: the night he had stormed off after Gene had slapped him down for being so disrespectful. Mickey, typically, had blamed Gene.

§

Mickey had clutched her breast and, still trembling, slowly sat down. "Are you happy now?"

"Me? I didn't start it," Gene had protested.

"You did start it."

"Did you hear the way he talked to me? I won't have him talking to me that way. If I ever talked to my father like that, I wouldn't be able to walk for a week!"

They heard an engine growl followed by the screech of balding tires as Bobby's '63 Chevy Impala sped away.

"You goaded him, Gene. You deliberately said things you knew would rankle him."

Gene looked away sheepishly. "You don't know what you're talking about."

"I do know. You know how I know? Because I know you better than anybody, Gene Coyle. You don't even believe the things you just said to him."

"About what?"

"About all of it. You told me you think this is an awful war. You said we've no business being there. You said it was a waste, all these young boys dying over there. You told me you voted for Nixon because he promised to end it."

"So what?"

"So you don't believe those children at Kent State deserve to be dead any more than you believe in the Man in the Moon. And did you stop to think about Bobby being in the National Guard? What if he gets called up? Do you want *him* killing hippies? One Coyle with nightmares in this house is enough."

Gene blushed and looked away. "You know everything, don't you?" He turned and left the room.

§

Mickey gave a contrite, downward glance. "I'm sorry, darling. I shouldn't have said that. It wasn't fair." A moment later, she heard the back door softly open and close. She sat on the couch and wondered what had become of her happy family.

She knew that her husband didn't really have nightmares. It was worse than that. Gene Coyle had horrible memories of a real event, sometimes in his sleep. He had spoken of it only once, briefly, to Mickey. She'd gotten the details from Gene's mother, who had taken her aside after their engagement. She told Mickey about the nightmares and depression she'd witnessed in Gene. "There's been a wonderful change for the better since you came into his life, dear. He'll never ask, but he'll still need your help and understanding from time to time."

Mickey's future mother-in-law then recounted the story for her. Nineteen-year-old Gene and his pal Eddy had stood side-by-side in a fierce firefight on a French battlefield. A Nazi bullet pierced Eddy's heart. Gene caught him as he fell, held him in his arms as a pietà, and screamed, "Medic! Medic!" while he tried to stop the bleeding.

Eddy had looked at Gene serenely and said, "Your eyes are so clear, Gene." Then Eddy stared at the cloudy sky. Gene followed his pal's gaze, but saw nothing. Eddy whispered something unintelligible and then was gone. Moments later, three Nazi bullets entered Gene's torso, missing vital organs. Somehow, with Eddy lying lifeless in his lap, he continued to fight, firing his M1 rifle until he exhausted his ammunition and lost consciousness.

B. ROBERT SHARRY

The quiet of the house and Mickey's reminiscence were interrupted by the shrill ring of the weighty, black desk phone on the front hall table. She lifted the hefty receiver, connected to its base by a thick, fabric-covered cord, and listened to instructions that would forever change the Coyles' lives: *By order of the Governor of Massachusetts, Private Robert M. Coyle is to report for active duty at 5:00 a.m. tomorrow, Tuesday, May 5, 1970.*

Bobby returned late that night. Mickey told him about the call. Then she told him about his father. "I wish you could remember the look on your father's face when he held you in his arms for the first time. Have you forgotten how much he loves you and how good he's been to you?"

"He started it."

"I know. But before you make another 'big-war-hero' snide remark to your father, there are some things you should know, my dear boy. You should know what was happening to him when he was your age, just nineteen."

Chapter 15

ADAM PAYNE ARRIVED in Montreal at eight the following evening. He checked in to a small, nondescript hotel on Rue Sherbrooke Ouest in the Westmount neighborhood, and paid with Canadian cash. He sat at the foot of the bed and surveyed the tiny, modest room; it was a far cry from the luxury of the Hilton at Place Bonaventure he had enjoyed on his last trip to Montreal.

§

At Adam's suggestion, Mary Chapman had called to inform her parents that she wouldn't be coming home for Christmas break; she would be staying in Amherst as a volunteer preparing holiday meals for the less fortunate.

Instead, Adam and Mary had driven to Montreal and registered as Mr. and Mrs. Smith at the new Hilton. After three hours in the throes of passion, the couple spent time in the heated rooftop pool. Thick fog rose from the surface of the warm water surrounding their submerged bodies while fat snowflakes floated from the night sky onto their nuzzling faces.

Later, dressed to the nines, they walked two blocks briskly through the winter cold for a gourmet evening at the famous Beaver Club. The maître d' seated them at an inside corner Adam had requested in advance. The table was for four, but the couple sat together on an upholstered sofa with its back against the dark, wood-paneled wall. A diminutive electric lamp and a slender garnet vase with elegant Calla Lilies surrounded by bone china and silver service sat atop a white linen cloth whose skirt fell in pleats, almost touching the plush patterned carpet.

Dinner began with champagne and seared foie gras. Next came a chateaubriand for two with white asparagus and truffled au gratin potatoes accompanied by a smooth Chateauneuf-du-Pape.

By the time their chocolate mousse and a digestif of Grand Marnier Cuvée du Centenaire had arrived, Adam had slid his fingers inside Mary's lingerie and was tracing gentle circles on her wet entrance.

Adam continued to rub while the waiter placed the dessert and cognac on the table.

"Merci, Alphonse." Adam added a nod of appreciation and Alphonse withdrew with a slight bow.

"Oh, God," Mary whispered, "Do you think he knows?"

"Oh, he *knows*." Adam rubbed faster.

Mary put an elbow on the table and covered her flushed face with her hand. After a moment, she reached down with her other hand and Adam was sure that she would discreetly remove his. Instead, she took his fingers in hers, changed their position ever-so-slightly and began guiding his strokes.

"Oh, God," she breathed. They were the same words she'd spoken moments ago but their meaning had changed along with her breathy inflection.

She pressed her fingers down on his, adding pressure, coaxing them to move in a new direction, up and down.

"Oh, God."

Beneath the table, Adam felt her moving her pelvis back and forth now. He rubbed faster, in rhythm with her movement, up and down, up and down.

Up and down.

A whispered scream.

"Oh, God!"

She stilled his hand and squeezed her thighs tight. She took in a quick breath and held it. Adam felt warm pulses caress his soaked fingers. He watched her breast swiftly rise and fall as she began to breathe again.

The throbbing subsided and her breaths became regular. Mary lifted her hand from her face but still used it to shade her eyes from the other diners.

Like an ostrich, Adam thought, *If she can't see them...*

Mary gave a sideways glance Adam's way, gasping, "God, the things you make me do."

Adam flashed a sly grin. Then he took a spoonful of chocolate mousse with his free hand and brought it to her lips.

§

The next morning, Adam had awakened with a start. He glanced at the bedside clock.

"Shit," he muttered, and jumped out of bed.

"What's the matter?" Mary had murmured sleepily.

"I'm late. Remember, I'm meeting an old colleague this morning at McGill?"

"Mmm," was all Mary could manage.

Adam dropped some cash on the nightstand. "Here's some money. Buy a new minidress for dinner tonight.

"I'll be back later this afternoon."

But Adam hadn't gone to McGill University. He went to a row house in a nearby neighborhood known as the McGill Ghetto. The "old colleague" was a former student of Payne's named Chuck Barber.

Barber had developed a heroin addiction while at UMass. He'd flunked out in 1968 and spent the next year living in friends' dorm rooms and on the street. On December 1, 1969, the first draft lottery since World War II was held. Barber's number was six.

Barber had turned to Adam Payne for help. Payne would ordinarily have told him to "get bent." However, Barber related an anecdote that got Payne's attention: Barber had attended a party where a friend got very drunk and depressed. Sobbing, she had told Barber about an affair she'd had with a professor, which had culminated in an illegal abortion. Barber said she now referred to her former lover as "The Prick."

Payne got the hint. He had not used condoms with that one because she was on the pill. But she neglected to mention that she had stopped taking the prescription because she didn't like the way the drug made her feel. When she finally mustered the courage to tell him, he could see that she felt guilty about her deception. Payne had put on a great show of indignation, and had no problem getting her to agree to an abortion.

But the bitch couldn't keep it to herself, and now Barber was blackmailing him. Barber needed to get to Canada, but lacked money and transportation. Payne quickly drove the junkie to Montreal, found him an apartment, given him some cash, and promised to check in on him from time to time.

Payne approached the row house. The scent of him and Mary together seemed trapped in his nostrils. He wondered if Barber would smell it too, and decided he didn't care.

Led Zeppelin's "Whole Lotta Love" seeped from Barber's basement apartment. Without knocking, Adam opened the front door and stepped inside. Immediately, the residual scent of him and Mary Chapman was overpowered by the smells of must, stale cigarette butts, and empty beer cans. His eyes adjusted to the dimness. Barber sat on the floor with his back against the far wall. His eyes were closed. Payne had to step around a young black man and a naked teenaged girl, both sleeping on the floor, to reach Barber. He thought to himself that if there weren't other people in the room, he wouldn't mind strangling the little shit and being done with him once and for all. He squatted down.

"Chuck," Payne said in a pleasant tone.

Barber's eyes opened slowly. He shrank from the brash light of morning like a vampire. Then he recognized Adam Payne and grinned. "The Prick! Qué pasa, man?"

B. ROBERT SHARRY

Payne inclined his head toward the naked teenager. "Are you babysitting?"

Chuck leered at her. "You know my motto, man: *If it moves, fuck it. If it doesn't move, fuck it anyway; it might be asleep.*"

Payne then nodded toward the young black man. "Do you own him? Or are you just renting?"

Barber chuckled. "Willy? He's okay, man. A little fucked up from 'Nam, but he's okay."

"He's American?"

"Well, sort of. He's from Mississippi." Barber snorted at his own joke.

Payne had managed some small talk, then dropped a wad of money in Barber's lap and returned to the Hilton.

Adam stepped into the hotel room. Mary stood at the window with her back to him. She wore a sleeveless, paisley minidress with the price tag still attached. She turned to face him, her white-coated lips spread in an enigmatic smile.

Adam cocked his head to one side. "What?"

"Another first for me," she said.

"Oh?" He was smiling now, too.

"I walked around the city all day, shopping and…" She paused.

"*And?*"

"And feeling like you were still inside me. I woke up feeling that way, and I still do. It feels like you *are* still inside me, right now."

Adam locked eyes with her and crossed the room slowly. He ripped the new dress from her body and let it fall to the floor.

IN THE DOORYARD BLOOM'D

§

Adam shook the memory of Mary Chapman's perfect body from his mind. He tossed his valise on the bed and left the small Westmount hotel. He found the nearest pay phone and called Chuck Barber. No answer. He tried again, just to make sure he'd dialed the number correctly. Still, no answer.

Hailing a taxi to take him the dozens of blocks he needed to travel proved easy. Within minutes he stood at the corner of University and Sherbrooke.

He walked one block north on University and took a right on Milton. Another block and he turned the corner at Lorne Avenue. Warily, he continued on Lorne until he stood in front of Barber's apartment. The place sat in total darkness. He had just started up the short walk to the building when a young woman came bounding down the exterior stairs from the apartment above. She gave a startled gasp when she saw Payne standing in the darkness.

"Oh my God, you scared me!"

"I'm sorry," said Payne. "I didn't mean to."

She breathed a sigh of relief. "My condolences; are you family?" she asked.

"Family?" *Barber did it! Bobby Coyle is dead!*

"Of Chuck's?"

"Chuck?!"

"Oh God, you didn't know? Oh my God, I feel so stupid. I'm sorry."

"What are you talking about?"

"I shouldn't be the one telling you this. Chuck died. Somebody found him on the sidewalk early this morning. The police were here all day. I'm sure they can give you more information. I'm, like, really sorry."

Think fast. Doing his best to look confused, Payne said, "I'm sorry, too, Miss. But I don't know any Chuck. I'm just a tourist. I took a wrong turn and got a little lost." *What's near here?* "I'm just trying to find Park Avenue."

The girl's brow furrowed. "I could have sworn I'd seen you here before. Now I'm, like, really, *really* sorry."

Shaking her head to clear it, she raised a finger and pointed. "Just go up to the next corner. That's Prince-Arthur. Take a right, and that will take you to Park Avenue."

Payne pondered whether he needed to kill the young woman who thought she recognized him. He decided he didn't.

"Thanks," said Payne. "Sorry about your neighbor," he added as he walked away.

The coed watched Payne as he ambled up the street. Then she shrugged and headed in the opposite direction.

Payne followed the young girl's directions to Park Avenue, although he hadn't needed them. He had come to know the city quite well over the years.

Questions seemed to chase each other through his mind as he walked. *What happened to Barber? Is Coyle still alive? If he is, where is he? And how can I find him?*

He would learn nothing more tonight, he knew. He hailed a taxi and headed back to Westmount. After an excellent meal of braised caribou with

IN THE DOORYARD BLOOM'D

cognac sauce, he walked back to his hotel room. He got into bed and fell asleep quickly.

The next morning he bought a copy of the *Gazette*, Montreal's English newspaper. Settling in at a sidewalk café, he ordered a toasted baguette and a bowl of hot chocolate with espresso. He combed the newspaper for anything that might relate to Barber. By the time his order arrived, he'd found the article. Police were investigating what appeared to be a drug overdose in the McGill University neighborhood. A local resident performing an early-morning dog-walk had found the body and called police. It was thought that the deceased was an American expatriate whose identity was being withheld pending notification of next-of-kin. Police suspected the deceased might have been selling drugs, because they had recovered over four thousand American dollars from the deceased's belongings.

Fucking junkie. There goes my money. But this still doesn't tell me anything about Coyle. Shit.

Had Adam Payne been watching the crowd rather than reading his newspaper, he'd have seen two young men—one black, one white—walk past the café on their way to Old Montreal.

Chapter 16

THE ASSAULT AND desertion charges against Private Coyle were a low priority for Jack McTeague. Still, the case gnawed at him. True, the murder investigation was none of his business, but… *Something's just not right.* Jack's gut told him that Professor Payne had lied, and that bothered him.

During his June monthly guard duty, Jack decided to interview Bobby's parents. When he called them to ask for a meeting, Gene Coyle was reticent and referred McTeague to his lawyer, Dan Lewis.

McTeague called Lewis. He introduced himself using his military rank, Captain John McTeague. The more McTeague explained to Dan about his desire to interview the Coyles, the more convinced Dan became that he recognized the voice. "You ever go by the alias Jack McTeague?" Dan asked.

"You know, I thought your name was familiar, and your voice, too. Are you the same Dan Lewis who worked as a prosecutor in Beantown?"

"About a hundred years ago. How've you been, Jack?"

"Me? I'm just peachy. I'm still catchin' bad guys in Boston. I'm acting here in my weekend warrior capacity. When did you go over to the other side?" McTeague teased.

"Long time ago," said Dan.

They caught up on each other's lives and reminisced about a few of the cases they'd worked on together. There was one case, though, that neither man mentioned: The one that had changed the course of both their lives.

§

In 1964, Jack McTeague and Dan Lewis were just two of dozens assigned to a special task force whose purpose it was to find The Boston Strangler.   In October of that year, Albert DeSalvo confessed. As some seasoned detectives on the task force, Jack wasn't convinced they had the right man. But Jack was a rookie detective and had made the rookie mistake of voicing his doubts within earshot of a reporter for a large Boston daily newspaper. His comments had proved embarrassing to his superiors. Jack McTeague went from rising star to persona non grata in no time, and had been marking time to early retirement ever since.

As for Dan Lewis, it was the climate of fear and hysteria surrounding the case that had convinced his wife, Miriam, that Boston was not the place for them to settle and raise a family.

§

McTeague came back around to the purpose of his call.

"I don't know, Jack. To be honest, I don't see how this can possibly benefit my clients."

"I hear ya." McTeague hesitated, then said, "I shouldn't be saying anything..."

"But?" Dan's lawyerly instincts kicked in. He sat up straight.

"Hell, this isn't even my case—the dead girl part, I mean. But something just doesn't add up.

Don't quote me on this, 'cause I'll deny it to my grave, but I don't think your boy did the girl. That's just my gut talking, you understand. I don't have anything solid that you could use; something just tells me the kid didn't do it."

"You think she jumped?"

"No, definitely not," McTeague said without missing a beat.

"Why *definitely* not?" asked Dan.

"Because I saw where she landed. Her body was so far away from the building, I don't think she jumped. I can't picture her literally taking a flying leap unless she was high as a kite and, from what I hear, the autopsy found no drugs or alcohol present. If she was despondent and wanted to kill herself, she'd just kind of step off, or let herself fall headfirst, but not get a running start like she was in some broad-jump competition—you know what I mean?

"I don't even think she was pushed. I think somebody, or somebodies, really *pitched* her off of that roof using a whole lotta force."

"Interesting," said Dan, while thinking he didn't see how this information could help Bobby Coyle, who was young and strong and certainly could have brought *a whole lotta force* to that rooftop.

"Well, for whatever that's worth," McTeague said.

"Jack, this isn't just another client to me. Gene Coyle is my best friend. I've known Bobby since he was a boy. He's almost like a son to me. You know better than most that I've dealt with my share of killers. Bobby Coyle's no killer, Jack.

"The staties are betting he's in Canada, probably Montreal. If you ever come across something that you can let me know without compromising yourself or your duty, I'd really appreciate it."

Dan and McTeague said their goodbyes to each other with obligatory talk about getting together sometime under more pleasant circumstances.

Chapter 17

LIFE ON THE STREETS of Montreal would have been much worse for Bobby Coyle if not for two things: Beautiful weather that summer and the tutelage of Willy Maze.

Willy taught Bobby how to forage for food at the dumpsters of some of the finest restaurants in the city. "You feel like Italian tonight?" became a standing joke.

He also taught Bobby how to make small amounts of cash. One way was to squeegee the windshields of captive cars in the few minutes spent waiting for the traffic light to change. This was hit-or-miss: Most people rolled up their windows and locked their doors when they saw the grungy, hippie-ish window washers.

If Bobby was lucky, some would crack their windows just enough to pass a twenty-five-cent coin through. If he was really lucky, someone might donate a loonie. "Loonie," Willy explained, was the nickname Canadians gave their dollar coin because of the loon bird depicted on it.

One of the more profitable scams for Bobby became the "bus home" routine. Willy taught him to pick out middle-aged American tourists and explain that he was a young American student tourist who'd been mugged and lost everything. He needed a "loan" of eighteen dollars for the bus ride home. He knew it was a lot to ask, but, if his benefactors would just write down their names and addresses, he promised that his parents would repay them by mail as soon as he got back home. This required some acting ability, as it worked best if Bobby appeared vulnerable, afraid, and embarrassed.

The men were often skeptical, but oh, that motherly instinct of their better halves could almost always be relied upon. With an "Ohhhh," they'd give an imploring look to their husbands, as if to say, *What if this were our boy?* More often than not, the husband would fork over a twenty with a muttered "Keep the change."

Bobby would thank them profusely. Smiling and sighing with relief, he directed his gushing thanks to the wife. Then he would disappear around the next corner, and flash a big grin to Willy while crumpling up the paper with the names and address of his marks and tossing it into the gutter.

After his second successful con job, an ebullient Bobby turned to Willy and remarked, "This is so easy, man—how come you never do it?"

Willy just stared at him.

"What?"

"Come here," Willy said, as he walked up the street.

"What?" Bobby repeated.

When they reached the next intersection, Willy said, "Watch this."

He approached a middle-aged couple much like the one Bobby had just scammed. He smiled and addressed them in his most polite voice: "Excuse me, sir, ma'am?"

B. ROBERT SHARRY

The couple's faces filled with fear. The wife clutched tightly to her pocketbook, and the husband clutched tightly to his wife. "We're not interested," the husband said, as he whisked his wife in the opposite direction.

Willy sauntered back to Bobby with an exaggerated look of mock confusion. "Now why you suppose them nice people didn't wanna talk to me? They musta been in a hurry, is all. The way they split so fast, they must be late for an appointment, right?"

"I'm sorry, man," Bobby said.

There were other skills Willy taught Bobby, like how to stuff newspaper in his clothing for insulation on cooler nights, and the best places to sleep. He taught him to go down to the docks and get day-laborer work as a longshoreman. If he approached the right businessman, he would be paid a lot less than a union worker, but wages would be in cash, and there would be no record.

Willy pointed out the "crazy bastards" who lived on the streets and told him who was harmless and who was a psycho. Bobby learned the best public toilets to use for sponge baths and the best times to use them.

Willy took Bobby to the Yellow Door, a basement coffeehouse on Aylmer Street, just a block from Chuck Barber's. Willy said it was a good place to meet other Americans, get a cheap meal, and sometimes hear some pretty decent live music.

"There's people upstairs from the café that can maybe help you get landed. They're workin' on me now," Willy said.

"'Landed'?"

"Yeah, man, you know. That's what they call it when you legal here. You *landed*. Then you safe, man."

"Safe—I'm not sure I know how that feels anymore," Bobby said.

Willy explained that *landed immigrant status* was the path to obtaining Canadian citizenship. It was based on a point system in which so many points were given for job skills, so many for speaking French or English, so many for level of education, and so on. Enough points, and the applicant could legally stay.

After they ate their fill at the Yellow Door, Willy led Bobby upstairs to the makeshift offices of the Montreal Council to Aid War Resisters.

A young man who resembled Allen Ginsberg smiled when he spotted Willy. "Willy Maze. How you hittin' 'em, man?"

"I'm doin' real good, my man." Willy shook his hand. "I'll be doin' better when I'm landed."

The man shot a suspicious glance at Bobby. "Who's your friend?" he asked.

"Oh, this is my man Bobby. He's cool, man. Bobby, meet my man Freddy."

"Hi," Bobby said, extending his hand.

"Bobby *what*?" Freddy kept his hands at his sides.

Bobby looked to Willy for instruction.

"It's okay, man. Freddy's cool."

"Bobby Coyle."

"Can't help you."

"Qué pasa, man?" Willy said. "Why you do him like that?"

"I can't help him."

After a long pause, Freddy sighed. "Look, we help who we can here. We try to get housing, jobs, and landed status for anybody who's a war resister or deserter."

"That's my man," said Willy, as he motioned to Bobby.

"No, this is different. Your man's wanted for murder."

"I didn't kill anybody."

"Well, whether you did or not, they think you did, and that brings heat that we just can't afford. We already have to deal with the FBI undercovers they send up here. The Canadians are sympathetic to us, but there are limits. We can't be seen as harboring someone wanted for murder.

"Besides, we help people of conscience, man, not criminals who wanna exploit us so they can hide from the pigs. Ironically, the Establishment labels us criminals because we refuse to hurt people."

Willy broke in: "How you know so much about this, man?"

Freddy sighed again and went to a high stack of *Boston Globes* piled on the floor next to a higher stack of *New York Times* in the corner of his office. He dug through them until he found the particular

Globe issue he sought. Once he spotted the article he sought, he folded the paper and handed it to Willy.

"Here," he said.

Willy took the paper and held it so that Bobby could read it simultaneously. The paper's account described what was believed to have happened at UMass more than a month before.

After several moments of scanning the article in silence, Bobby read the name "Mary Chapman" aloud. His knees buckled, and Willy had to grab his arm to stop him from going down. Bobby stared off in shock.

"You know her, man? Who is she?" Willy asked.

Bobby, still in a stupor, nodded his head. "She was my friend. We dated for a while."

Willy looked to Freddy, who shrugged.

Then, still holding Bobby by the arm, Willy led him toward the stairs and propped him against the wall. "Be right back."

He walked back to Freddy. "Bobby ain't like that, you dig? He didn't kill nobody."

"How can you be so certain?"

"'Cause I'd see it in his eyes. Killin' changes a man's eyes." More to himself than to Freddy, he added, "Jesus knows, my eyes is changed."

§

Freddy regarded Willy with compassion. He liked Willy. He saw something noble in the gentle giant. The way Willy carried himself suggested a kind of pride and dignity that Freddy admired. If Willy had faith in Bobby, well, maybe it was well placed.

B. ROBERT SHARRY

"Willy, tell him not to call home. Tell him not to contact anybody back home. It could make it miserable for his family and maybe lead the fuzz to him. They're probably watching his house, maybe even tapping the phone. I don't know about the locals, but if they bring in the FBI for this... well, they're a lot more corrupt and a lot sneakier than most people realize."

§

Willy nodded his head and then returned to Bobby. Together, they wandered the streets in silence.

After an hour, Bobby abruptly halted. "I saw him," he said.

Willy had shot ahead two paces before hearing Bobby and turning around. He looked around to see who Bobby was talking about, but didn't recognize anyone on the street.

"Who? Who'd you see?"

"Payne! When I went to his office, after I clocked my sergeant, I saw him. It didn't hit me till just now. When I got to the hallway on the top floor, he was just coming through the door that leads to the roof!"

"I don't get it."

"Willy, that's where Mary Chapman was before she... She was on the roof of that building! And so was *he*!"

IN THE DOORYARD BLOOM'D

Chapter 18

MARY CHAPMAN HAD broken one of his rules and, much to the professor's annoyance, shown up at his apartment, uninvited.

She made nervous small talk while she built up her courage. "There's talk that Dr. J may go pro."

Payne smelled baby powder and Juicy Fruit gum. There was a time when he had found the scent of her enticing; now he felt as if he might choke on it. "I have no idea what you're talking about."

"Dr. J? Julius Erving? He's our star basketball player?"

Payne had zero interest in sports. "Oh. Good for him."

Payne's phone was ringing.

Mary took a deep breath. "I need to talk to you."

This should be mind-numbing.

"I haven't been having my friend."

What the hell are you blabbering about? He was about to pick up the phone.

"So, I went to the doctor…"

It sunk in midsentence. Payne spun around and glared at her. "Oh Christ! Oh Jesus! Goddamn it! How could you let this happen?"

"Me? You're the one with the Trojans!"

The phone continued to ring.

"Are you sure? How can you be certain? Maybe you just think you are." Payne's face became redder by the moment.

Mary shrank. "The doctor did a Wampole test."

The ringing had stopped.

B. ROBERT SHARRY

Payne turned away. "Shit! This is all I need," he said, more to himself than to Mary.

"All *you* need? Excuse me, but I'm the one who's pregnant... with your baby!"

"How do you even know it's mine? I always use a rubber!"

"What do you think I am? I haven't been with anybody else!"

I know exactly what you are.

"What about Bobby?" Payne had just assumed all along that Bobby Coyle was still screwing her, too.

"How can you even say that? I broke up with him for you. I haven't been with anyone else since before Montreal."

This isn't getting me anywhere. "Okay, okay. I'm sorry. I shouldn't have said that. Don't worry. Everything's going to be fine."

"Really?"

"Really." Payne threw a gentle smile at her.

"Oh, Adam," she sighed as she fell into his arms.

"I know a doctor, a real doctor. I'll set it up and pay for everything. Don't worry."

She pulled away from him. "I can't do that. I could *never* do that. It's a mortal sin. We would both go to hell!"

I'm already there. "You have to. What else can you do?"

"*We* can have a beautiful baby together and love it. And love each other."

There was a knock at the front door.

IN THE DOORYARD BLOOM'D

Looking out his window, he saw a Chevy Impala parked on the street. Mary had followed behind him. "Shit. That's Bobby's car." She backed away from the window. "What's he doing here?"

"I have no idea," Payne said anxiously. "Have you told him anything?"

"No. Nothing."

"Could someone else have told him?"

"No. Nobody else knows."

Through clenched teeth, Payne said, "This is extremely important: Have you said anything to anybody about us?"

"No!"

"About...?" he pointed to her stomach.

"It's not exactly something a single woman wants people to know."

It occurred to Payne that Bobby's arrival would be an excuse to get rid of Mary until he could come up with a plan. "All right, listen: I'm going downstairs to answer the door."

"No. He can't see me here!"

"He won't. When you hear us coming up the front stairs, you go out the back door. Trust me. He'll never know you were here."

"Are you sure?"

"Trust me. Come to my office at Herter tomorrow at 12:30. With all this protest and strike stuff going on, there'll be no one else there. They'll all be out watching the action. We can talk then."

With all the sincerity he could pretend, Payne smiled and added, "And, Mary? I'm sorry for the way I acted. Of course, we'll do the right thing. Don't worry. Everything's going to be fine."

"I love you, Adam Payne."

"Me, too." *You fucking shiksa.*

Payne slowly descended the stairs, partly to give Mary time to get to the back door and partly because he'd convinced himself that Bobby knew the truth and would sucker punch him as soon as the door opened. But Payne had to know. One way or another, he had to know if Bobby Coyle knew.

Payne was relieved when he opened the door and Bobby launched into an apology for coming by unannounced. Then he was astonished when Bobby explained the events that had brought him there for advice.

This schmuck thinks I'm his friend. He didn't come to punch me out; he came to cry on my shoulder.

Bobby talked of the Kent State massacre and how, as a guardsman, he didn't know what he would do if activated. He couldn't shoot other students.

Payne told him he had only one choice: to follow his conscience and do the right thing. It was no excuse to say, *I was just following orders.*

After an excruciating two hours of listening to Bobby Coyle talk about his petty problems, Payne was happy when Bobby finally left.

Now Payne could concentrate fully on a solution to his own problem. Of course he'd considered the possibility of a pregnancy. He always did, especially since that last episode. He had no illusions. If he couldn't convince the bitch to get an abortion, he would be ruined. His career would be over. Everything he'd worked and planned for, gone. There would be no department chair in his future. Hell, he'd be lucky to have any kind of future.

Please don't misunderstand me, Dr. Payne. We were thrilled to receive such an impressive résumé here at Backwater Junior College, but what prompted you to leave your position at UMass?

Oh, you know, it was just one of those 'I was screwing one of my students and she got knocked up' things. You know how awkward that can be. I thought it best to move on.

And forget about Judy Rosen. There would be no wedding, no father-in-law on the university board of trustees. Oh, Judy would probably forgive him and marry him anyway. But her father wouldn't forgive or forget. There was no point in marrying frumpy Judy if there was no career to advance.

No, this had to be dealt with quickly and permanently.

Chapter 19

MARY CHAPMAN REACHED the seventh-floor landing at Herter Hall and stopped to examine herself. She hadn't had time this morning to wash her hair. She'd sprinkled a little baby powder on it and brushed it through.

She pulled out a small compact mirror to check her face. *Damn, a zit.* A dab of cover on the pimple, a quick curling of the eyelashes, a fresh coat of white lipstick; it would have to do.

Mary took the stairs in Herter Hall two at a time. She'd read that this was extraordinarily good exercise, so she bypassed the elevator. After all, this wasn't the Empire State Building, just seven stories. She needed to start taking better care of herself. She'd already stopped smoking. She'd never acquired a taste for coffee, and she'd loaded up her dorm room with fresh fruit. Besides, for Adam, she wanted to get her figure back quickly after the birth.

She would become the ideal college professor's wife. She envisioned their perfect future together: the large, stately home in Amherst, romantic evenings by the fireplace, travels in Europe. She imagined how she and Adam would host perfect garden parties at their magnificent home for their college professor friends and spouses. As a couple, they would be popular and admired, perhaps a little envied. Above all, she would make Adam Payne deliriously happy. *Dr. and Mrs. Adam Payne.*

Should she bother finishing college? She certainly wouldn't need to work, but she didn't want to be an embarrassment to Adam. He would want his wife to be an educated woman. Yes, she would go back to school after the baby was born.

She took a deep breath, opened the door to the hallway, and walked toward Adam Payne's office.

What should she call him now? *Sweetie* sounded like something grandmothers say. She liked *Darling* but was afraid it sounded too old-fashioned; same for *Sweetheart*. *Honey* sounded like her mother talking. One thing she knew: She would never refer to him as *my old man*.

She arrived at Adam's office door and took another deep breath before opening it. Adam's broad smile instantly put her at ease. "Hi, darling."

He called me "darling"!

Adam kissed her. "I have a surprise for you."

"A surprise?" *Are we eloping?*

"There's something I want to show you."

A ring?

"Come with me, darling."

"Darling." That settles it.

Adam took Mary's hand in his. He led her to a door at the end of the hallway, and ushered her through.

"What are you up to?" Mary giggled.

"This leads to the roof."

"I know *that*! But why?"

"It's a surprise."

"Should I close my eyes?"

"Um, sure."

Mary closed her eyes and let Adam lead her by the hand. The moment she stepped outside, she felt the warmth of the May sun on her face, heard chickadees calling in the distance, and smelled the heated asphalt of the flat rooftop.

Has he planned a romantic picnic on the roof? That would be just like Adam. Or maybe he'll make love to me.

She sensed that Adam's position had shifted. Perhaps he was on bended knee. *Dr. and Mrs. Adam Payne.*

§

At five seconds: Cool knuckles pressed on the nape of her neck and against the small of her back. She detected a slight tug at the back of her hip-huggers. The front waistband tightened against her hips and lower abdomen.

At four seconds: Once lifted, Mary felt the tips of her toes perpendicular to the level plane of the roof, as a ballerina flitting en pointe.

At three seconds: Mary took flight and opened her eyes. The initial thrust caused her long, blonde hair to float from the sides of her face. In half a second, the brief flight ended and descent began. For an instant her stomach felt as if it had just crested on a rollercoaster.

At two seconds: Mary had plunged sixteen feet and was gaining speed.

At one second: Her body had surrendered another sixty-four feet to gravity. From Mary's perspective, it appeared that the ground raced to meet her instead of the other way around.

At .5 seconds: Mary Chapman had time for one final thought: *My baby.*

§

IN THE DOORYARD BLOOM'D

Payne resisted the urge to peer over the parapet, and headed toward his office. He'd thought it all out very carefully, even taking the precaution of wearing Hush Puppies. He would not go outside. Instead, he would pretend to work in his office until someone interrupted him with the awful news.

Mary Chapman? Suicide? I can't believe it! She was in one of my classes! Dear God, what a waste. Such a beautiful young girl with her whole life ahead of her. It just doesn't make sense! What a crazy world we live in!

Yes, that was best. For a moment he pondered whether he should telephone someone, have a casual conversation. That person would then remember him as being in good spirits and not at all acting strangely. But whom should he call and under what pretext? *Judy Rosen. I'll call Judy. A little small talk, maybe ask if she'd like to have dinner at the Lord Jeffery Inn...*

He reached the bottom of the stairway, slowly pulled the door open, and peaked from one end of the hallway to the other. Empty.

Payne slithered through the stairway door and took a step toward his office. Bobby Coyle burst in from the other end of the hallway and spotted him.

Chapter 20

WILLY GAVE BOBBY an *I told you* so look. "Son of a bitch. Didn't I tell you you can't trust that honkey? Didn't I tell you that, son? Barber didn't trust him none, and I told you you shouldn't neither, didn't I?"

Bobby's mind was racing. He hadn't paid attention to Willy.

"Hey!" said Willy.

"Hmm?"

"I told you you can't trust him, didn't I?"

"Yeah."

"And I told you he probably had somethin' to do with Chuck tryin' to kill you, didn't I?"

"Yeah."

"That's right. I told you."

"What do I do now?"

"Ain't nothin' you can do."

"I have to go back and clear my name."

"No! No, you don't. No, you can't."

"But if he killed Mary…"

"Are you outta your tree, man? You don't know that. Well, maybe you *know* that, but you ain't got no proof. You go back there, what you gonna say?"

"I'll tell them the truth."

"What truth? The one about you seen him comin' through a door? And what if he denies it? Then who they gonna believe, you or the big-time college professor? Hmm? Who they gonna believe, Bobby?"

"I'll just have to take my chances."

IN THE DOORYARD BLOOM'D

"That's what I'm tryin' to tell you. You ain't got no chances. You go back there, they're gonna throw your sorry ass in jail and throw away the key. You ain't got no proof, and you ain't got no chance."

"You don't know that."

"I do know that! You think you're the onliest one? What do you think I'm doin' here? Why you think I had to run?"

"You told me. That's different."

"I didn't tell you everything." Willy pulled the palm of his hand across his face, from forehead to chin. "My lieutenant was a real badass, a real motherfuckin' badass. He liked killin'. We all killed, but mostly we killed just so we wouldn't get killed. But he liked it.

"We were spread out in a village, and it was just me and him at this one hooch. He threw a grenade in, and when it cleared, we went in. We heard cryin', and there was a young girl in there, and she was hurt bad in the back. And then she rolled, and I seen she had a baby in front of her she was protectin'. I think it was her baby, but she was so young, it coulda been her baby sister—I don't know.

"I started to go to them, and he shot from behind me. He shot 'em dead, the girl and the baby, too. And I just turned back and stared at him, like. And he was smilin'. And then he puts his finger to my head, like it's a gun? And goes *Boom*. And then he laughs, and he turns around, and he walks out. And then he torches the hooch."

"Jesus, Willy."

B. ROBERT SHARRY

"So I tell my sarge, and you know what he says? He says, *What proof you got?* I says, *I know what I seen*, and he says, *That ain't good enough. Who you think they're gonna believe: some nigger grunt, or a officer and a gentleman?*

"So I made up my mind right then and there, next leave I got, I was gone. The onliest thing I regret is that I didn't frag that motherfucker's ass before I left.

"It don't matter what you seen or what you think you know, Bobby. You ain't got enough, so you can't go home. I ain't sayin' it's fair; I'm just tellin' you like it is."

Chapter 21

JUDY HAD REMINDED Adam that she wanted the home address of his colleague in Montreal so she could mail an invitation.

"Tell you what," he'd said, "I'll just take this one with me and address it myself, make sure it gets out."

"You promise? Honestly, Adam, sometimes you're so forgetful. What am I going to do with you?"

Probably nag me to death. "I'll try to do better, darling. Thanks for putting up with this absent-minded professor." When he got home, he tossed the invitation in the trash.

Judy devoted her time to the wedding plans, enjoying the details—the choosing of venue, food, flowers, dresses. Most of all, she savored the time spent with her mother. Their planning was often done over pleasant lunches punctuated by frequent laughter. Even though her father ribbed her about the wedding putting him in the poorhouse, he had said early on that no expense was to be spared.

"'Nothing's too good for our little girl' were his exact words," Ruth Rosen told her daughter.

What Adam Payne looked forward to most about his wedding was the week before the ceremony that he could spend in peace without Judy hanging on him like an albatross. He wanted a break from listening to her animated descriptions of every boring detail. Feigning interest and excitement was exhausting.

§

On her wedding day, Judy wore a Victorian-style, full-length white silk gown with long sleeves and high neckline. The sight of Judy and Adam beneath the chuppah brought tears to Harry Rosen's eyes. "She's always beautiful," Harry choked out to Ruth, "but today, she's absolutely radiant."

Adam brought his right foot down heavily on the glass and smiled broadly for the audience.

The reception was luxurious and tasteful. Of the 150 in attendance, only a handful were Adam's guests: His father and a few other relatives from the Boston area whom he hadn't seen in years, his colleague, Ed Stein and wife, Cathy. Payne had invited department chair Dr. Charles Dugway because he thought it politically expedient. The rest of the guests were Rosen family and friends; dignitaries, university trustees, and other crème de la crème from the Rosens' extensive roster of peers.

Harry and Ruth Rosen had commandeered the entire Lord Jeffery Inn at Amherst to celebrate their daughter's nuptials.

Harry Rosen beamed as he twirled Judy around the dance floor. He nuzzled her, saying "I love you" over and over as they danced. Judy, eyes overflowing, pleaded, "Daddy, stop. I love you so much, but you're ruining my makeup."

Later Harry took Adam aside, shook his hand, and welcomed him with genuine warmth to the family. This he followed up with a good-natured tease about how Adam had "better take good care of my little girl."

Then the two men stood in awkward silence for a time, sipping their cocktails while they surveyed the dance floor. "I hate to bring up business at a time like this," said Harry finally, "but when you get back from your honeymoon, I'd like to sit down with you and talk about a project that's pretty dear to me."

"Of course, Harry. Anything I can do to help. You can count on me."

"Thank you. It's a small public radio station that's just not making it. I'm one of the trustees."

Adam started to respond, but Harry cut him off. "When you get back, son. I shouldn't have brought it up now." Harry scanned the dance floor and spotted Charles Dugway gliding gracefully with his wife. "It's nice that the Dugways could attend."

Adam saw the opportunity to plant a seed. "I suppose so," he said, and waited for Harry to take the bait.

Harry looked at Payne, then at the Dugways, then back to Payne. "Why do you say it like that?"

"Oh, I don't know. I get the feeling that he doesn't quite cotton to me."

"You think he doesn't *like* you?"

"Well..."

"But why? Why would Dr. Dugway dislike you? Judy tells me you're one of the most popular and respected professors on campus. Dugway's lucky to have you in his department."

"It's just a feeling I have. Let's just call it 'cultural differences.' I'm probably just being paranoid..." Adam paused, letting the words dangle in the air. "Well, I've got to get back to my beautiful bride." Adam walked across the dance floor in the direction of the long, white, flowing silk.

Harry was eyeing Charles Dugway with different expression on his face, one of puzzlement tinged with anger.

§

Adam knelt on aquamarine carpet and peered through the open, sliding glass door of his hotel room. He saw Judy turn the page of her paperback as she lie, sunbathing, on pink sands, far below. He chuckled and brought his attention back to the woman in the room with him.

Geneva was a chambermaid who had caught Adam's eye as soon as he had checked in at the Pink Grotto resort. A thin twenty-something with large, heavy breasts and an ass like a shelf. Her smile was enormous and showcased perfect white teeth. A pink maid's uniform with white apron set off the patina of dull copper that was her skin. Adam began flirting immediately.

Now he knelt behind Geneva, pounding into her in rhythm with the surf. She smelled like no other woman he'd had before. Her clean scent combined smells of the sea with musk. She was uninhibited, practically feral. It was her idea for Adam to enter her from behind. After rough foreplay that had left their bodies slick with sweat, she had dropped to her hands and knees and presented herself to him, like an animal.

She made noises like an animal, too; a guttural squeal each time Adam's pelvis smacked against her buttocks. Her pendulous breasts swayed beneath her with each savage thrust. Adam couldn't remember being so hard since he was a teenager.

§

Judy would never dare to have sex like that, and in broad daylight. She was too repressed, too *Judy*. Adam didn't mind screwing her nearly so much as what came after. Invariably, she would want to "cuddle". Payne was convinced that she'd be perfectly satisfied to skip the sex and move straight to the "hold me" crap.

§

A few days later, he sent Judy into town on a shopping spree to buy some island clothes. "You deserve it," he said. "Besides, I want my wife to be the envy of all the women on Bermuda."

He had Geneva all afternoon.

When they'd scheduled a sightseeing tour to the Crystal Caves, Payne feigned an upset stomach and insisted that Judy go on without him. "No sense in both of us missing out on the fun. You go ahead. I'll be fine."

"Maybe we should go to the hospital," Judy had said with concern.

"Don't be silly. It's probably just something I ate. I'll take it easy today, and by dinnertime I bet I'll be right as rain."

He did take it easy, having Geneva only once that day; his dick was starting to feel sore.

Toward the end of his two-week honeymoon, on Geneva's day off, Adam left the hotel to play golf. After the round, he met her at the clubhouse for lunch. They had crab salad and a couple of rum swizzles. When it was time for dessert, Adam led her to a secluded fence covered with morning glories near the sixteenth hole.

Chapter 22

BOBBY COYLE AND Willy Maze spent the rest of the summer and part of the fall of 1970 living hand-to-mouth on the streets of Montreal. Between the colder turn of the season and Willy's need to stop and "cook" every several hours, living by their wits became increasingly difficult.

Freddy, from the Montreal Council to Aid War Resisters, had come up with a somewhat risky plan to get Willy landed status, but it would hinge on Willy getting clean of his heroin habit and improving his French language skills. Freddy said he could then get him housing and a job. Then would come the risky part: Extra points would be given toward landed immigrant status if Willy made his application at the border. This would require that Willy to pass through U.S. Customs, travel a short distance into the United States, then turn around and return to Canada via a Canadian customs station where he could make his application.

Freddy would supply forged Canadian identification and a sympathetic Canadian citizen to escort Willy on the trip. Willy had only to keep his cool at U.S. Customs. The ploy had worked for others many times in the past, and there was no reason to think it wouldn't work again.

The most difficult part of this plan was the part where Willy had to get off heroin. He began by cutting down on his dose, hoping that would ease the withdrawal. He set a date two weeks out for stopping altogether. The reduced dosage caused him to be irritable and lose his appetite.

Bobby learned to read Willy's mood. He could sense when Willy would be receptive to soft-spoken words of encouragement. But he also knew when Willy was likely to turn on him like a vicious dog if he said the wrong thing. But even the times when Willy snapped at Bobby were soon followed by a bear hug and a plea for forgiveness. That was Willy's nature.

Willy took his last injection at midnight on October 14, 1970. After the final dose, he put the drug paraphernalia back in his "skag bag" and ceremoniously pitched it into the middle of Beaver Lake at Parc du Mont-Royal.

An Indian summer had brought welcome warmth that made sleeping under the stars almost palatable. Bobby awoke at sunrise and looked around for Willy. He spotted him sitting by the water's edge, staring wistfully at the spot in the lake where they had watched his "skag bag" sink.

Bobby wiped the sleep from his eyes and padded over to Willy. "I don't know about you, man, but I'm starving. Let's get us some breakfast."

Willy tried to be upbeat. He smiled and said, "Sure thing, man. Let's chow down."

Although Willy barely made a dent in his food, that first morning seemed to go pretty well in Bobby's estimation. By noon, though, Willy had begun to show flulike symptoms—a runny nose, watery eyes, and chills. And he was irritable, but no worse than Bobby had seen before.

IN THE DOORYARD BLOOM'D

He can do this, Bobby thought.

By midnight of the fifteenth, Willy's condition had worsened. He started vomiting around the same time the diarrhea started. Although this night was cooler than the night before, sweat poured from Willy. Soon after, he shivered uncontrollably. He couldn't sleep. When he wasn't puking or shitting or sweating or shivering, he paced around like a caged animal, and muttered to himself.

Bobby didn't sleep either that night. He kept watch on Willy, and wondered what he could do if Willy faltered and tried to score some heroin.

After dawn Willy settled down a bit. He lay in a fetal position on the ground, often trembling uncontrollably. He slept some, albeit fitfully. As the sun rose higher and the park warmed, he became even calmer. Throughout the day Bobby napped but awoke often to make sure the addict had not bolted.

Although Willy refused to eat, Bobby encouraged him to sip some water occasionally to stave off dehydration. But every time he drank, he puked it up shortly afterward.

In the calm of the warm afternoon, Bobby again reassured himself, *He can do this*. But two hours after sunset, Willy, who'd hardly spoken all day, stood and began to walk determinedly in the direction of downtown Montreal.

"Where you goin', man?" Bobby called.

Willy didn't answer.

Bobby jogged after him. "Come on, man — where you goin'?"

Willy kept walking but turned his head enough to deliver an icy stare that made Bobby stop in his tracks. He took a deep breath, sprinted to Willy. "No! You're not gonna do this!"

Willy stopped this time and gave Bobby a dismissive up-and-down once-over. "Who gonna stop me?"

Bobby gulped. "I am."

"Hah! Don't make me hurt you, boy."

With his open hand, Willy shoved Bobby's chest hard, throwing him back several feet until he lost his balance and fell backward. Then the big black man pointed a finger at Bobby, as if to warn him to stay down. With a quick pivot, the muscular legs resumed their powerful strides.

But Bobby ignored the warning. He got up and ran as fast as he could, and when he was close enough, he dove low, wrapped his skinny white arms around those tree-trunk calves, and tightened as hard as he could. Willy was felled like a black sequoia, and hit the ground hard.

"Muthafucka!" Willy freed one leg and kicked Bobby in the face with enough force to send him rolling a good three yards. Willy rose, shaking and sweating, and pointed again. "I warned you, didn't I?"

Willy turned and started walking.

Bobby shook his head to clear it, and tasted blood. Head pounding, he rolled over to his stomach, pushed himself up, and charged again. At the last second Willy whipped his arm backward and caught the side of Bobby's head with the back of his fist. Bobby landed hard and rolled again. Once more, he pushed himself up and charged.

Willy let out a primal roar and charged back. The impact was like a head-on collision between a VW and a Mack truck. Willy landed atop Bobby, knocking the wind out of him. He screamed with the blind rage of a wounded animal as he delivered fist after fist to Bobby's face.

In time, Willy tired. His blows diminished in frequency and intensity. His feral screams morphed into childlike sobs. His distorted face was drenched with his own sweat, mucus, and tears... and Bobby Coyle's blood.

The big black man let out one final scream of anguish. Willy Maze cradled his friend's limp body in his arms and sobbed himself to sleep.

Chapter 23

DETECTIVE SERGEANT DAVID Long of the Massachusetts State Police had solved the murder of Mary Chapman. He had everything he needed: motive, opportunity, witnesses, and physical evidence. But Long's tidy package was missing one thing: the perpetrator.

He had obtained an arrest warrant and put out an APB for Coyle. But his attempts to locate Coyle had failed. A young man had come forward after seeing a newspaper article accompanied by Bobby's photo. He had reported picking up a hitchhiker matching Coyle's description shortly after Mary Chapman's plunge from the roof of Herter Hall.

Judging from the location where the young man had dropped off his hitchhiker—and Canada's reputation for easy entry- —Long surmised that Bobby Coyle had fled north. But when he sought assistance from the Royal Canadian Mounted Police, their response amounted to *So, we're looking for a young American male with long hair? That narrows it down. We'll get back to you.*

Now it was a waiting game. Long hoped that Coyle might be picked up for another offense, a traffic violation, something. Since Coyle was in the National Guard, his fingerprints were on file.

Jack McTeague had called Long a couple of times, ostensibly as a courtesy to keep Long abreast of his investigation. But Long had been around long enough to know when he was being pumped for information. He gave McTeague very little, and what he did give was given grudgingly. He made it clear that McTeague's help was unneeded and unwelcome. Oblivious to McTeague's career as a Boston homicide detective, Long was loath to have interference from a weekend warrior, a Sherlock Holmes wannabe.

One question McTeague asked did gnaw at him, though: "How many good prints did you get from the rooftop?" The truth was, he didn't have any. He had Coyle's prints from Payne's office and the stairway door on the seventh floor, and he had them on Coyle's equipment, but nothing from the rooftop stairway, rooftop door, or any surface on the roof itself.

Long shrugged it off. It would have been nice to have found fingerprints on the roof, but that wasn't crucial to his case.

No, Long had all the evidence he would need. Patience was what was required, and he had plenty of that.

Chapter 24

WHEN WILLY MAZE awoke at dawn, he noticed that Bobby's chest was expanding and contracting. *Breathing!* The second thing he noticed was Bobby's arms gripped around his left leg.

"Oh, sweet Jesus. Thank you, Lord. Thank you, Jesus."

Bobby stirred and awoke with a start, tightening his scrawny vise on Willy's leg.

"No, no, it's okay. I ain't goin' nowhere, man. Oh, praise Jesus you alive. I thought sure I kilt you, Bobby. Praise Jesus. I'm so sorry. I'm so sorry."

Bobby raised his head and looked up at him. Willy gasped at the sight of the swollen pulp of bruises and dried blood on Bobby's face.

"You're not gonna try to get away again?" Bobby rasped.

"Oh, Jesus, no, man, no. I'm feelin' better now. Not good, but better. I'm gonna do this, man. I think the worst is over."

Bobby gave a weak nod. "Good. I'd hate to have to kick your ass again."

Willy laughed and cried at the same time. He reached forward and gently pulled Bobby by his underarms, cradling him in his lap.

"I gotta go back to sleep now, okay?" Bobby rested his head on Willy's chest.

"Yeah, man, you go to sleep." Willy stroked the top of Bobby's head. "Thank you, Jesus. Thank you, Lord."

§

IN THE DOORYARD BLOOM'D

Willy had been right: The worst was over. Though flulike symptoms and painful stomach cramps plagued him, each successive day became more tolerable.

He repeatedly apologized to Bobby, who always responded, "Forget about it." After several days the swelling in his face had diminished, while the dark purple bruising had become more pronounced. Willy apologized yet again.

"Just don't make me laugh," Bobby said. "It hurts when I laugh. And I laugh almost every time I see your ugly face."

"Me, ugly? I got news for you. You can't see 'cause you ain't got no mirror, but your face is so dark from them bruises, you could be my twin brother." Willy laughed so heartily at his own joke, it made Bobby laugh, too.

"I told you, don't make me laugh. Ow! God, that hurts."

Willy struggled daily to stay heroin-free, but it helped that Freddy kept his promises. First, he arranged for under-the-table jobs in a tourist-trap restaurant on Crescent Street. The sympathetic employer hired both Willy and Bobby to work in the kitchen.

Next, Freddy found Willy a furnished one-bedroom apartment in the McGill ghetto, within blocks of Barber's old place. Bobby made his bed on the couch in the living room. Both men avoided Lorne Avenue, and they never spoke of the night Chuck Barber died.

B. ROBERT SHARRY

After a time, Willy obtained landed status. As a deserter he wasn't eligible, so a new identity was established with phony U.S. documents. Wilson Johns, deserter, "legally" became Willy Maze, draft evader. Freddy had recruited an understanding black couple who agreed to escort Willy across the border into the United States. Willy sat in the back seat and held his breath while a U.S. Customs agent at the New York crossing at Champlain studied his fake Canadian documents. The agent stared sternly at Willy for a long moment. Then he waved them through.

They drove a few miles south, turned around in Plattsburgh, and headed straight for the Canadian border station known as Saint-Bernard-de-Lacolle. There, Willy made application for landed status, picking up the necessary bonus points for applying at the border.

Willy felt a sense of hope he hadn't known for a long time. He began attending one of Montreal's Baptist churches for Sunday services. He starting dating a French girl named Justine, a student at the University of Quebec at Montreal (UQAM) and part-time waitress at the tourist trap. Sporting a perpetual smile on his face, he exuded a new-found peace of mind. Bobby would sometimes study his friend's face and see the little boy in him.

But Willy's cheerful disposition also intensified Bobby's feelings of isolation and loneliness. He was happy for Willy, but he knew he could never attain the same legitimacy.

IN THE DOORYARD BLOOM'D

One evening, as Willy readied himself for a date with Justine, he danced around the apartment to the "Theme from Shaft", grinning and pantomiming as a smiling Bobby looked on. When the song ended, Willy turned the radio volume down and looked in the mirror. "You have blessed me, Lord. I don't deserve it, but You have blessed me. Thank You for all my blessin's. Thank You for Justine. Thank You for my church and my friends. Thank You for helpin' me stay clean. Thank You for my job and my home, and thank You for life." Willy turned away from the mirror and grinned at Bobby. "And thank You for Bobby Coyle, Lord. Amen!"

"I'm happy for you, man," Bobby said. "And, by the way, you *do* deserve it."

Willy came at Bobby with soft, playful punches. "Can I get a 'amen' from you? I said: Can I get a 'amen'?"

"Amen!" Bobby covered up to the fake punches. Willy wrestled him to the couch.

"Good things is comin' for you, my man. I feel it. Hey, why don't you get dressed and come out with me and Justine? We ain't doin' nothin' special."

"Thanks, man, but I'll pass. I got a good book I'm reading."

"A good book is fine and all, man, but when you gonna get you a good woman? A good woman makes all the difference in a man's life, my friend. How come you never go on a date? You ain't as ugly as all that. There gotta be some mama out there willin' to be seen with you."

"It's complicated."

"What do you mean, 'complicated'? You find a woman who's hungry the same time you is, and you say, 'You wanna get somethin' to eat?'"

Bobby laughed. "It's not that. It's what comes after that. After a while, girls expect... something more. What do I have to offer a girl? I really am happy for you, man, but I can never have what you have. My situation's different. Did you forget that I'm wanted for murder? I can never get landed, like you. I can never be legitimate. That's not fair to any girl."

"So what you gonna do, be a monk the rest of your life?"

"I don't think the monks would have me, either." Signaling an end to the discussion, Bobby added, "You better get a move on. Justine's waiting."

Chapter 25

AFTER RETURNING FROM his honeymoon, Adam Payne called on his father-in-law to discuss the fate of the small public radio station that weighed so heavily on Harry Rosen's mind. Before calling on the old man, Adam had spent hours listening to the station. What he heard was classical music, and more classical music. And just when he thought he would scream? More classical music.

Harry Rosen was a die-hard classical music fan. That meant Payne would have to dance around the obvious solution to the problem. *Harry, you dinosaur, stop playing the classical shit.* He would have to stroke the old man. "You know, Harry, I love the format. I could listen to it all day long. The problem is there simply aren't enough cultured people in this small market to support it by themselves."

"Any ideas, Adam?"

"Well, yes. First, appeal to the current base audience. Tell them the truth. I believe in always telling the truth. Explain that, in order to preserve the gem of the format—classical music—you need to expand the format to draw in a wider audience and thus more donors. Tell them: *It's do or die.* At least, that's what I'd do."

"Would you? Would you do it? Take over the reins of the station and try to save it?"

Oh, shit. "But, Harry, I don't know anything about broadcasting. You need someone with experience. I'm afraid I'd muck it up."

B. ROBERT SHARRY

"Forget about the technical stuff. We've got people to handle that. We need some new blood, somebody young with his fingers on the pulse of the community."

Someone to raise money for you, you con artist. You set me up. "Harry…"

"I'd sure owe you one, son."

You bet your ass you will. "Well, if it were anybody but you, Harry… I'll do my best. But if this is going to work, I need carte blanche. I don't want to be fighting with other members of the board."

"You leave them to me."

"And there's my workload at the university. I can dump only so much on my grad students."

"You just tell me what you need, and I'll make sure the administration does it for you."

Adam Payne was cornered. He cocked his head to one side and smiled. "Well, I guess I'm in the radio business."

"Thanks, Adam. I knew I could count on you."

The next day Payne recruited Ed Stein to share his misery. On the drive to the station, Stein looked at his friend and said, "Adam, I've been meaning to ask you something. I couldn't help but overhear you at your wedding. You said something to Harry Rosen about Dugway. What did you mean by 'cultural differences'?"

Payne had been unaware of Stein standing behind him when he planted the seed with Harry. "Oh, come on, Ed. Don't tell me you haven't noticed."

"Noticed what?"

"That Dugway's an anti-Semite."

"What?"

"Are you going to sit there and tell me you've never picked up on those vibes from him?"

"No, never. I've known him a long time. He can be distant, maybe even pompous, but not *that*."

Payne gave a sardonic laugh. "I guess he's got you snowed."

Neither spoke for the rest of the drive. When they reached the tiny radio station, the two men made their way around and introduced themselves. Payne guessed from their body language that the small staff had been clued in to management changes and were anxious about what changes might lie ahead.

Payne and Stein listened to speakers in an adjacent room while Rodney Pick conducted the annual fund drive.

Payne shook his head. "This guy, Rodney, probably knows more about classical music than any other dweeb on the planet, but his monotone is enough to put a coffee-gulping speed-freak into a coma."

"You woke me up to tell me that?" Stein deadpanned.

Rodney Pick would play some classical music and then invite listeners to participate in the drive. Then he'd play some more classical music. After an hour, only three calls had come in. One call didn't even involve a donation. The two other calls raised a grand total of twenty dollars.

"Okay, I've had about enough of this shit," Payne said to Stein. He strode into the studio to the strains of Richard Wagner.

"Rodney, if you don't mind, I'd like to say a few words to our audience... both of them."

Pick looked flustered for a moment. Unaccustomed to interruption in his insulated sanctum, he could not hide his resentment. "Well, I *do* mind. I still have another hour and a half to go," he said.

Payne gave an icy stare. "Let me put it another way." He leaned in close to Rodney. "Get the fuck outta here and wait in the other room."

Pick jumped from his seat, scooped up his program notes, and tried to regain some composure. Then he exited in an artist's huff, glancing behind a few times in case Payne was following.

"Stay close by. I'll call you if I need anything," Payne said. "And, Rodney? Don't ever play anything by that piece of shit Wagner again."

Through the studio window, Payne smiled and winked at the young, pimply-faced engineer giggling in the adjacent room. He needed the kid.

He sat down and looked around the studio to get his bearings, then told Stein to sit by the telephone. The young engineer's disembodied voice came to Adam over the intercom. "That was cool."

"Thanks. Listen, ah..."

"Theo."

"Right, Theo. I'm going to need all the help I can get here, man. We've got to raise some bread, or else we've got to sign off. So I need to convince people to open their wallets. What button do I push to talk on this thing?"

"Hang on." A few seconds later, Theo bounded into the studio and showed Payne some basics. "The cardinal rule? No dead air. Keep talking even if you've got nothing to say. Something is always better than nothing in this business. Try not to say *ah* and *um*. Keep the mic about this far from your mouth. Hit this button when you wanna talk. I'll be right over there." He pointed to the engineer's room. "I'll help you any way I can."

"Thanks, Theo. Now let's kick some classical ass."

Payne lifted the arm from the turntable, bringing an abrupt halt to Wagner, and began to address an invisible audience. "Sorry for the interruption, folks. This is Dr. Adam Payne, and I've got some bad news for you: The station is closing, and this will be our final broadcast. Sorry, folks, but we just can't stay on the air anymore… without your help. You see, we don't have enough money to pay the bills. It's as simple as that. So we have to pull the plug and close the doors… unless you ride to the rescue. You see, free radio isn't free. With commercial radio you have the advertisers to make it free. We don't. We have you, and that's it.

"So if you don't care enough, the lights go out and the music stops. We have to raise over five thousand dollars or we can't operate. Simple as that. When we raise five thousand, the music comes back. If we don't, this truly will be the day the music died. It's all up to you."

B. ROBERT SHARRY

The phone began to ring. Stein took the calls, recorded the donor information, and kept a running tally. Adam Payne kept talking all through the day and evening, and all through the next day and evening.

When they locked up that first night, Payne said, "Tomorrow, Ed, if they pledge five, get them to go to ten, ten to twenty, and so on. Plead with them. Make them feel guilty."

By the end of the second evening, they had raised more than their goal of five thousand dollars. Payne signed off by congratulating the listeners as heroes and playing Rossini's rousing *"William Tell Overture"* to conclude the fund drive.

"You know, Eddy," Payne said as they left that night, "there just might be some future in this public broadcasting stuff." *Money and clout, too.*

"Future? It's a tiny nonprofit."

"Non*profit* doesn't mean non-*money*," Payne said. Then, with a wry smile, he added, "'Broadcast or perish' is what I always say."

Chapter 26

A CONSIDERABLE RIFT had developed between Gene and Mickey Coyle. Gene had disowned Bobby, and Mickey grieved for him. These cross-purposes caused a span of resentment so wide that bridging it seemed impossible. An unpleasant quiet permeated the house.

It had been such a happy home, once.

§

Gene, after graduating from college, had gone to work selling insurance for a small agency in Mount Plain. Mickey had graduated from the Massachusetts State Teachers College at Westfield.

The young couple had moved into their new house just before Bobby was born. A friend had made a baby shower gift of a book called *The Common Sense Book of Baby and Child Care*, written by a pediatrician named Spock.

Mickey's newfangled approach to parenting sparked a few minor arguments with her husband. Gene said, "My father took me to the woodshed more than once, and I turned out okay," and, "Why should we reward Bobby for doing the right thing? Shouldn't we just punish him when he does the wrong thing?"

Theirs was a neighborhood of three-bedroom Cape Cod houses that were planted, almost at once, upon a tract of farmland during the postwar housing boom.

For fifteen years their lives were picture perfect. But by 1967, when Bobby was sixteen, his relationship with his father changed. No more the superhero who could do no wrong, Gene Coyle was flawed and, perhaps worse, uncool. No more the perfect son, Bobby now questioned what his father said, often launching disagreement for its own sake. When once the two had discussed everything ponderable, they had very little to say to each other now. When they did speak, the conversation was apt to be quarrelsome. Mickey looked on helplessly while husband and son engaged in a series of arguments that lasted the better part of the late 1960s.

Just when it seemed the generation gap couldn't get any wider, a dramatic wave of change washed over the country. The year 1967 brought the Summer of Love in San Francisco. Thousands of young people, drawn by news of the Human Be-In in January, piled in cars, hitchhiked, or took buses headed for California. Their ultimate destination: the Haight-Ashbury neighborhood of Frisco and the burgeoning hippie scene.

In June the Beatles released *Sgt. Pepper's Lonely Hearts Club Band*. A few weeks later, the Monterey International Pop Festival blared. Over fifty thousand people, mostly teenagers, came to groove on Simon & Garfunkel, Jefferson Airplane, Janis Joplin, Jimi Hendrix, and others. They called it a "Happening."

In November a new magazine called *Rolling Stone* published its first issue, with a helmeted John Lennon on the cover.

IN THE DOORYARD BLOOM'D

Bobby's appearance numbered among the radical changes that year. His dirty-blond hair grew from a Beatle mop to shoulder-length and wavy. His wardrobe of chinos, oxford button-downs, and desert boots had become faded jeans, paisley shirts, and sandals. Strings of beads encircled his neck and wrists, and he spent an inordinate amount of time alone in his room.

§

Now Mickey spent her time crocheting, taking classes, gardening, reading, and going on long walks. Gene went fishing and golfing, watched television, and puttered in his workshop for hours. Any walks he took were in the opposite direction.

Dan and Miriam Lewis invited the Coyles to dinners, movies, and other events, but acceptances were infrequent. When the Coyles did agree to join them, the conversation was sparse and strained, as with a couple in the midst of an argument who try to conceal it in public. They are cordial but not affectionate. They think they've fooled their friends, but they haven't.

Chapter 27

ON JANUARY 21, 1977, his first day in office, Jimmy Carter fulfilled a campaign promise and unconditionally pardoned hundreds of thousands of Vietnam-era draft evaders. Close to one hundred thousand of them had settled in Canada.

Bobby had been a fugitive for almost seven years. He didn't dwell on it, but in the back of his mind he was always aware that a tap on his shoulder could come at any time.

What he did dwell on was the limbo that was his life. He was neither American nor Canadian, father nor son, husband nor lover. His entire existence was underground, off the books, under the table; a lost soul surviving in a haze, with no compass. Loneliness and desperation had been banished years ago, and replaced by numbness.

He remembered a short story that he'd read in high school. Edward Everett Hale's "The Man Without a Country" told the story of Philip Nolan, a young, impetuous military officer who fell in with the purportedly treasonous Aaron Burr.

At trial, when asked if he had anything to say that would prove he'd always been faithful to the United States, Nolan replied, "Damn the United States! I wish I may never hear of the United States again!" The court granted his wish and spirited him off to a navy vessel to spend his remaining fifty years at sea. Nolan went from one ship to another, remorseful and ashamed. But he used the time to secretly glean information about his former country and ultimately became an ardent patriot.

And now, Bobby Coyle was the Man Without a Country, the Man Without a Family, the Man Without an Identity, the Man Without a Life.

When it came time to choose an alias, Bobby chose *Philip Nolan*. He could never hope to have a legitimate status. He would never be *landed*, never be a real Canadian citizen. The best he could do, with Freddy's help, was to obtain forged Canadian identification.

When he'd arrived in Montreal, Bobby was desperate to survive. Now, without hopes or dreams, only guilt and regret, he didn't much care one way or the other. Hurting his parents was his greatest regret. When he recalled his last months with them—the spiteful way he'd behaved, the vile language he'd used, the selfish attitude of entitlement with which he accepted their generosity —shame formed a lump in his throat. He wanted to go home and beg forgiveness.

Bobby kept to himself, even at work. Freddy had placed him with a sympathetic French construction contractor. Bobby had learned the basics of carpentry from his father. But he learned the artistry of finish carpentry from Jacques Fournier, the bear of a man who was his boss.

Bobby was the ideal worker. He was always on time, worked hard, never complained, and, most importantly to Monsieur Fournier, took pride in his craft. Fournier knew that *Philip Nolan* was not Bobby's real name, but never asked questions.

B. ROBERT SHARRY

As for Willy, Bobby rarely saw him these days. The fault was not Willy's or Justine's. They had been generous with their time and genuinely enjoyed Bobby's company.

No, it was Bobby who decided that he was a third wheel. He convinced himself that they were better off without him. Bobby Coyle convinced himself that everyone was better off without him.

Chapter 28

ON THE NIGHT OF Friday, June 16, 1978, Bobby couldn't sleep. He reached for his wallet on the nightstand and removed the miniature watercolor Lilas Bellefontaine had presented to him eight years before.

The cream parchment was now dirty and water-stained, the blossom's purple color had faded, and the lilac scent had dissipated. But just looking at the picture transported him. He could close his eyes and smell its sweet, powdery aroma and feel the warm spring sun on his face just as he had when he and Lilas lay on the grass at Bellefontaine farm and held hands.

Like a child's favorite stuffed animal, the lilac miniature had brought him comfort over the years. He considered buying perfume and re-scenting it, but decided it wouldn't be the same. This night, as on so many nights before, the cherished keepsake soothed his troubled mind and helped him sleep.

§

He awoke early the next morning. Jacques Fournier didn't believe in working weekends. He coveted leisure time with his family and encouraged his men to do likewise. "We won't be like the Anglos," Jacques would say. "They live to work. We work to live."

The morning was cool but the sky cloudless, and the French TV meteo report promised a warm, sunny afternoon. Bobby packed some food in the Igloo Playmate cooler he used for work, grabbed a book, and walked to the Place-d'Armes metro station on the Orange Line. He would switch to the Green Line at Berri-UQAM and continue to Station Viau. From there it would be a short walk to Parc Maisonneuve.

Bobby loved the parks of Montreal, especially the more expansive ones. He'd never gone back to Parc du Mont-Royal with its Beaver Lake after he and Willy had hit rock bottom. But there were plenty of other parks in Montreal, all offering a beauty and solitude rare in most large cities. He would pick a spot by a maple tree where he could choose sun or shade throughout the day.

He entered the Green Line train at Berri-UQAM and found a single seat facing the aisle. Although the ride to Viau would take only seven stops, he opened his book and started reading. Something made him look up. Diagonally across the aisle from him sat a bespectacled young woman. She, too, held a book in her lap and smiled broadly in his direction. When he realized she was smiling at him, he gave a sheepish half-smile and returned to his book.

The first stop was Beaudry Station. An elderly woman boarded the train, carrying a bag of groceries in each arm.

Bobby stood to offer his seat. "S'il vous plaît, Madame."

The old woman was delighted. "Je vois que votre mère vous a bien enseigné. Merci, Monsieur." *I see that your mother has taught you well. Thank you, sir.*

IN THE DOORYARD BLOOM'D

To steady himself in his standing position, Bobby grabbed hold of the handrail running along the ceiling. He couldn't help but glance at the young woman again and found that her eyes and smile had followed him. Then, she spoke. "Votre français est beaucoup amélioré, Monsieur." *Your French is much improved.*

True enough. Immersion in the language had worked wonders for Bobby in the eight years he'd been in Canada. But how could this beautiful young woman know that his French had ever needed improvement? Could he have worked with her at the tourist trap? No, he would have remembered her. She was stunning, with black, shoulder-length hair; a perfect complexion; and clear, walnut-colored eyes. No, she had just seen how Anglo he looked and made a logical deduction. Even so, there was something familiar about her.

Still smiling, she shook her head. "Vous ne vous rappelez pas de moi, n'est-ce pas?" *You don't remember me, do you?*

I don't know how I could forget someone like you, Bobby thought. *You look like… like an angel.*

Bobby's knees started to buckle. He gripped tighter on the rail above to keep from collapsing. A whisper of recognition barely escaped his lips. "Lilas?"

Chapter 29

ON THE DAY OF HIS daughter's birth, Adam Payne had gone to a large flea market in South Hadley. With cash, he bought a .30 caliber Springfield M10903 sniper rifle with telescopic sight from a World War II veteran. He brought the gun to the large Victorian where he and Judy now made their home, and, along with gun oil and cloths procured from a gun shop, wrapped it in light canvas and secreted it in the attic rafters of the carriage house.

Judy Rosen Payne had given birth to a baby girl. She named her Shayna, a Hebrew name meaning "beautiful." For Adam, Shayna's arrival presented just an expected complication, something to be tolerated. The infant's only value was that she might keep Judy occupied enough so that she'd be less of a drag on him.

Several weeks had passed when something bizarre happened. Judy hadn't been feeling well since giving birth. Her obstetrician determined that she was suffering from some minor complication related to the birth and that a surgery would be necessary to correct it. When she told Adam she would be in the hospital for a few days and wanted him to take care of their baby, he suggested that her parents take "the kid." In a rare display of defiance, Judy vetoed the idea, insisting that her parents were too old to cope with the demands of an infant.

"All of Shayna's things are here, everything that's needed," she said. "Besides, it wouldn't kill you to spend a little time with your daughter."

Her reaction surprised and mildly irritated Payne. Yet the part about her parents being too old was probably true, and he would gain nothing by engaging in an argument he couldn't win.

It's just a few days. Payne smiled. "Of course, you're right. You just go ahead and don't worry about a thing. Shayna and I will get along famously."

The first day was intolerable. Shayna was cranky, she wouldn't eat, and she went through one diaper after another. Although he rigorously followed Judy's detailed listing of the baby's daily schedule, he could not stop her crying. This pissed him off. He had done everything as instructed, when instructed to, and still the little rug rat wasn't satisfied. *Typical female.*

"Are all kids this much of a pain in the ass, or just Jewish princesses?" he muttered.

At 7:15 p.m. he consulted the homemade instruction manual again. *7:30 Tubby (baby shampoo on sink-top) (watch temp.), 7:45 bottle (burp), 8:00 bedtime.*

"Thank God," said Payne as he crooked the screaming baby in his left arm and filled the kitchen sink, checking the water temperature often. He undressed the still-screaming Shayna and eased her into the warm bath. Miraculously, the earsplitting screams subsided.

B. ROBERT SHARRY

"Finally, a little civility," Payne said. He looked at his daughter's eyes, really looked, for the first time. Huge blue saucers studied his face. He knew those eyes, he thought, but he hadn't seen them since he himself was a child.

Supporting Shayna's tiny back and head with his left hand, he scooped tepid water with his right hand, pouring over her chest and shoulders to keep the exposed parts of her little body warm. "You like that? You do, don't you?" He continued speaking to his daughter in soft tones, all the while afraid that the piercing shrieks would recommence once the bath was over. But they didn't.

He swaddled her in a soft towel, dried her, and then diapered and dressed her for bed. After heating her formula and checking the temperature on his wrist, he settled into the living room rocker to give her the bottle. Finally, he lifted her to his shoulder and gingerly rubbed and patted her tiny back. She let out a great belch, and her head nodded around like a bobblehead doll.

"Where is your etiquette, young lady? What would Emily Post think?"

He rose from the antique rocking chair and carried her to her crib. As he lay her down on her back, it occurred to him that Shayna's big, beautiful eyes had not stopped studying him since that first moment in the bath.

"You've been a good girl for your daddy — yes, you have. Sweet dreams, Princess."

Payne went back to the living room rocker and sat down heavily. He thought about his daughter's eyes—eyes she owed to a grandmother she would never know.

§

Adam Payne had been born in 1942 in New York City, to Russian-American Jews whose parents had immigrated at the turn of the century. Parents and grandparents alike had infused him with the history of his people: the awful prejudice and discrimination at the hands of their fellow Russians; the isolated existence of the shtetl; the violence, murder, and barbarity of the pogroms, followed by forced relocations, more humiliation, and more death.

When he was a toddler, Adam's family moved to a tenement in South Boston at his father's insistence. Adam had emerged bright and eager to learn, imbued with what his mother called a "sunny disposition." He discovered early on how to enthrall family and friends and win their approval.

Precisely when he stopped giggling through the days would be impossible to pinpoint. He couldn't trace it to a single incident, but rather to a series of indignities that began with his enrollment in public school.

As any young innocent, Adam had been ignorant of the invisible difference that distinguished him from his equally unaware classmates. But some parents and some teachers had wasted no time in making the other students aware of the imperceptible. The students, in turn, pointed it out to Adam through their relentless taunts, spittle, and beatings. On occasion, they held him down while they searched his scalp for devil horns.

Adam's mother begged for his transfer to a Jewish day school, but his father insisted that that would just delay the inevitable and that the earlier he was exposed to anti-Semitism, the sooner he would adapt and toughen. Thus, public school would become Adam Payne's primer for life as a Jew among Gentiles.

Eventually, he learned to deny his adolescent tormentors the satisfaction of seeing his tears. He saved them for the long walk home. But when his mother died soon after he entered the sixth grade, any chance Adam Payne had for a normal life went with her.

He became hardened. Through a diet and weight-lifting regimen that would satisfy a drill sergeant, he developed and toughened his body. Through books and the help of an older Jewish boy in his building, he armed himself with self-defense tactics and steely resolve.

Then he went on the offensive. With a suckering glare, he dared his tormentors to take their best shots. Bullies soon learned there would be a heavy price to pay for prodding Adam Payne.

In time there were no more taunts and no more tears. But neither was there any sense of joy. He had lost his spirit and soul. He was changed, but not broken. Adam Payne promised himself that, no matter what it took, he would have his day.

Chapter 30

BY THE TIME THE train reached Frontenac Station, the seat next to Lilas had been vacated. She looked at Bobby and patted the empty seat with her hand. The moment he sat next to her, he smelled the scent that his lilac miniature had once given off.

"Where are you going?" she asked in English.

"Parc Maisonneuve."

"Ah, this is very near where I work at the Botanical Garden. Jardin Botanique is part of Parc Maisonneuve, but they are managed separately. You must come with me to see where I work first. Then you can cut right through the gardens to the park."

"All right," he said. Then, taking a deep breath, he added, "It's good to see you, Lilas."

They exited the subway at Station Pie-IX and walked up the boulevard. Lilas did something so natural that it would seem unremarkable to most people—she took Bobby's hand in hers. The gesture and the warmth of her hand stirred him, a reminder of how he felt when she would take his hand during walks on the farm. To hide his glistening eyes, he looked away from her, pretending to survey the other side of the street.

They reached Jardin Botanique and passed through the gate to a chorus of "Bonjour, Lilas" from employees manning the entrance booths. Once inside, Lilas explained that this was not a *real* job for her yet. She was a horticulture graduate student at the University of Montreal, and this was an internship. Once she graduated, she would become an employee. She would have to. "My garden is here, and so I must be, too."

"*Your* garden?"

"Oui! Come—you'll see." She led Bobby by the hand, eventually stopping in front of a sign that read *Collection des Lilas*. Lilac Collection.

"Ah!" said Bobby. "Now I see why it is *your* garden."

"Since I was a little girl, my parents take me here every year when the lilacs are blooming, and they say, *You see the sign, Lilas? This is your garden.*" She laughed the same laugh as the sixteen-year-old girl Bobby remembered. "I believed them. They are my parents; I was a little girl. Of course I believed them."

"I think you still do."

"Shh." Lilas held her index finger to her smiling lips and whispered, "I do, but I don't want others to be envious. So it must be our secret."

She tugged again on his hand, and they entered Lilas's garden. There were lilac bushes everywhere, as far as the eye could see. Almost an acre full of every color and scent variation imaginable stood before them in full bloom. The fragrance was intoxicating.

They ambled through the garden, arm in arm, in a lazy zigzag. Lilas rattled off facts and figures about the blossoming bushes. The passion with which she spoke captivated him.

The private tour took a full hour, and then they sat for another hour beneath one of her favorite bushes. Bobby wanted to freeze the moment, thinking that he would be content to sit there, gaze upon her, and listen to her voice for eternity. Then he remembered something. "Now, I have a surprise for you."

"For me? But how? You didn't even remember me until today."

"That's not true." Bobby slipped the tattered, faded parchment from his wallet and handed it to her.

Her eyes flashed with recognition, and then filled with tears.

Chapter 31

WHEN ADAM PAYNE WASN'T doting on Shayna, he was concentrating on expanding his small broadcasting empire. He found that, through salary and perquisites as executive officer, the little nonprofit could be very profitable indeed.

One day, Payne sat in his Herter Hall office with his feet propped on his desk. Next to his feet sat a Pet Rock that one of his students had given him.

Ed Stein walked into the office, picked up the stone, and asked, "What have we here?"

"That, my friend, is unequivocal proof that P. T. Barnum was right: There *is* a sucker born every minute."

Ed took a seat across the desk from Payne. "You rang?"

"We need to raise more money at the station."

"But how? I think we've reached the saturation point with our listeners."

"Exactly. That's why we need different listeners."

"Who? Anyone who likes classical music is already in the choir."

"Forget classical music. What do we have more of in this area than just about anyplace else?"

"I don't know, but I'm sure you're going to tell me," Stein said.

"Colleges… and freaks, man, a lot of freaks. Guilt-ridden freaks who are searching for themselves. They'll practice any religion but their own, embrace any culture but their own. People who are dying to buck the Establishment. They want to run into the jungle and play Che Guevara. And while they're in the jungle, they want to hug every tree so they can free the planet and save it at the same time. And those are just the teachers!" he laughed. "You know how impressionable students are. They may not have much money now, but someday…

"Hey, even a counterculture has to buy stuff. We should look at *The Village Voice* and… what's that local one? Somebody's got to be reading that crap. See who's advertising in those papers, get some leads."

Payne reasoned that the more competitive pressure he could put on small, local commercial stations, the easier it would be to devour them. But the commercial stations had the advantage of the almighty advertising dollar. He wanted a share of that.

"You know we're not allowed to accept advertising," said Stein.

"It's not called advertising. It's called *underwriting*. Is there anything wrong with accepting a corporate donation?"

"Well, no, but…"

"And is there anything wrong with acknowledging a donor? We do it all the time."

"Yes, but I still don't see…"

"All we have to do is mention what the donor *does* when we gratefully acknowledge their contribution."

"Then it's just semantics?"

"Exactly."

A few minutes later, Charles Dugway walked into Payne's office and found the two men discussing public radio business. A look of exasperation spread across his face. "Gentlemen, I am in favor of the arts as much as anyone, and I applaud your sense of noblesse oblige, but I am concerned that the amount of time you two are spending on this project is having a detrimental effect on the ability of this department to fulfill its mission.

"I need you two to keep this radio business to a minimum while you're at work here. It's become too much of a distraction."

Payne kept his feet on his desk. "Have you discussed this with the administration, Charles?"

Dugway was momentarily nonplussed. But bewilderment gave way to indignation, his grey eyes narrowed and his patrician posture gained height. Enunciating every word and punctuating each with a staccato pause, he said, "What.do.you.mean?"

In a tone designed to goad the starchy old man, Payne answered, "It's a fairly straightforward question, Charles. I simply asked if you had discussed this with the administration."

"Listen here, Payne. I am the head of this department. I don't need to discuss this with the administration. I'm well aware of my responsibilities to the administration, and of yours to me. It is entirely within the scope of my authority to take remedial action in the interest of protecting the quality of education at this university. You people are spending entirely too much time away from your responsibilities and the students are suffering for it. Have I made myself clear?"

"Absolutely, Charles—especially the part about 'you people.'"

Dugway appeared confused. He looked to Stein for some clarification, but Stein offered none. Dugway turned back to Payne. "What *are* you blabbering about?"

"I take it that by 'you people,' you mean Jews?"

Dugway, flummoxed for the third time in as many minutes, recovered as best he could. "I won't even dignify that with a response. You've gone too far this time, Payne," he spat. He spun around on his heel and stormed out of Payne's office.

Stein watched Dugway pound down the hallway. When he was certain the old man was out of earshot, he turned to Payne. "Are you insane?"

"Fuck him. I'm tired of these condescending WASPs and their arrogant, holier-than-thou bullshit."

Stein shook his head. "Dugway is a pompous snob, but he didn't deserve that."

Payne gritted his teeth, pulled his feet off the desk, and slammed his fist on it. "Fuck him! Fuck them all! Now it's our turn!"

Stein was visibly shaken by Payne's violent outburst. "'Our turn'?" he asked, trembling. "And just who are you including in that, Adam? Because if it's me, count me out. I want my turn, but not this way. I'm not going to help you destroy a man's reputation for the sake of ambition."

As Stein left his office, Payne thought, *He'll come around.* He rose and closed his office door and telephoned Harry Rosen. He wanted to speak to him about the incident before anyone else did.

Rosen was completely taken in. Here was his son-in-law telling him that the head of the history department at the commonwealth's university despised Jews. Payne quoted Dugway as spitting the words "you people" at him and Stein with such contempt that Payne would no longer continue to work in such a poisonous atmosphere.

No, this wasn't the first time, Payne told Harry. This was just the latest of spiteful remarks. He couldn't speak for Stein, but, as for him, he was resigning and wanted to let Harry know as a courtesy.

The archetypal absentminded Professor Charles Dugway never had a chance. He'd never fought in the gutter, wouldn't know how. Having never encountered a situation such as this, he just assumed that the absurd allegation would be seen for what it was, and that his unblemished reputation was all the defense he needed, if indeed he needed a defense at all. So when confronted by Rosen, he assumed the same arrogant, aristocratic posture he had with Payne. "I won't dignify that with a response," he said in a condescending tone.

"That's not good enough. Sometimes *we people* insist on a response," Rosen countered.

IN THE DOORYARD BLOOM'D

Dugway "retired" soon after. A month later, the history department at UMass Amherst had a new chairman. Adam Payne.

Chapter 32

AT AN OUTDOOR CAFÉ near the University of Quebec at Montreal, Bobby Coyle and Lilas Bellefontaine sipped red wine. The mild air of a late-June evening carried the aromas of a city cleansed by springtime and eager for the warmth of summer.

They had been talking for hours about what had happened in their lives in the eight years since they had parted. Bobby had omitted anything that happened before Willy had attained landed status. In truth, Lilas had done most of the talking, but Bobby was perfectly content to listen to the sound of her voice and study her lovely face.

Lilas yawned. "I'm sorry—I must get some sleep. I hate to leave, but I need to be back at the garden by eight in the morning."

"I understand. It is late."

"Call me tomorrow?" Lilas asked as she rose from the table.

Bobby hesitated. "Lilas, I don't know if that's such a good idea. There are things you don't know… reasons you shouldn't become too close to me."

"Then tell me, so there won't be things I don't know," Lilas answered, as if to say, *Problem solved.*

"It's not that simple."

Lilas leaned forward and put her palms on the table. "But it *is* that simple. After all these years, God has brought you back to me. You have to trust me." She gazed into his eyes, waiting for his response.

But he said only, "I'm sorry, Lilas." The look of hurt in her eyes stung him. He watched her walk away, and his heart sank.

§

Bobby walked the streets of Montreal through the night. At dawn he found himself watching the sunrise over the waterfront. He was tired: tired of not being able to have the things others took for granted, tired of being alone, tired of thinking, tired of being tired. He couldn't stop thinking about Lilas. The thought of never seeing her again tormented him. But how could he put the weight of his circumstances on a carefree twenty-four-year-old woman? It wouldn't be fair to her.

He walked aimlessly through the cobblestone streets of Vieux-Montréal, the Old City, and then took to the path that ran alongside the Lachine Canal. At four in the afternoon, he found himself at the Atwater Market.

Suddenly, everything became clear to him, and he stopped walking. *I won't live this way anymore. It may be selfish, but I will not let her go. I want to be with her.*

§

He hurried to the nearest metro station and caught a train to Station Pie-IX. He ran to Jardin Botanique. He fumbled for the price of admission and then hustled to Lilas's garden. When he found her, he took her in his arms, kissed her, and held her so tightly he was afraid he might hurt her.

Then he told her everything—everything that had happened to bring him to Bellefontaine Farm in the first place. He told her about the anti-war protests at UMass, about what he had done to Sgt. Chip Visky, and why he had fled and then been shot by police. Then he told her everything that had happened once he had left the farm: Chuck Barber trying to murder him, Willy Maze saving his life, living on the streets of Montreal, learning of Mary Chapman's death and that he had been blamed for it. Then he told her why: Adam Payne. He told her of making a life for himself, underground, as Philip Nolan, and how he could never go home again. He warned her that life with him would *never* be normal.

Chapter 33

IT WAS SUNSET NOW in the lilac garden.

"How do you feel now, Bobby?"

"Like I haven't felt in more than eight long years. I feel something I thought I'd never feel again, that I even forgot how to feel. I feel… hope. That's it: I feel full of hope."

A long, comfortable silence settled between them. They lay on soft, green grass. A sunken Jackson Pollock sun spattered dusty rose and violet across the western horizon. Evening grosbeaks gave a concert with cardinals as chorus. And fragrance: everywhere the stimulating scent of lilac. All of these, and man and woman together on a warm, June twilight.

"Make love to me," she whispered. "Take me in my garden."

Bobby stood, held out his hands to Lilas, and helped her rise to her feet. He cupped her face in his hands and drank in the beauty of her eyes. He moved closer and kissed her, tasting a sweetness he had never tasted before. Closing his arms around her, he pulled her closer and kissed her eagerly. He took one step back, then slowly undressed her while they searched each other's eyes. When Lilas was naked, he moved his eyes to her body and marveled at her loveliness and perfection.

He drew her in close, wrapping her body in his. Heat radiated through his shirt, and she felt warm and protected. Within the cocoon of his embrace, Lilas unbuttoned his shirt. Soon he was naked, too.

Their senses were blazing, stoked by mutual wonder,– the taste and scent of the other, gazes of love, the softness of her, and the hardness of him. They lay on the warm grass.

"I need to feel you inside me."

She guided him with her hand, slowly taking him in until he was completely enveloped in her warmth.

"I love you, Lilas."

"And I love you."

Chapter 34

ADAM PAYNE DROPPED seven-year-old Shayna at her ballet class. "Have fun, my prima ballerina. Mommy will pick you up after class, okay?"

"Uh-huh."

"Now give your old daddy a big hug and a kiss."

Shayna happily obliged. She threw her arms around her stooping father's neck and kissed his lips. "Bye, Daddy."

"Bye, Princess." His lips spread into a loving smile as he watched her join the other girls. *There goes the next Margot Fonteyn.*

He drove to New World Public Radio's main office and studio in Amherst. New World was now composed of six strategically located stations that reached listeners as far east as Worcester; north to Southern Vermont and New Hampshire; south to Hartford, Connecticut; and west to the Berkshire Hills.

He couldn't be late for his on-air interview with Olivia Collingwood, Ph.D., professor of women's studies at Smith College. He had developed a loyal following among the faculty and students of Smith. They sent a lot of money his way. He'd treat Ms. Collingwood with the deference he knew she craved—schlep coffee for her and stroke her ego.

Ollie Collingwood wore her usual mannish attire. Her short hair was combed back and gelled. She had incorporated sideburns into her coiffure.

Whatever breasts she had, Payne noticed, she went to great lengths to conceal beneath her suit coat.

"I hope I got this right." Payne smiled as he slid the coffee toward her. "Cream, no sugar?"

"You remembered. You're good, Adam."

"We have only a few minutes to airtime. Sally's going to join us, so it'll be more like a three-way discussion, okay?"

Sally Barker was Payne's top news personality now. She had interned for him as a communications major. Although she was young, Payne had helped develop her natural talent and made her better.

And she worshipped Payne. In her attempts to win favor with him, she fawned over him, even on-air, sometimes to the point of Payne's embarrassment. During fund drives, her flowery praise of Payne had prompted Ed Stein to remark, "Sometimes, if I close my eyes and listen to the radio closely enough, I swear I can hear the sound of her lips smacking your buttocks."

Sally Barker entered the studio.

"Hey, Sal, can I get you some coffee?" Payne asked.

Sally looked a little surprised. When it was just the two of them, Payne would jiggle his empty mug as a signal for Sally to refill it.

"No, thanks—I've had my limit for the day."

"Well, if you change your mind, just let me know."

"Thanks."

"Hi, Sally. How are you?" Ollie asked in a sugary voice.

"I'm great, Ollie. How're you?" Sally responded, a little too sweetly.

Payne jumped in. "Sal, I was just saying to Professor Collingwood…"

"Ollie——please, call me Ollie." Then she added, "Off-air."

"Thank you," *you dyke*. "I was just saying to Ollie that we should keep this in a conversational mode. Ollie, I'll begin by asking you about progress in women's rights. Then we'll let you take it from there, and Sally and I will follow your lead and jump in from time to time. We'll do about twenty-five minutes, okay?"

Payne had advised Sally earlier that she'd have to take off her reporter's cap. There would be just the softest of softball questions.

Into his microphone, Payne introduced "one of the most highly regarded authorities in the field of women's studies, and someone considered a beacon in the struggle for women's equality, and an example for young women everywhere, Dr. Olivia Collingwood, professor of women's studies at Smith College. Thank you for taking the time to sit down with us, Professor Collingwood."

"It's a pleasure to be here, Adam."

"You know, we here at New World Public Radio are known for our objectivity and independence, but I've got to tell you, I'm a little biased. I'm not ashamed to say it: I am a feminist. There, I said it. But I felt I had to in the interests of full disclosure, as the lawyers say. Integrity demands that I reveal any biases. I'm a feminist, and I don't care who knows it. Now that we've got that out of the way, Professor Collingwood, please tell our listeners what the state of progress is in the women's movement."

§

When the staff had gone home at the end of the day, Sally approached Payne in his office, put her arms around his waist, and said, "You were brilliant today."

"I was, wasn't I? That ought to get a few more flannel shirts to call come pledge time."

"You're *awful*."

"Can you believe that dyke?"

"Adam..."

"I'm sorry, but come on! That cunt-lapper looks like a caricature. I kept waiting for a Snap-on tool truck to pull up outside the studio."

"Adam, you are *so* bad," she said with a giggle.

"I know." Payne unzipped his pants, pulled out his penis, and stroked it. "Now shut up and suck me."

§

Judy greeted Payne cheerfully that night, as she always did. She knew he worked long, hard hours, and she wanted to be supportive.

"Shayna wanted to wait up for you, but it just got too late. I had to put her to bed."

"I know. I'm sorry to be so late. I'll just go in and give her a kiss."

Payne stood beside Shayna's bed, watching her sleep. He bent down, stroked her hair, and planted the softest of kisses on her cherubic cheek. "Sweet dreams, Princess. Daddy loves you."

When he returned to the kitchen, Judy had a scotch on the rocks waiting. As she handed it to him, she said, "I heard you on the radio with Ollie Collingwood today. It was a great show."

"Thanks, honey." Adam was smiling contentedly. He always was when coming from tucking Shayna in for the night.

Judy stood at the kitchen island and sipped white wine. "You know, it got me thinking: Maybe Shayna could go to Smith."

Payne's smile evaporated. "Not in a million years."

"But why not? We want the best for her. And when I heard you today, I was so proud of you standing up for women's rights. And Smith's one of the best schools anywhere."

"Used to be." Adam said dismissively. "I deal with Smithies all the time. They don't just want equality; they want revenge. There's an underlying premise in everything they do that the white male is the enemy. Do you really think I would spend a hundred thousand dollars so some hairy Amazons can teach my own daughter to hate me?"

Adam moved from the kitchen to the dining room. He pulled out his chair at the head of the table and flopped down.

Judy stood in the kitchen, stunned, and stared at his back.

"Where's my supper?" he called over his shoulder.

Chapter 35

ON THE MONDAY morning following his reunion with Lilas, Bobby Coyle arrived late to work for the first time ever.

He walked onto the job site more than two hours late with a new-found spring in his step. Instead of a hangdog look and feeble excuse, Bobby just smiled, wished everyone a good day, and literally whistled while he worked.

His fellow construction workers had looked to the boss, anticipating he would launch the same tirade on Bobby as he had on others when they were late for work. But the bear did not growl that day. His coworkers looked at each other in astonishment as Bobby, who'd never been heard to utter more than "Bonjour" in the morning and "Au revoir" at night, talked a blue streak all day long.

In the afternoon, Jacques Fournier, that bearded bear of a man, playfully wagged his thick index finger at Bobby. "You have found a woman."

"No," Bobby beamed. "She has found me!"

"Either way, I can tell she is good for you, my friend. Hold on to her, if she is French." Then, with a stern look, he added, "But tell her not to make you late for work again."

Bobby grinned, came to attention, and saluted. "Oui, Monsieur L'ours." *Yes, Mr. Bear.*

§

Lilas and Bobby spent every possible moment together that summer, doing the things that lovers do. During his years of an almost monastic existence, Bobby had saved a lot of cash and now had reason to spend it. There were romantic horse-drawn carriage rides, bike rides and picnic lunches, al fresco dinners, disco dancing, lazy museum Sundays, day trips to Mont-Tremblant or the Eastern Townships near where Lilas grew up, and weekends in Quebec City.

In the fall Lilas entered her second year as a graduate student at university. Growing up on a farm, she had an ingrained appreciation of plants and nature and their cycles. After graduation she intended to work at the Jardin Botanique for the rest of her life. She was never happier than when among the gardens there. None, though, gave her more happiness or had more meaning than the Lilac Collection, which had been planted in the 1930s and nurtured and expanded throughout the years.

§

Late that summer, Elaine Bellefontaine arrived in Montreal to take her daughter out for lunch and some shopping. Lilas had given her the impression that she had someone in her life, but Elaine didn't know who. Lilas wanted Bobby to join them for lunch.

"I don't know, mon Coeur. She doesn't know anything about you and me, does she?"

"She will know I love you. Then she will love you, too." Lilas smiled.

Her beautiful smile was Lilas's secret weapon, though she didn't know it. "All right, mon Coeur, just tell me where and when. I'll be there."

B. ROBERT SHARRY

They planned to meet at a Bishop Street restaurant. Elaine arrived first, secured a sidewalk terrace table, ordered a glass of white wine, and waited for her daughter. Happy and relaxed, she looked forward to a pleasant lunch and an afternoon of shopping and girl talk about the goings-on at home and Giselle's college experiences, among other topics.

She sipped her wine and perused the menu. A smile came to her face when she heard, "Bonjour, Moman!"

Elaine rose and hugged her daughter, kissing alternate cheeks. "Ma Pêche, I'm so happy to see you," she said in French. She turned her attention to Lilas's companion. A flash of recognition, then her smile faded.

"Mon Dieu." She dropped down to her seat.

The next thirty minutes were awkward. No one ate much. Bobby guessed that Elaine was silently preparing all the questions she would ask Lilas the moment they were alone together.

He said he couldn't stay longer, and needed to get back to the job site, which was several blocks away. Making his exit with as much grace as possible, he shook Elaine's hand and said how nice it was to see her again.

As soon as Bobby was out of earshot, Elaine turned to Lilas. Flustered and shaking her head, she said, "Mon Dieu, ma Pêche. Your father, he will have a heart attack! What are you thinking?"

IN THE DOORYARD BLOOM'D

"I'm thinking I love him, Moman," Lilas said with a calm smile. She put her hand on her mother's in a comforting gesture.

"But, Lilas, how can you know that so soon?"

"I've always known, Moman."

"Oh, Mon Dieu."

Chapter 36

DETECTIVE LIEUTENANT David Long of the Massachusetts State Police periodically reviewed his open files. There were several unsolved homicides, mostly drug hits, which he doubted would ever be solved. He would evaluate the files, make some notations, and then put them back for another year or so.

Mary Chapman's case was among the perennials. Ten years old now, this case received more attention than others, chiefly because the Chapman family was known socially and politically to the Hampshire County District Attorney.

On the Chapmans' behalf, the DA's office made occasional inquiries into the status of the state police investigation. Long's response was always the same: They had their suspect; they just didn't *have* their suspect. All Long could do was try to shift the focus of the Chapmans' frustration to the lack of cooperation from Canadian law enforcement.

There were few approaches Long could take to the case. He had neither the authority nor the jurisdiction to order a manhunt in Montreal, and there was no way that he could think of to draw Coyle out of hiding. As far as Long knew, Coyle had never contacted family or friends in ten years.

The witness list was short. There were the people who had heard, more than seen, Mary Chapman collide with the pavement, but what more could they add? Only two witnesses had seen Coyle after Mary's death — the student with whom Coyle had hitchhiked and Coyle's professor, Dr. Adam Payne. But there was no new information that either could bring to the investigation. Even so, there existed the possibility that Coyle might contact his old mentor sometime. Who knew? Coyle might suddenly be overcome with remorse and need to talk to someone.

So, in order to document his file, Detective Long would make a periodic call to Payne. He always kept it short; he didn't want to annoy Payne.

Payne was always gracious, telling Long he could call as often as he liked, and that he would call Long if Bobby Coyle ever contacted him.

"Boy, the army is certainly tenacious, aren't they?" said Payne.

"What do you mean?"

"Well, it's just that I continue to get calls similar to yours from Major McTeague. No matter which of you calls, I always get hopeful that there's been some kind of breakthrough. But I guess he just has to do the same thing you do: show that the case hasn't been forgotten. Say, just curious, do you two ever talk?"

"No, not in years."

"Ah, well, everyone's got a job to do, I suppose. Call anytime, Detective. You're never a bother. It's always a pleasure."

"Thanks, Professor."

While Long made his note in the Chapman file detailing his latest conversation with Professor Payne, he noticed another notation he'd made years before, based on something Jack McTeague had brought up. He had written *no fingerprints on the roof/stairway?* and circled it.

He closed the file and returned it to its alphabetical home among the unsolved.

IN THE DOORYARD BLOOM'D

Chapter 37

ALMOST TWO YEARS had elapsed since Bobby and Lilas had reunited. Lilas had just completed her graduate studies at the University of Montreal and would spend the summer interning again at Jardin Botanique.

The couple was together constantly, falling further in love with each passing day. Bobby rose every morning thankful for his life, his work, and, more than anything, his love. He remembered Willy Maze looking at his own reflection in the mirror and thanking God for all of his blessings. *Now I understand how you felt, Willy.*

Bobby began to visit dozens of jewelry stores in the city in search of the perfect engagement ring. On June 1, 1980, he found it in a small jewelry store in Montreal's Westmount section. Bobby stepped inside the bijouterie, and a small bell on the door jingled. The woman behind the counter looked thin and fragile, with grey-streaked hair worn in a bun, and slate-grey eyes. "May I help you find something?"

"I'm looking for an engagement ring."

The old woman's eyes twinkled. "May I make just one suggestion, young man?"

"Of course."

"Don't exclude the old. Some of the most beautiful things in this world are not brand-new. Oh, new can be beautiful, and perhaps that's what you'll fancy, but don't just reject the old out of hand. You might be surprised."

"You mean a used ring?" Bobby asked.

"Perhaps."

"But wouldn't a woman be offended by that?"

"Perhaps. Some girls would, certainly, but others appreciate the beauty of the past." She waved her hand over a display case with a graceful gesture.

Bobby peered into the case from above, pretending to be interested, just so as not to offend the old lady. Then something caught his eye. "What's that?"

"You mean the one with two stones — one diamond, one sapphire?"

"Yes."

"The French call that setting Toi et Moi, *You and Me*," she translated. "A flawless diamond and a beautiful, old, dark blue Burmese sapphire set together forever. These two have been side by side for over one hundred years now."

Sold.

The old woman placed the ring in a square, sterling silver antique ring box lined with black velour.

"Good luck, young man," she called as Bobby left the shop.

With the ring tucked in his front pocket, Bobby headed back to work. He thought ahead now. There were arrangements to make.

IN THE DOORYARD BLOOM'D

Chapter 38

MONDAY, JUNE 9, 1980, marked Lilas's twenty-sixth birthday. They had agreed that Bobby would pick her up from work at Jardin Botanique at 9:00 p.m. Bobby told her he had made special plans for her birthday dinner and had a 9:30 reservation.

"Is it dressy?"

"Very."

"Then I'll bring a dress and shoes with me to work and change there."

"That's a great idea."

People were always nice to Lilas, but today everyone seemed even nicer, because of her birthday, she guessed, although she didn't remember telling anyone about it. And as friendly and smiling as her fellow employees were, she'd noticed a few who whispered and giggled with each other whenever she passed by.

Just before nine o'clock she slipped into the ladies' toilette in the administration building, taking the change of clothes with her. Bobby's special dinner plans had inspired her to splurge on a classic black cocktail dress and matching shoes. She changed quickly, fixed her hair and makeup, applied a small amount of lilac cologne, and turned sideways to look in the mirror.

Satisfied with her appearance, she headed out to meet Bobby at the Pie IX Street gate. She was almost to the front door of the building when a familiar voice called her name.

"Lilas."

B. ROBERT SHARRY

She turned and smiled at Guillaume Lefevre. Guillaume was the horticulturalist in charge of the arboretum, which made him Lilas's boss. The two had become good friends as well as mentor and student. Guillaume knew that Lilas intended to have his job someday, and someday she would, with his blessing.

"Bonsoir, Guillaume. Ça va?"

"Bonsoir, Lilas. Yes, everything is well, but there is something in the Lilac Collection that I'm concerned about. Perhaps you noticed. The new variety that we grafted last week does not look good."

"Oh, no," Lilas said. She'd been by it earlier in the day and hadn't noticed anything, but she didn't doubt Guillaume for a moment. In her experience, he had forgotten more than most specialists learn in a lifetime.

"But you look so beautiful. I hate to ask you…"

"What?"

"No, I can't. I can see that you are ready for a night on the town."

"Perhaps tomorrow, then?" Lilas felt relieved.

"But, of course."

"Bonne soirée," Lilas called as she pulled the front door open.

"And yet…"

Lilas turned back toward him.

"And yet, if you could spare just a moment, I would really like you to take a look at it."

IN THE DOORYARD BLOOM'D

Lilas glanced toward the front door again and then back to Monsieur Lefevre. "Of course, Guillaume—let's go."

"Here, take my arm," Guillaume said. "You have those high heels on, and I would never forgive myself if you fell."

Arm-in-arm they walked together into the blackness that cloaked the Lilac Collection.

Guillaume felt Lilas tense as they entered the darkened copse. "I brought a small flashlight," he said, clicking it on and pointing the beam to the ground just in front of their feet.

The grafted bush that her mentor had described grew at the back of the garden. It would be slow going and take much longer than she'd anticipated. She hoped Bobby wouldn't be worried or upset.

When they reached the middle of the darkened grove, Lilas noticed a flicker of illumination on the periphery. She turned in the direction of the light. What she observed seemed so out of place that it momentarily confused her.

There, nestled among a quartet of lilac bushes, were two Queen Anne chairs and a formally set dining table, complete with white linen cloth extending to the ground, fine china, crystal goblets, and polished silverware. A single red, tapered candle glowed saffron through its hurricane chimney. A bouquet of lilacs—amethyst, white, and pink—huddled in a crystal vase in the center of the table.

Bobby, dressed in a tuxedo, stepped from behind one of the lilac bushes. "I'm glad you could make it."

"Mon Dieu!" Lilas covered her mouth with cupped hands. She looked from Bobby to Guillaume. "You are a naughty boy, Monsieur."

"Forgive me, Lilas." Guillaume kissed her cheek and escorted her to Bobby, then disappeared into the darkness.

Bobby took Lilas's hand, led her to the table, and beckoned her sit.

"Merci," she said.

Presently, two women appeared from the shadows. Lilas recognized them as employees from the Jardin Botanique restaurant, the same two who had been whispering and giggling when she passed them that morning.

"This is all beautiful, mon Coeur, but there is one thing I must ask you."

"Anything, my love."

"How is it possible to get so many French women to keep a secret?"

"It wasn't me," Bobby said. "Word came down from the director that anyone who spoiled the surprise for Lilas would be looking for a new job tomorrow."

"Non!"

"Oui!" Bobby laughed.

"Oui! It's true!" said one of the women as she poured champagne.

Violin and cello music began to play. Lilas searched for the source. She could barely make out the silhouette of the two musicians seated in the background.

The young lovers' dinner began with a pâté de foie gras. Lobster chunks in butter sauce accompanied by a spinach soufflé followed. Between courses, they danced slowly beneath the starlit sky to the string music. Lilas, shoeless now, took pleasure in feeling the cool grass beneath her bare feet.

Midnight brought crème brûlée, Lilas's favorite dessert. The servers and musicians departed, leaving the young lovers alone.

Lilas reached across the table for Bobby's hand. "Ce soir était magique, mon Coeur."

"It's not over yet." He stood and reached into his pocket, pulling out the sterling silver package. Then he walked over to Lilas and placed it before her on the linen tablecloth.

Lilas looked at the filigreed silver box. "Oh, but you've done so much. This is already the best birthday I've ever had. I will remember it forever."

Bobby took her hands in his and planted one knee on the grass. "Lilas Bellefontaine, I know I don't deserve you. I doubt if I truly ever will. But, if you'll have me, I will spend my life trying to be worthy of you." He reached over and opened the silver lid. "Will you marry me, mon Coeur?"

Lilas looked at the ring and back to Bobby. Tears welled in her eyes.

"Oui. Oh, oui."

He kissed her softly, and then placed the ring on her finger.

B. ROBERT SHARRY

Lilas held out her left hand and admired the ring. "Toi et moi, mon Coeur. Toi et moi toujours." *You and me forever.*

Chapter 39

JUST AS HER MOTHER had, Shayna Payne attended a Jewish day school with grades K through eight.

If Judy Payne thought she might get an argument from her husband, a product of the public school system, she was mistaken. In fact, Adam had been insistent that his daughter not attend public schools. At Shayna's dance and piano recitals, Judy would lean back in her seat and glance at Adam, his face beaming with love and pride. Afterward, Adam would lavish hugs and kisses on Shayna and allow her to choose a restaurant for celebration. It was after these joyous family events that Judy was most likely to have some intimacy with Adam.

§

Adam had become dean of the College of Humanities and Fine Arts at the university. He'd also managed to add another station to his burgeoning radio empire. As he had predicted, in time he was able to draw quite a large salary as president of the nonprofit.

By 1982 he had discovered a new sexual smorgasbord. He joined a local health club for the exercise, but soon discovered that if he worked out in the late morning, he would be surrounded by bored, oversexed-but-underserved housewives of local professionals. After depositing their children at school or day care, the unfulfilled hausfraus looked for ways to relieve the monotony of their privileged lives.

Shopping would allay the tedium for just so long. What they really needed, Payne determined, was to Fuck Till They Dropped.

He never felt sorry for the cuckolded. At Rotary Club luncheons, Adam would pretend to listen attentively while an acquaintance droned on about something or other. He'd smile, look him straight in the eye, and think: *I just had your wife yesterday. I may well have her tomorrow, too.*

For all of his dalliances, Adam never gave a second thought to anybody else screwing his own wife. Judy wasn't the type. She was too cerebral, too plain, too *Judy.*

Chapter 40

GIL BELLEFONTAINE ROARED. "No! I will not have that Rosbif for a son-in-law."

Guiltily, Elaine had concealed what she knew of Lilas and Bobby's relationship. Even after Lilas had thrust her engagement ring before her mother's eyes, Elaine held out hope that the affair would run its course and save her the strife of informing her husband. But when Lilas began planning the wedding for June of 1982, Elaine knew the talk with Gil could be delayed no longer.

Lilas had told her mother everything she knew about Bobby, except the part about Mary Chapman.

"We don't know anything about him," Gil said, while pacing the kitchen like a caged wildcat.

"We know she loves him." Elaine sat at the kitchen table and followed Gil with her eyes.

"Love? What does she know of love? She is just a girl."

"Just a girl who is older than I was when we married."

"Bah. You knew me. We knew each other all our lives. Our parents knew each other. How do we know he's not just using her?"

"For what?"

"So that he can stay in Canada."

"Gil, she is an adult. There is nothing we can do to stop her, so we must love her and help her."

"Maybe a call to Immigration would help her."

"If you do that, she will find out. She will be hurt, she will never trust you again, and she will never forgive you. Is that what you want?"

After an hour of back-and-forth, Gil sighed in resignation. "Do what you want; I don't care. But don't come crying to me when he hurts her."

Round one went to Elaine. This was not the time to discuss Lilas's desire to have the ceremony at the farm, or the type of tuxedo that Gil would wear when he gave his daughter away. She anticipated many more rounds in this contest and needed to conserve her strength. During the next several weeks, Elaine alternated her time between planning the wedding with Lilas and patiently leading her husband to acceptance.

§

The wedding was a simple and charming affair, just as Lilas had always dreamed. With Willy Maze by his side, Bobby stood to the right of the outdoor, makeshift altar and marveled as Lilas walked the grass aisle on the arm of her father. She was radiant in a simple V-neck white satin gown. Through the veil, Bobby could see the pearl necklace that had been a wedding present from Gil to Elaine. Glancing across the aisle, he saw Giselle, maid of honor to her sister, trying to blot the tears that would spoil her makeup.

He looked again at Lilas. *You are so beautiful. You are perfection. I'll never understand why you chose me, but I'll do my best to make you happy, to be the man you deserve.* Then he thought of his parents. *I wish you were here. I know you would love her as much as I do.*

IN THE DOORYARD BLOOM'D

How could you not? Look at her! Then he thought of Adam Payne. *I should hate you, and I do. But if they found me now, convicted me, and threw me in jail for the rest of my life, it would be worth it for the time I've had with Lilas.*

Bobby felt Willy's large hand on his shoulder. He turned to see the big, black man wearing a broad smile. "Thanks for standing up for me, Willy."

"I love you, man," Willy whispered. "I'm just so happy for you both. You deserve this, Bobby."

When the time came, Gil Bellefontaine grudgingly delivered his precious daughter to Bobby Coyle.

After the ceremony, guests milled about or sat at long tables near the farmhouse. Gil interrupted a group in conversation. "Will you give an old man a moment with his new son?" Gil smiled as he led Bobby away by the arm. When they had reached some distance from the others, Gil tightened his grip on Bobby's bicep, causing him to wince.

"If you ever hurt her, Rosbif…" Gil said, his brown eyes boring into Bobby's blue ones.

Bobby trembled. "Oui, Monsieur."

Gil walked away and rejoined the guests. Moments later he laughed and toasted the circle of guests with a bottle of Labatt beer. He looked back to where Bobby still stood. The middle-aged farmer flashed an icy smile and raised his beer, as if to toast, in Bobby's direction.

Bobby Coyle gulped.

Chapter 41

GENE COYLE'S INSURANCE business declined over the years. At first, he attributed the loss of business to Bobby's crimes. Although cancellations after the incident were few, many clients took their business elsewhere when the policies came due for renewal.

But that was years ago. What caused the business to shrink further was Gene's reluctance to seek new customers out as he once had.

Dan Lewis noticed that Mickey showed more resilience. She had gone to work as a teacher in the regional school system. Although not the Mickey of old, she didn't seem as broken as Gene. When Dan commented on this to Miriam, she said, "That's because she's a woman. Women have always been stronger emotionally. We grieve over things, pick ourselves up, and move on. You want a man around when the house is on fire, but you want a woman there when the fire's out and it's time to rebuild."

Dan smiled. "How come you didn't tell me before we married that you were stronger and smarter than I? You could have saved me years of humiliation."

"Because if I'd told you then, you wouldn't have believed it. You're only now coming out of denial," Miriam said, giving Dan a peck on the cheek.

Dan's smile faded. "I don't know what to do, Miriam. I'm sitting here, watching my friend waste away, and I don't know how to help him."

"Just be there for him, like he's been there for you. That's all you can do."

§

Dan was more determined than ever to help his old friend. He called Jack McTeague.

"What's shakin', counselor?" Jack asked when he recognized Dan's voice.

"Not much, Jack. I wanted to talk to you about Bobby Coyle."

"That was over ten years ago, wasn't it?"

"Closer to eleven now."

"Is there a new development?"

"I was hoping you might be able to tell me."

"Nothing that I know of. Sometimes you just gotta let it go, Dan."

"I know, but sometimes it's your best friend's kid."

"I hear ya."

"Can you think of anything that could resolve this, even if it's not in our favor?" Dan asked.

"Not really. If Bobby's dead and his body hasn't shown up by now, it ain't never gonna happen. If he's alive and doesn't want to be found…"

Dan sighed. "It's just so sad. I've known Bobby from the time he could walk. I just can't see him killing anyone, much less the mother of his baby."

"Was it ever conclusively established that Bobby was the father?"

McTeague's question hung in the air for a moment. Dan had never considered otherwise.

"You have reason to believe he wasn't?"

"Nope. Hey, I'm a detective. I'm just wondering if, at the time, there were any blood samples from Bobby available for HLA testing."

"I can't see how."

"That's what I figured. Too bad. There's something newer now and supposedly more accurate. It's called an RFLP DNA test. Don't ask me what that means, but it still requires a blood sample, so…"

"Well, I don't see that happening. Hey, if you get out this way and have time for lunch…"

"Thanks, but I like to stay in Massachusetts, mostly."

"What's that supposed to mean?"

"Hey, everybody knows our western border stops at Worcester." Jack laughed at his own joke.

"Some detective you are."

"Soon-to-be-retired detective."

"Retired? You dog! I'm envious."

"Hey, you should have stayed on the public payroll. Actually, I'm speaking a little prematurely. I've still got a couple more years. Seriously, though, if I do take a trip before I retire, I might just check out Montreal. Never been there. Hear good things about it, though. Maybe catch an Expos game. Hell, I'd up the bleachers crowd by fifty percent, just me alone."

"You'd do that?" asked Dan.

"Naw, probably be more like twenty percent."

"You know what I mean. You think you could find him?"

"Hey, I'm a detective. You never know. I'll need everything you've got, especially the most recent pictures. You got time for lunch next week?"

"For you, I'll make time."

Chapter 42

MADAME AND MONSIEUR Philip Nolan honeymooned on the island Republic of Cuba. With daily temperatures in the mid-eighties and nights cooler by ten degrees, they romped in the surf of Cojimar Beach by day, and took leisurely walks around Old Havana in the evenings.

Bobby and Lilas took many of their dinners at their hotel, but they did dine out a few times—twice at a romantic garden paladar where the traditional Cuban dish of ropa vieja was highly recommended, once at the famous La Bodeguita del Medio near Cathedral Square, and once at the infamous Club Tropicana, where the food paled in comparison to the scantily clad dancers.

The Tropicana show was spectacular. The newlyweds sat at a long table with Europeans and Canadians, watching as the showgirls cascaded into the audience and dragged men at random onto the dance floor. One of them targeted Bobby, gave a sultry smile, and beckoned him with her index finger. He looked to Lilas for permission. She kissed him and pushed him up from his seat as the showgirl took him by the hand.

"Just don't go falling in love with her. I've heard about these Latin women and the spells they cast on men," Lilas called after him.

"You've already done that to me. She doesn't stand a chance."

Lilas applauded and laughed as Bobby clumsily followed the showgirl's lead on the dance floor.

IN THE DOORYARD BLOOM'D

Once he got the hang of Mambo, though, he was quite good. After his lesson, Bobby took Lilas by the hand and led her to the dance floor.

The tropical night air and the Latin music beats just wouldn't allow them to sit. They moved together well. Giddy from rum, they danced and laughed for hours. It was after three in the morning when they returned to their hotel room. They stood on their balcony and gazed at a star-filled sky.

"Are you happy, Madame?"

"How could I not be?" she whispered as she kissed him. "And you, Monsieur—are you as happy as I am?"

"I didn't realize it was possible to be this happy. My heart is so full, I'm afraid it might burst. You saved my life, you know."

Lilas gazed questioningly.

Bobby groped for the right words. "Before you, I didn't have a life, just an existence. I was just going through the motions from one awful day to the next. Since you came back to me, I'm living. I hear the birds now; I smell the flowers; I see the sunrises and sunsets—the simplest of things. But most of all, I see you. You are the most beautiful thing in the world, and I love you so much I can barely stand it. I will love you forever."

Lilas took his hands in hers. "I will love you always, mon Coeur. Those terrible days are in the past now and will never return."

The young couple kissed passionately, slowly undressing each other by tropical moonlight. He knelt before his naked bride, wrapped his arms

B. ROBERT SHARRY

round her waist, and tenderly kissed her breasts. His fingertips lightly traced the hourglass of soft flesh from her ribs, to her waist, and down to her hips. Divining fingers dowsing through the heat of inner thighs found liquid warmth, and his touch made Lilas moan softly.

He rose, gazed into her moonlit eyes, kissed her, and carried her to bed.

They made love until the sun rose, and then fell asleep in each other's arms.

IN THE DOORYARD BLOOM'D

Chapter 43

IN 1985 SHAYNA PAYNE became a bat mitzvah. The ceremony was held at a temple that Adam Payne had visited only once before. Adam looked on with pride as his daughter recited the haphtarah. When Judy wept, Adam poked at her playfully, mocking her tears while holding back his own. He hadn't cried since sixth grade and wasn't about to start now.

The Paynes celebrated at the Lord Jeffery Inn. The festive party soon developed its own personality, one of fun and letting loose. The banquet room reverberated with laughter, music, and dancing.

Judy, as ever, bathed in the overflow of Payne's affection for Shayna. He danced with Judy, joked with her, smiled at her. Like a cactus flower that must live with a paucity of rain, Judy soaked up every drop of contentment she could, while she could, and made it last.

§

Harry and Ruth Rosen were in their seventies now, but as active and loving as ever. Harry had retired from the law firm the previous year. He had all but decided to retire from the university board of trustees until Adam convinced him to stay on.

Adam surveyed the sea of guests. His eyes settled on Sally Barker, his chief on-air radio personality. She sat next to her new husband, but smiled seductively at Adam. He had tired of sex with her but didn't expect she would cause him any trouble. Incredibly ambitious, she still needed him to further her career.

Seeing Sally made Adam think of his network. He had just negotiated the addition of another radio station to the constellation surrounding WRTH: *Earth* Radio, as he had redubbed the station. But the political landscape had changed; a Republican president sat in Washington, and more frequent rumblings about cutting government funding for public broadcasting were heard. Republicans didn't like what they saw as the left-leaning tendencies of NPR and were loath to spend money to support the enemy. To offset the decrease in government funding, Payne calculated that the station would need to maintain a constituency of liberal groups who would increase donations and underwriting income.

A young intern had joined the station. Emily was Asian and exotic. Her silky hair and almond-shaped eyes were black as coal, and her skin tawny. She was petite, with small breasts and a tiny ass.

Adam imagined himself screwing her standing up. She would be perched on his cock with her legs wrapped around his waist. She was small enough that he could cup her ass in his hands and slide her whole, tight little body up and down his length.

Something interrupted Adam's fantasy. Judy had taken his hand in hers. He looked down at their joined hands in his lap, and then to his wife's face. Judy beamed at him with an expression that Adam concluded was adoration.

IN THE DOORYARD BLOOM'D

Chapter 44

WITHIN A YEAR OF marrying, Bobby and Lilas had purchased a run-down stone row house near Marché Jean-Talon in the Petite-Italie neighborhood of Montreal. Willy and Justine, accompanied by their newborn daughter, Roberta, helped them move in.

With Lilas working full-time now at the Jardin Botanique, Bobby began the renovation and restoration of the house. He completed one room at a time, sealing each room off from the rest of the house with large sheets of plastic to reduce the migration of construction dust to other rooms.

It took almost a full year to complete, but the transformation was startling. Bobby had made their home look new while preserving antique details that gave the house its charm.

The tiny backyard became a beautiful terrace, lush with perennials, thanks to the skill and imagination of its resident horticulturist. Lilas combined natural beauty with comfort to create an inviting outdoor room where she and Bobby had candlelit dinners, or just sipped wine and relaxed.

Two rescued kittens named Toi and Moi provided hours of entertainment with their *chantics,* as Bobby called them.

The Mazes were frequent guests. Willy, now chef de cuisine at the restaurant, often prepared five-star meals for them. Conversation flowed easily among the two couples. Inevitably, though, Bobby would talk of the United States. Like his assumed namesake, Philip Nolan, he took interest in everything American.

Lilas noticed that Bobby became more emotional at the beginning of July. Fête du Canada, or Canada Day, is the national holiday celebrating the establishment of Canada with its new constitution on July 1, 1867. Quebecers also celebrate Moving Day on the same date. In order to prevent landlords from evicting their tenants during harsh winter months, most leases expire on July 1.

This annual celebration would remind Bobby that the American Independence Day was just around the corner.

Determined to do something special to lift Bobby's spirits, Lilas planned a surprise Fourth of July party. She invited a large crowd of family and friends, including her coworkers from the Botanical Garden and Bobby's from Jacques Fournier's construction company. She enlisted Willy as technical adviser and menu coordinator, telling him that she wanted to host an authentic American Fourth of July celebration. Everyone was sworn to secrecy.

The Fourth fell on a workday for Bobby. Lilas, Willy, and Justine spent the entire day decorating the backyard terrace and preparing food.

Without explanation, Jacques Fournier ordered Bobby to work two hours overtime at the job site. Bobby didn't see the sense of it, especially since no one else had been told to stay. But Jacques had been so stern when he gave the order that Bobby thought it best not to question The Bear.

IN THE DOORYARD BLOOM'D

It was after seven that hot evening when he trudged through the front door. "Bonjour, mon Coeur," he called as he walked the hallway toward the kitchen. "Sorry I'm late. Don't ask me why, but Jacques had me stay and work some overtime while everyone else got to go home."

Lilas appeared in the kitchen doorway. "My poor baby. That Jacques Fournier is very mean. I will have a talk with him, mon Coeur."

"Please, don't."

Lilas smiled and kissed him. "I know what you need: a tall beer and a good dinner."

"That sounds wonderful."

"I have cold beer waiting on the terrace." Lilas took him by the hand and led him toward the back of the house.

"I knew there was a reason I love you so much."

They stepped out the back kitchen door and started down the steps leading to the backyard. Bobby halted in amazement at the sea of familiar faces before him. The entire wooden fence surrounding the yard was draped in red, white, and blue bunting. Dozens of small American flags festooned the entire yard.

Willy manned the grill. The smell of hot dogs and hamburgers cooking filled the air. Long folding tables covered with red, white, and blue tablecloths dotted the backyard. Each guest held a drink in one hand and a piece of paper in the other. When Bobby's eyes landed on Jacques Fournier, The Bear flashed an enormous grin.

Then the music Bobby knew so well started to play. The opening bars of "The Star-Spangled Banner" cued the guests to refer to the papers they held. Every one of the guests began to sing, with the exception of Gil Bellefontaine, who looked annoyed.

"Oh, zay can you zee by zhe dawn's early light..."

By the time they finished the traditional first stanza in their beautiful French accents, Bobby's eyes had welled with tears. He tried to join the chorus, but could choke out just a few lines.

When the music stopped, Bobby looked for Willy and saw that his old friend's eyes streamed tears. Seeing the two men's reaction, the crowd fell silent, unsure of what to do. Lilas wondered if throwing the party had been a mistake. She had wanted only to make him happy.

Then Bobby smiled, cleared his throat and began to sing. *"O Canada!"*

A collective whoop sprung from the crowd. Then they joined him in song. *"Terre de nos aïeux, Ton front est ceint de fleurons glorieux..."*

As the French version of the Canadian anthem ended, someone lit a string of firecrackers, and an enormous cheer rose.

Chapter 45

THREE MONTHS AFTER the Fourth of July party, Bobby and Lilas sat by the stone fireplace on the candlelit terrace, holding hands and sipping wine. Bobby watched in amusement as Toi and Moi bounded around the terrace on the trail of a fluttering moth. Lilas studied his face lovingly while she traced his forearm with her fingertips. Then she leaned in close. "Mon Coeur, our little family is about to get larger."

Bobby continued to follow the cats' movements. "Oh, Lilas, I love the cats, but don't you think two are enough?"

"I'm not talking about a kitten, my love."

"What, then, a dog? A bird? What now?" Bobby asked. When Lilas didn't respond, he turned to face her.

Lilas was beaming. When the moment of realization came, Bobby tilted his head to one side.

"No...," he said.

Lilas's smile broadened. She raised her eyebrows and nodded her head quickly.

"Oh, mon Coeur, un bébé?"

"Oui."

Bobby slid from his chair and knelt beside his wife, embracing and kissing her.

"How far along?"

"Ten weeks."

"So..."

"April 15."

Bobby frowned. "That doesn't give me much time."

"Time for what?"

"Time to build the most beautiful nursery any baby has ever had." He kissed his wife tenderly and whispered, "I love you so much."

Chapter 46

JACK MCTEAGUE MADE his first trip to Montreal. The local police had no interest in helping him find Bobby Coyle. They treated him with disdain, dismissing him with a reminder that he was a guest in a foreign country and had no police powers in Canada. When he tried to snoop around on his own among the American expatriate community, he met a similar wall of hindrance and suspicion.

He had made the rounds of several known hangouts for Americans and shown Bobby Coyle's high school graduation picture, but all he got was a cold shoulder and an occasional obscene gesture thrown his way.

But one woman, a waitress at a coffeehouse called the Yellow Door, conveyed something with her eyes. Jack detected a flash of recognition when she saw Bobby's photo.

Her forceful "Fuck off, pig!" drew the attention of all the other patrons and staff, who turned and glared at McTeague.

"Everything okay, Linda?" a big guy called while keeping an eye on Jack.

Jack threw up his hands and said, "Okay, okay. I'm going. I'm not looking for trouble."

He walked down to Rue Sherbrooke and stopped at the sidewalk terrace of one of the big chain hotels. Taking a seat at a table covered by a Cinzano umbrella, he ordered black coffee, lit a Marlboro, and thought about what he'd learned.

Once he'd rested awhile, Jack hit the pavement again. After running into a few more dead ends, he got discouraged and drove back to Boston.

He hated to disappoint Dan Lewis. Ever since they'd reconnected over the Coyle case, he remembered how much he'd liked and respected Lewis in the old days. Lewis had been a tough prosecutor, but always fair and honest.

Much as he hated letting Dan Lewis down, though, he was mad at himself for failing. His gut had told him from the start that some things about this case didn't add up. Unless he found Bobby Coyle, he'd never be able to prove it.

Chapter 47

ADAM PAYNE HAD SET his sights on becoming the provost and senior vice chancellor of the university. It would mean ruffling the feathers of a few superiors, but he'd been positioning himself socially and politically since the day he'd become a dean. And now he had a winning combination: He controlled the most popular radio outlet in the market and had forged alliances with the local daily newspapers and a network TV affiliate. He had the power of the press. And, of course, he had Harry Rosen.

There would be grumbling about favoritism and nepotism, but only in hushed tones. Anyone who dared to cross Payne did so at his own peril. He was just too powerful now. Even the current chancellor, a seasoned politician who had wangled the chancellorship as his own golden-parachute retirement from the statehouse, treated Payne with deference. Taking Payne under his wing, the chancellor had confided to his wife, "Keep your friends close and your enemies closer." Although he knew Payne would eventually have his job, he wanted to hang on a few more years to increase his pension.

The worst part for the chancellor wasn't the secret humiliation he felt knowing that Payne was more powerful than he. The worst part was knowing that Payne knew, and the feeling that Payne held him in contempt and was just tolerating him, temporarily, out of necessity.

B. ROBERT SHARRY

WRTH *Earth* Radio continued to expand. The addition of each new station to the network increased Payne's power and arrogance. Even Ed Stein, who fancied himself Payne's close confidante, could find himself on the receiving end of the boss's wrath. They were in Payne's office at WRTH. Payne sat at his desk and perused reports, while Ed stood on the other side of the desk, trying to make his case for an investigative report the station was producing on local pollution. Stein was frustrated by Payne's insistence that they not be critical of a local manufacturer who was one of the worst offenders, but also a major WRTH underwriter.

"Whatever happened to *taking on the Establishment*? You know, *fighting the good fight*?" Ed pleaded.

Payne peered over reading glasses at Stein and sneered. "We *are* the Establishment now, you moron."

Ed's eyes registered shock, and then sought the floor. Payne backpedaled. "Look, what I mean is, we have an obligation to present both sides of the story, and that includes the manufacturer's side, and the fact that a lot of people depend on the company for their livelihoods.

"If you must rake someone over the coals to keep the tree-huggers happy, choose a company that's not an underwriter. It's easy for these fucking trust-fund dilettantes to run their mouths off for the cause du jour. They already *have* their money, passed down to them from one robber baron or another. Now they want the little guy to suffer so they can assuage their guilt."

The hurt look disappeared from Stein's face. "We have only one environment, Adam — one earth. We need to take care of it. You've said so yourself."

"On the *radio*," Payne said dismissively.

"But…"

"Oh, please, Ed. If Rachel Carson were alive and living in my neighborhood, she'd need fucking earplugs. No matter how much is done, it will never be enough for those wackos." Payne returned to his paperwork, a signal that the conversation was over. He was preparing for a public media conference he would attend in Washington, D.C., in a few days.

§

Stein turned to leave with shoulders drooping. He was probably the one person who understood the dichotomy that was Adam Payne: the teacher who hated students, the dean who hated teachers, the feminist who hated women, the broadcaster who hated his audience, the Democrat who hated liberals, the humanist who hated people. Payne was an equal-opportunity disdainer. As far as Ed Stein could tell, the only other human Payne *didn't* detest was his daughter, Shayna.

§

When Stein opened the door to leave the office, Payne's secretary, Emily, stuck her head in and quietly announced, "Your three o'clock is waiting." Payne looked at her quizzically.

"Two gentlemen from the Mount Plain Savings Bank."

"Oh, right. Make them wait another ten minutes, then show them in."

Payne remembered that someone had called the station a few weeks prior to summon him to the bank president's office the following day to discuss advertising. When his director of corporate underwriting had relayed the request, Payne had scoffed, "Fuck 'em. If some tight-ass bank president wants to see me, let him come to me at my convenience."

Payne knew exactly what type of man this bank president would be; a grownup version of one of Payne's childhood tormenters.

§

His secretary closed his office door without a sound. Payne went back to his paperwork, but his thoughts soon turned to Ed Stein. He regretted snapping at him—a tactical error. He resolved to make it up to him.

One thought led to another, and Adam remembered how they'd first met: a faculty get-together when they were both newly appointed associate professors. Stein had been incredibly nervous, while Adam remained characteristically calm and collected. Adam had talked Ed down from his near panic. After that, the two met for lunch often at the faculty lounge, discussing all manner of things.

Payne remembered a particular incident that brought a crooked smile to his face. Payne's first lecture of the semester had been titled "Founding Fathers: Heroes of the Revolution or Racist Pigs?"

IN THE DOORYARD BLOOM'D

His students had sat in awe of the hip young professor who challenged the Establishment propaganda. Payne studied their adoring faces and chuckled to himself.

Later, in the faculty lounge, he joked about it with Stein.

"You should have seen their faces, Ed. They're so impressionable. These kids are like pretzel dough that I can twist into any shape I want."

"They're young adults, Adam. They're searching to find their identities."

"Don't kid yourself, Ed. They think they're adults, but they're just children in bigger clothes. Some of them are so dense that it makes me wonder how they ever got into college in the first place."

"I don't think you give them enough credit."

"I think you give them too much credit, Eddy-boy. I'm telling you, I can get these kids to think or do anything I want them to."

Payne and Stein left the lounge and walked across campus through bright sunshine and crisp autumn air. Payne saw an opportunity to make his point. Annie Boucher was one of his fawning sprites, but a homely one. The rhythmic swish of chunky, corduroyed thighs heralded her approach.

"Watch this," Adam murmured from the corner of his mouth.

"Hi, Dr. Payne," Annie gushed.

"Well, hi there. Annie, isn't it?" Payne smelled bubblegum.

"Yes!"

She's flattered that I remembered her name. "Annie, this is Professor Stein."

"How do you do, Annie?" said Stein.

"Fine, thank you." Annie didn't even glance at Stein. Adam held her attention with a hypnotic gaze.

"So, Annie, have you decided on a major yet?" asked Payne.

"Well, I'd like a career in environmental science. Ever since I read *Silent Spring*, I've wanted to do something about all the pollution."

You and about a million others. "Good for you," said Payne in a tone one might use with a toddler. "Thank God, someone will save the Earth."

Annie Boucher blushed. As her cheeks flushed, the expression on Payne's face turned serious. "You're probably as upset as I am about the new sidewalk they're putting in on the other side of campus."

"New sidewalk?"

"They just don't get it, Annie. They don't care that every shovelful of dirt they disturb contains insects, worms, and millions of tiny organisms that are just as alive as you or I. And for what? So we don't have to get our shoes a little muddy? And they won't care until somebody has the guts to stand up to them and protest.

"Oh, there're plenty of people to speak for whales and gorillas, but who will speak for the weakest and smallest? They may not be the cutest, but they have just as much right to live as the rest of us."

Payne paused for a few beats. "Well, nice to talk to you, Annie. See you in class."

As they walked away, Stein murmured, "You can't really think she's that stupid."

"We'll see," said Payne.

The following week, Payne sauntered into Stein's office sporting a smug grin. He dropped the latest edition of the *Daily Collegian* on Stein's desk. A photo's caption read *Students Protest Sidewalk Construction*. The photo showed three student protestors at the sidewalk site. They lay on their backs with their bodies stretched across the intended path. Annie Boucher, wearing a bandana and granny glasses, held a megaphone to her mouth.

"I don't believe it," Stein said. "It seems I owe you an apology, Professor *Higgins*."

"I'm just an *ordinary* man," Payne had replied, doing a flawless impersonation of Rex Harrison.

§

Emily knocked softly on his door before entering with the two bankers in tow. "Dr. Payne, this is Mr. Schmidt, president of the Mount Plain Savings Bank, and Mr. Warren, vice president of marketing at the bank."

Karl Schmidt smiled insincerely, stuck out his hand, and said, "Mr. Payne, it's a pleasure to meet you in person. I've heard you so many times on the radio; it's nice to finally put a face with the voice."

"Nice to meet you, and it's *Dr.* Payne."

The bank president looked uncomfortably to his vice president and then back to Payne. "Of course, *Dr.* Payne."

Payne motioned with his hand and said, "Have a seat, gentlemen. What can I do for you?"

"Well, actually, I think it's what we can do for you. You see, at Mount Plain Savings we've always been civic-minded and supported local nonprofits. We'd like to discuss supporting yours."

You've discovered that our audience is enormous and that you're missing the boat by not advertising with us. I bet you want to "support" us during the prime drive-times.

"Yes, well, that's marvelous. We always welcome new members to the Earth Radio family. Do you have a check for me?"

Vice President Warren cleared his throat. "Well, actually, we thought of supporting you through our advertising budget."

"Oh, I see. There's just one problem: we don't accept advertising. You see, as public radio, we're not allowed to." Payne had dealt with these kinds of egotistic assholes his whole life, and he rather enjoyed watching them squirm. He didn't need them; they needed him.

"I believe they call it 'underwriting,'" the young banker explained to President Schmidt.

"Well, whatever they call it, we want the best drive-time spots," Schmidt said as he rose from his seat. "I'll leave my man here with you to work out the details."

Payne smiled and said, "Unfortunately, those spots are spoken for... by your competition, if I'm not mistaken."

With a tinge of anger, Schmidt said, "Perhaps we could make a larger donation."

Payne pulled an exorbitant figure out of the air and quoted it.

"But that's more than twice the going rate for advertising!" said Warren.

Payne was enjoying this. "That may be. I have no idea. We don't accept advertising."

"Wait outside," Schmidt said curtly to his vice president.

As soon as Warren was out of the office, Schmidt said, "Who do you think you're talking to? Do you know who I am?"

"An arrogant, WASP piece of shit?" asked Payne.

"You think you're hot stuff, don't you, *Doctor*? Just remember: at the end of the day, you're still just a Jew—another smug, money-grubbing Jew. Have a nice day, Hymie. Excuse me... I mean *Dr*. Hymie."

Schmidt watched Payne's face turn progressively darker shades of scarlet, and then scurried through the office door. Payne grabbed one of the radio awards trophies from his desk and launched it at the closing door.

§

Several days later, two underlings traveled with Payne to the public media conference in D.C.: Sally Barker and the newly appointed Berkshires correspondent, Tina Malinowski.

Tina was new to broadcasting. When Adam met her, she was the Berkshires stringer for one of the Western Massachusetts dailies. Their flirting began instantly. She had majored in journalism, but had gotten married to her college sweetheart right after graduation and started popping out offspring. She was thirty now, and, for the first time, all three kids were in school full-time.

Sally was miffed at Payne. Not only was his interest in her waning, but he was showering flattery and attention on Tina, who was younger than her by ten years. She was in no position to complain, however. Everyone knew the power Adam had. She'd just have to accept the situation for what it was.

Adam had instructed his secretary, Emily, to book rooms at the Mayflower Hotel — a Jacuzzi suite for him, and a double for Sally and Tina to share. Emily also arranged for a limo to pick them up at Washington National Airport at 11:00 a.m. and take them to the hotel. After they checked in, the trio agreed to spend the afternoon resting and meet for cocktails in the hotel bar at six.

"Oh, let's dress up tonight. I have a killer new cocktail dress I've been dying to wear," Tina said, batting her eyes at Payne.

Payne shrugged. "Okay with you, Sal?"

"Sure." Sally forced a smile. "Sounds like fun."

"It's settled, then," said Payne. "We'll all dress up like adults. They have a fantastic restaurant here in the hotel. I'll make a dinner reservation and meet you girls in the bar at six."

IN THE DOORYARD BLOOM'D

After a nap, followed by a long, hot shower, Payne dressed for the evening and called home before heading out. Judy answered the phone with a cheery voice. "I've been waiting for your call. I'm glad you arrived safe and sound. How's your room?"

Payne glanced around at the sitting area, the wet bar, and the pink marble Jacuzzi. "It's okay, for a hotel room."

He talked to his wife for the minimum time he considered necessary, then said, "Put Shayna on."

"She's right here. I love you and miss you, Adam."

"Me, too," said Payne.

His demeanor changed as soon as he heard his daughter's voice. They spoke for several minutes, laughing often. Shayna finally signed off, explaining she had "tons of homework."

"Your old dad can take a hint. You have sweet dreams tonight, Princess. I love you."

"I love you too, Daddy. You wanna talk to Mom again?"

"No, that's okay. Just tell her I'll call again tomorrow night."

When Payne arrived at the cocktail lounge, he chose a low table with four comfortable chairs on rollers. He ordered a single malt scotch on the rocks and lit a cigarette. And then he waited. At 6:30, the waiter placed his second cocktail before him. His irritation at being kept waiting turned to mild amusement when Sally and Tina sashayed into the bar. He leaned toward the waiter and muttered, "Is the hotel holding some kind of sluttiest-dressed contest?"

He smiled amiably and rose to greet his employees. He kissed each on the cheek, taking in her scent. Alcohol flowed freely for the next hour and a half. Though both women were flirtatious, Tina mostly gawked adoringly at Adam, while Sally peppered her conversation with double entendres.

The banter continued through dinner and two bottles of champagne.

§

Sally had decided that if she couldn't stop Adam Payne from having Tina, she could at least keep herself in the picture. Tonight, she would engineer a threesome, and Adam, she hoped, would be grateful.

IN THE DOORYARD BLOOM'D

Chapter 48

ON APRIL 10, 1985, Gil and Elaine Bellefontaine and daughter Giselle sat with Bobby in the hospital waiting room, along with Willy and Justine Maze.

Elaine and Giselle had greeted Bobby with hugs and kisses. Gil had grunted out his usual taunt, "Bonjour, Rosbif," and then grabbed the first magazine he saw and sat down.

No matter what the occasion, Bobby's attempts to make conversation with his father-in-law either went unanswered or were met with a curt response that usually included the word *Rosbif.* Lilas had once explained the slur to him. There were two schools of thought: Some attributed the moniker to the English propensity for eating roast beef, while others thought it referred to the similarity of an Englishman's complexion to the pink interior of a rare-done roast. Everyone, however, agreed that *Rosbif* was meant to offend.

Elaine tried her best to facilitate conversation between the two, but it wasn't working. Bobby was willing; Gil was not.

§

Gil regretted finding Bobby all those years ago. If he hadn't, his daughter would have married a local farm boy. Gil would have built a house for the young couple on Bellefontaine land. His French son-in-law would be working alongside Gil in the orchards and would love Lilas the way she deserved to be loved. He would never hurt her, and would never let the land leave the family. Lilas and her farm prince would produce many loving grandchildren for Mémé and Pépé Bellefontaine to spoil.

§

Elaine gave up. She turned her attention to Giselle, discussing how they would help Lilas once the baby arrived.

When Lilas's doctor entered the waiting room, Elaine spotted the grave look on his face. She stood up quickly. "What is it?" she demanded.

The doctor faced Bobby. "We have complications."

Again, it was Elaine who spoke. "What complications? Tell us."

The doctor took a deep breath. "It's what we call an amniotic fluid embolism. It means that some amniotic fluid has entered Lilas's bloodstream and settled in her lungs. I won't minimize it: this is very dangerous for Lilas. Her heartbeat is erratic, and there is a risk of cardiac arrest." The doctor didn't tell them that the survival rate was only sixty percent.

"I don't understand," said Bobby. "We did everything we were supposed to do."

The doctor spoke with compassion. "It's nothing you did or didn't do. Sometimes these things just happen. We will do an abdominal delivery. Then, as soon as we have delivered the baby, we'll transfer Lilas to the intensive care unit. I'll come back as soon as I have something more to tell you."

"Doctor," Gil called, stopping him just as he reached the halfway point through the heavy swinging doors. Staring at Bobby as he addressed the physician, Gil said, "Make sure my daughter has the best of everything, whether it's covered or not. It will be taken care of. Do you understand?"

Not everything was covered under Canada's national healthcare system. The doctor understood that Gil would pay privately for whatever his daughter needed.

"Mais oui, Monsieur," the doctor replied. Then he disappeared into the long hallway as the doors swung closed behind him.

Gil shot a look to Bobby as he brushed past him and spoke softly enough that Elaine wouldn't hear him. "That's what you should have said to the doctor, *Rosbif*."

Bobby ignored the jab, and the family settled into waiting. When he could sit still no longer, Bobby stood up and began to pace.

The doctor reappeared after an hour and a half. "You have a beautiful baby girl," he said to Bobby.

Bobby sighed with relief. "My wife? What about Lilas?"

"We won't know for a while. She's in intensive care." He turned to Gil. "We're doing everything we can to stabilize her condition, but, until then, we just won't know. Our main concern right now is bleeding. This condition carries with it a reduced ability for her blood to clot. She may be anemic. I assume there is no objection to transfusion?"

"Doctor! Lilas and I are the same blood type," said Elaine. "I can give blood for her!"

B. ROBERT SHARRY

"Thank you, Madame. We are in good supply at the moment, but I shall certainly call on you if need be."

"Thank you, Doctor. We will be here for as long as it takes. Only, please, keep us informed," Elaine pleaded.

"Of course, Madame." The long hallway again swallowed the physician.

Giselle rested her head on her mother's shoulder. Elaine made the sign of the cross and began to pray.

Chapter 49

THE WAIT LASTED almost two days. Bobby and his in-laws never left the hospital. Elaine sent Giselle home on the pretext that someone needed to be at the farm. She wanted to spare her the agony of waiting and promised to call with any news.

Besides being a pillar of strength for Lilas, Elaine had the added burden of enduring the presence of two men who were under stress, did not like each other, and were in the same room.

She'd already formulated a plan to intercede if an altercation between the two ensued. She knew that if anything like that happened, it would likely be instigated by Gil. She would make it her mission to reduce tension between the two.

She separated them as often as possible by sending them on errands. Never before had she requested so much coffee. She alternately asked Gil and Bobby if they would mind fetching a cup for her from the cafeteria. When Gil pointed out a vending machine just a few yards away, she claimed she just couldn't tolerate instant coffee from a machine. A trip to the cafeteria would take at least twenty minutes, maybe thirty if it was busy.

Elaine drank the first two cups. After that, she poured her coffee little by little into a hapless dwarf ficus tree when the men weren't looking.

The anxiety of waiting for news of Lilas was relieved by visits to the nursery. Elaine suggested that she and Gil alternate visits with Bobby so that someone would always be in the waiting room in case news of Lilas came.

§

Gil and Elaine stood and peered through the nursery window at their granddaughter. The new parents had chosen the name Aimée, meaning "loved." Although the joy surrounding her arrival was tempered by the overriding concern for her mother, there was much cooing done by father and grandparents alike. Elaine decided that Aimée Nolan had her mother's eyes and nose, and her father's determined chin.

"Maybe so," Gil said over the baby's crying, "but I think she has her aunt Giselle's lungs."

Elaine smiled and grabbed hold of Gil's arm. "You think so, Pépé?"

Gil put his arm around Elaine and pulled her close. "That's right—I'm a Pépé now. That means you're a Mémé, old woman."

"I may be getting older, but I'm not so old as you, Pépé." She tapped his chest lightly. "You know what I think?"

"No, what do you think, Mémé?"

"I think little Aimée screams for her mother. I think once she is reunited with Lilas, the screaming will stop."

Gil nodded his head and pulled Elaine even closer to him.

§

The minutes and hours passed with agonizing slowness. Faithful about stopping in often to update the family, the grim-faced doctor could say only that he was doing everything possible for Lilas, and that time would tell.

Elaine noticed how carefully the physician seemed to avoid any optimism. After each of his visits, Elaine sat stoically and prayed.

Late in the evening of the second day, the doctor appeared with a weary smile on his face. "The worst is over, I think. Lilas is improving." He turned to Bobby. "She has been asking for you and the baby all along, but I couldn't permit it till now. She just wasn't strong enough. I hope you understand."

"So I can see her now?"

"Oui. Follow me, Monsieur."

Bobby looked at the Bellefontaines, then back to the physician. "Doctor, is it all right for her parents to come, too?"

"Yes. But, please, no excitement. Just a brief visit, okay? She needs rest more than anything. And so do you. You all look terrible. So here's what we'll do: a short visit now, if you all promise to go home after. Then you can come back tomorrow morning. Agreed?"

The family nodded their heads and followed the doctor through a maze of corridors to the intensive care unit. Lilas lay with eyes closed, a series of wires and tubes connected to her. Bobby approached the hospital bed. His wife's face looked drawn and weary. He took her delicate hand in his rough carpenter's hands. Her eyes fluttered open, and she smiled weakly.

"Hi," Lilas said in a voice that was barely audible.

"Oh, mon Coeur, you had me so worried."

"Aimée?"

"She's fine. Don't worry. I see her all the time. They're taking wonderful care of her. And she's beautiful, mon Coeur, like you. But she wants her Moman."

Bobby remembered that the Bellefontaines were behind him. "Your parents are here," he said, stepping aside.

Lilas lifted her head a little as Gil and Elaine came forward.

"Bonjour, ma Pêche," Elaine said through tears.

"Moman, Popa. You look so tired."

"We are not tired," Gil said. "We are just happy to see our little girl."

Lilas's eyes began to close. "I'm so sorry. I'm just so weary I can't seem to stay awake."

Elaine said, "No, ma Pêche, don't be sorry. Sleep now. It is the best thing for you."

Bobby leaned in and kissed his wife on the lips. He whispered, "I will be here early tomorrow. I will always be here, mon Coeur. Je t'aime."

Chapter 50

"...AND MAY I INTRODUCE the newest and, I might add, youngest-ever chancellor of our flagship university, the University of Massachusetts Amherst, Dr. Adam Payne!"

The auditorium filled with the sounds of cheers and applause from the considerable crowd, which included state, national, and even world-renowned luminaries—this despite the dour countenance and polite applause of many of the faculty.

"Thank you from the bottom of my heart, my dear friends and colleagues," Payne began.

After recognizing the long list of dignitaries and extolling the virtues of higher education in general and the mission of UMass in particular, Payne wrapped up his remarks with, "I promise you that I will spend every day living up to the high expectations of integrity, honesty, loyalty, and devotion that this cherished office, which you have entrusted to me, demands. Thank you, and God bless."

§

Payne's family brimmed with pride. The act of installing him as chancellor of UMass Amherst had been Harry's last as outgoing chairman of the Board of Trustees. He'd engineered it as a parting gift to his son-in-law, even though decorum and appearances dictated that he abstain from the actual vote.

Harry had helped cull the list of candidates to a final half-dozen from around the nation, none of whom had the slightest inkling that his chances were nil. Besides, for all the pomp and circumstance surrounding the position of chancellor, the job was decidedly single-minded: Bring home the bacon. And when it came to separating money from those who had it, no one did it better than Adam Payne. Skewed selection process or not, the people of Massachusetts still got the best man for the job. At least that's what Harry Rosen told himself.

§

Ed Stein would agree. After an association of more than twenty years, Stein knew Payne better than anyone, at least as much as anyone *could* know Adam Payne. What Stein knew for certain was that Adam Payne was brilliant, manipulative, driven, and dangerous if you crossed him or got in his way.

As for Payne's new position as chancellor, he had already proved his ability to raise money. The tiny radio station that was dying when Payne arrived at the scene was proof enough. Now his audio-baby, WRTH Earth Radio, comprised a dozen stations that covered the biggest population centers in Western New England. It had become a force with which local commercial stations just couldn't afford to compete.

One by one, the stations that Payne chose not to annex were forced to sell out to media conglomerates or file for bankruptcy.

Earth Radio now had tens of thousands of loyal listeners, and that translated into millions annually in donations and underwriting revenue. Payne exhibited the brilliance and tactical acumen of a born businessman.

§

At the reception following his installation, Chancellor Payne held cocktail court with various fawning dignitaries. His predecessor huddled in a corner with his wife and a few close friends, nursing his cocktail and shunning the limelight for the first time in his career. He told his friends about the new sailboat he and his wife had just ordered.

Payne felt a gentle tap on his shoulder and turned around.

"Daddy, I am so proud of you!" Shayna gushed. She kissed him and threw her arms around his neck.

Payne's face brightened. He brought his daughter close to him in a tight hug and whispered, "Thank you, Princess. That means more to me than anything. If I had to choose between having all these people or just you here, you know who I'd choose, don't you? I love you so much."

As father and daughter broke their embrace, Payne noticed his wife for the first time since before the ceremony began.

"We're both so proud of you." Judy rushed forward to hug Adam. But if she hoped Adam's response to her would be the same as to their daughter, her hope was dashed.

After hugging his wife lightly and patting her back, he broke the embrace and said, "Thanks a lot, honey." Then he looked at Shayna and said, "This calls for a Lord Jeffery dinner later, ladies— don't you think?"

Judy smoothed her dress and hid her disappointment- —something she'd become adept at. "Absolutely. What do you think, Shayn'?"

"Sounds good."

"Great. I'll be a little while longer here. Why don't you girls go on ahead and get us a good table. Ask your mom and dad to join us, honey, and order some champagne, too. Let's do it up right."

Payne headed back into the crowd for a little more schmoozing. Tina Malinowski caught his eye as she approached "Don't forget, Dr. Payne, you promised me an exclusive in the new chancellor's office."

"Don't worry, you'll get it, but it will have to be a quickie."

Tina pouted in mock disappointment.

Adam grinned. "I promise I'll give it to you more in-depth at a later date."

"I'm a skilled journalist, you know. I won't stop till I get it out of you."

Twenty minutes later, Dr. Adam Payne sat behind his new chancellor's desk for the first time. Tina Malinowksi knelt in the chair-well beneath the desk. Adam moaned with satisfaction. "Baby, you could suck the chrome off a trailer hitch."

When he arrived at the Lord Jeffery Inn, Payne hurried to the table, kissed Shayna on the top of the head, and sat down between her and Judy.

"Sorry I'm late. It took me longer than I thought. Did I miss anything?"

Chapter 51

AIMÉE NOLAN BECAME the center of attention the moment her mother's health was out of danger.

With Lilas still weak from her ordeal, Elaine Bellefontaine came to stay at Bobby and Lilas's row house in La Petite-Italie. Elaine was determined to help her daughter get the rest and nutrition she needed to recover her strength. Every morning the new grand-mère walked two blocks to the Marché Jean-Talon to buy warm baguettes and fresh ingredients for meals.

The Bear, Jacques Fournier, had told Bobby to take as much time off as he needed. "After all, you are now an equal partner in the business."

"What?!"

"You have earned it, mon ami. You have worked hard and been loyal to me for many years. Besides, this will prevent you from going out on your own and becoming competition for me."

"Thank you, Jacques."

Willing but unskilled in the art of parenting, Bobby learned from his mother-in-law. Elaine taught him how to hold his new daughter, feed her, bathe her, change her, and watch over her. He did not have to be taught how to love Aimée, though.

By the end of the second week, Elaine decided the time had come to return to the farm. "Don't worry; I will be visiting my granddaughter often."

"Thank you for all that you've taught me," Bobby said. "You are always welcome here."

"I know. Take good care of my girls," Elaine said, hugging Bobby goodbye.

Bobby took one more week off after Elaine left. The young family didn't do anything special. They just *were*, and, somehow, that made everything special—feeding Aimée, lying together as a family on their bed after Aimée's nightly bath in the kitchen sink, pushing her in her carriage to the market while holding hands, sitting on the terrace and watching Aimée's eyes roam the sky as she listened to the songbirds.

On the last day of May, they took Aimée to "Moman's garden" at the Jardin Botanique. The lilacs were in full bloom, the air filled with their scent. The young family lay on the grass beneath an ancient white-blossomed bush, with Aimée sleeping face down on her mother's stomach. When the baby woke, Lilas carried her around the grove while speaking softly of lilacs--the planting, care, feeding, pruning, the different names, the different scents.

Bobby laughed. "You think she understands you, do you?"

"Maybe not the words, but she knows her moman loves lilacs and her moman loves her." Lilas nuzzled her baby.

He was so content to spend time with Lilas and Aimée that Bobby didn't want to go back to his job, but neither did he wish to take advantage of The Bear's generosity. Only when he felt certain that Lilas was strong enough and could reach him at any time on the job site did he return to work.

IN THE DOORYARD BLOOM'D

Lilas took almost four months of maternity leave before going back to the Jardin Botanique at three-quarters of her former full-time hours. Justine Maze, at home with her own two children, cared for Aimée during Lilas's work hours. At first, when she dropped off Aimée with Justine, Lilas cried all the way to work. When she'd pick up Aimée in the afternoon, she would smother her infant with affection, as if they'd been apart for ages. It took a full month for her to travel from Justine's to the Jardin Botanique without falling to pieces.

In time, the Nolans fell into a comfortable routine, and both parents reveled in the joy that came from watching their child develop. They were a family, a real family, and happier than Bobby had ever imagined possible.

Once, as Bobby sat on the terrace and watched Lilas teach their toddler that a particular *oiseau* was a red-winged blackbird, he recalled his years of despair and contrasted them with the joy he felt now. *This feeling will never change. I won't let it. We'll go on this way forever.*

Chapter 52

UMASS ENDOWMENTS had increased by more than fifty percent since Chancellor Payne had taken office. Funding from the commonwealth poured in and spurred a massive expansion on campus.

Even faculty members who despised Payne had to admire and be thankful for his success. After all, the torrent of money he generated couldn't help but trickle down. Everyone benefited, and everyone knew it. The usual slur — "he's a cold, mean bastard"--was tempered now by reluctant, trailing praise.

Payne took great pleasure in all he had accomplished, but it was Shayna who gave him the most joy. She had inherited his good looks, her mother's sweet disposition, and the intelligence of both. An unspoiled and friendly nature made her popular with peers. After an early acceptance to Harvard University, she had graduated from high school in June. She had yet to pinpoint her ultimate goals, but whatever she did would involve helping the environment. Of that, she was sure.

It mattered not to Payne what career path his daughter chose so long as she was happy. He would see to it — had already seen to it — that she would never want for anything. The Paynes were wealthy in their own right and would be wealthier still when Judy inherited her share of the Rosen fortune.

On the morning of her high school graduation, Adam and Judy intercepted Shayna when she bounded down the stairs and into the kitchen.

Adam covered her eyes with his hands, while Judy held her hand. Together, Adam and Judy led Shayna to the front lawn.

"Daddy, what are you up to?"

"I'm making sure you don't peek. This is supposed to be a surprise!"

Shayna, barefoot and in her nightclothes, smiled with anticipation.

"Okay, ready? Drum roll..." Adam removed his hands from her eyes. "Ta-da!"

Shayna gasped when she saw the two-seater roadster convertible. "Daddy, it's a Miata! How did you...These things are, like, so back-ordered, you can't even get one. How did you? Oh my God! A Miata!"

"Do you like it, princess?"

"Like it? I love it! Mom, you were in on this, too?"

"Well, I knew about it, sweetie, but Daddy made it happen. I don't know how, but he made all the arrangements."

Shayna threw her arms around her father's neck. "Oh, Daddy, thank you, thank you, thank you! But it's too much."

"There's no such thing when it comes to my princess. Now, give me one of those Eskimo kisses." Father and daughter rubbed noses as Judy, with arms hugging herself, looked on and smiled.

After the graduation ceremony, the Paynes hosted an elaborate celebration at their home. They still lived in the house they had bought after their wedding, but it wasn't the *same* house. The

B. ROBERT SHARRY

Victorian on one and a half acres had been meticulously renovated and expanded to almost twice its original size. There were now over five thousand square feet of living space in the main house. Outdoors was an in-ground swimming pool with fire-placed patio and pool house. Judy had been careful to preserve the mature oaks, maples, and birches that shaded the backyard.

A few large party tents, one with dance floor, had been erected to keep guests shaded or dry, depending on the weather. During the afternoon, the fare consisted of hors d'oeuvres, hot dogs and hamburgers, but as evening approached, the caterers switched to a buffet of side dishes with steaks, chicken, or swordfish cooked to order. A jazz trio provided live music.

Some of the last guests to arrive were staff from WRTH, many of whom worked that Sunday. Tina Malinowski remained as close to Adam as she dared without arousing suspicion. Sally Barker stayed in the background with her husband and drank martinis.

Their ménage a trois, which Sally had gone to great lengths and considerable self-loathing to arrange, had not been repeated after the D.C. trip. In fact, upon their return, Payne's succinct and businesslike interactions with her bordered on curt. This treatment, in turn, drew her attention to his shameless flirting with Tina.

Sally was sipping at her fourth martini by the time Adam, making the rounds of a good host, turned from a group of guests and almost bumped into her and her husband, Jim Albright. She sloshed a few drops of gin on her hand as she tried to avoid Payne's turning body. He locked on to Sally's eyes and smiled.

"Sal! I didn't even see you. When did you get here?"

"The same time Tina did."

Shit, the bitch is drunk. Shut up, Sally. Neither one of us wants a scene.

Fortunately, Sally's husband seemed oblivious. Payne took Albright's hand in his and shook it as he gave the same greeting he'd given to most everyone. "So nice to see you. We're so glad you folks could join us."

"Thanks for inviting us. You must be very proud of Shayna."

"We are. Thank you."

After enduring the usual talk about the great food, the beautiful house, Shayna's future plans, and the cooperation of the weather, Payne could finally excuse himself.

"Well, thanks again for coming. There's plenty of food, so help yourselves."

"Hope you've got plenty of gin!" Sally called after Payne as he walked away. Payne turned and chuckled, acting as though Sally had made a little joke. But he knew better.

This bitch has become an albatross. It's time for her to go.

Payne made a mental note to get Sally out of his line of sight, but not his sphere of influence, à la Howard Hughes. He remembered reading that

Hughes, afraid of disgruntled senior employees sharing his secrets, would say, "Fire him, but keep him on the payroll." Payne would use his considerable influence to get Sally Barker a new, better job, and out of his life. Maybe the local public television station would have a spot for her. Of course they would. Adam Payne would see to it.

TV – a step up. How could the ambitious bitch refuse?

IN THE DOORYARD BLOOM'D

Chapter 53

IN JULY 1989 THE Nolans hosted their sixth annual Fourth of July picnic. The guests, now twice the number of the original crowd, all looked forward to singing "The Star-Spangled Banner" and following it up with the French version of Canada's anthem. The last musical note sparked whistles, cheers, and the first of the fireworks.

As much as Lilas enjoyed the event, its planning and execution had developed into a Herculean task for her. In the days leading up to this year's celebration, she had been plagued by headaches, fatigue, and aches and pains, all of which she attributed to the work involved.

A little after midnight, upon the departure of the last guest, Lilas and Bobby started to clean up. She carried a tray, which Bobby loaded with various plates and utensils that had been scattered around the backyard terrace. She suddenly felt light-headed and lost her grip on the tray, dropping it on the patio bricks. Then her knees buckled and she started to fall as she fainted.

"Lilas!"Bobby called in alarm. He caught her in his arms. "Lilas, what's wrong? Lilas!"

Her eyes reopened. "I… I don't know, mon Coeur. I suddenly felt dizzy." She forced a small smile.

"I should take you to the hospital."

"No, no. I'm fine now. I think I need to eat something. I just wasn't hungry. Maybe I drank too much."

"Are you sure you're okay?"

"Yes. I just need to sit for a while."

They sat in silence on the terrace. Lilas rested, and Bobby kept a watchful eye on her.

After a time, Lilas smiled at Bobby and said, "Mon Dieu, mon Coeur, I'm so tired. I think you are married to an old woman."

"Time for bed?"

"Oui—it will feel so good to get into bed tonight."

"You go ahead. I'll finish cleaning up."

When they awoke the next morning, Lilas rose first and padded toward the bathroom. Bobby noticed bloodstains on the sheet and on the back of her short nightgown.

"Lilas," he called after her. "You must have your period."

"Ahhh," she sighed. Then calculating in her mind, she added, "But that can't be. I just ended it a week ago."

"Oh, no, you don't," Bobby said. "I've heard of wives who tell their husbands that it's one week off and three weeks on."

"Oh, mon Coeur, don't wish *that*. I'm still so tired. I feel like I haven't slept at all."

Lilas went into the bathroom, relieved herself, and retrieved a feminine napkin. Sometime during her toilette she discovered that the bleeding had not been vaginal. The blood had come from her rectum.

As days passed, the bleeding persisted. Her headaches increased in frequency and severity. She continued to feel weak and tired and had to force herself to eat something every day. Even though she'd been losing weight, her belly was distended, as when she'd begun to show with Aimée.

Chapter 54

THE SECOND TUESDAY of the June 1989 Mount Plain Rotary luncheon meeting deviated from the normal routine in that the scheduled speaker had cancelled at the last minute. Karl Schmidt approached the podium to announce the change of plans.

"However, in spite of this glitch, we will still be entertained," Karl said. "I don't know how many of you fellas have heard of this guy, but he's a breath of fresh air on the radio, tells it like it is. He's the perfect antidote to Dan Rather over at the Communist Broadcasting System. He's a young fella, but his head is on straight. Name's Rush Limbaugh. You can hear him every day at noon on WANT AM. So Al's gonna pipe today's broadcast in here. Give a listen. I think you'll find this young fella refreshing."

As Schmidt reclaimed his seat, Limbaugh's voice filled the room. The members didn't pay much attention at first, continuing to talk among themselves over lunch. But when Limbaugh raised his voice and railed against affirmative action, the members sat silent and attentive. After a few minutes, one of the Rotarians called out, "Louder!"

"Al, can you turn it up?" said Schmidt. "I told ya you'd like this guy. Am I right, or am I right?"

"You're dead-on, Karl! Finally, somebody on the radio who knows what he's talking about and not afraid to call a spade a spade," yelled a voice from the back of the room.

IN THE DOORYARD BLOOM'D

Most of the Rotarians cheered and applauded as they listened to the sweet sound of common sense. Finally, someone who spoke for them, the Silent Majority, as President Nixon had dubbed them. At last there could be heard a voice of reason in a world gone crazy with pandering.

Schmidt took a gulp of scotch, turned in his seat, and spoke to the young man seated to his right.

"These men have never been a burden on society, Chip," he said to Woodrow Charles Wilson II. "They've never gone looking for a handout. Most of us grew up during the Great Depression. Today's young good-for-nothings don't know what it's like to really suffer. The men in this room never got food stamps. If they were hungry, they worked for food. And when their country called them, by God, they answered the call without complaint.

"Most of this crap, like affirmative action, starts in California. Everybody knows that. Usually it's that bunch of commies at Berkeley. If Ronnie Reagan hadn't stood up to them when he was governor, California would be a satellite of the Soviet Union by now.

"You see that girl over there?" Karl nodded his head in the direction of a middle-aged woman seated near the back. She was the only woman in the room.

"Uh-huh," said Chip. "That's Peggy McCann. She's got her own real-estate agency."

"She's our token woman. We had to let one in. Guess why?" Karl took another quick gulp of scotch. "Because a couple years ago, some bitch sued Rotary International for not allowing women in the club, and she won! Guess where the suit started?"

"California?" Chip asked.

"You got it. And now this McCann bitch is whining that there should be more women in our club. That's what happens: You let one in, and bang, the floodgates open and you gotta have more. They're never satisfied."

Karl leaned closer to the young man and lowered his voice. "I saw the same thing happen with the Jews. It started with Lewis over there. That hebe lawyer moved to town in the fifties. The first thing he did was steal your father's best clients. Then he got in here somehow. Once he got in, he pushed and pushed until now we're infested with them.

"Lewis is the one who pushed us to let a woman in, too. That's the way they are—pushy. You'd think they'd be grateful we let them in, but they have no problem biting the hand that feeds them.

"Next, they'll probably wanna let fags in the club. There probably are some in California clubs already. I wouldn't doubt it."

Chapter 55

LILAS SAT ON THE SUNNY side, beneath a favorite lilac bush at Jardin Botanique.

The specialist she'd visited that morning had used the words *leukemia* and *cancer*. He'd used hundreds of other words, too, but *leukemia* and *cancer* were the ones that kept repeating in her mind. He'd used those words because of the blood test; something about a *high white blood cell count*. She needed another test right away, he'd said. They would take a sample of her bone marrow and test it for… things. She couldn't remember exactly what.

When she really concentrated, she remembered other words the specialist had used, like *acute*, *chronic*, *biopsy*, *chemotherapy*, *radiation*, *myelo…somethings*, *lymph nodes*. But, apparently, none of the other words mattered until her bone marrow was tested.

"How did this happen?" Lilas had asked him.

"We don't know how it happens. It's nothing you did. We just don't know," he said. "We know so many things, and yet we know so little about many things."

He had told her not to worry; that there was no sense in worrying until "we know for certain what we are dealing with." He had told her *leukemia* and *cancer* and then told her not to worry. *You really do know very little about some things*, Lilas thought.

"Thank you," she had told the doctor as she left.

In the elevator, on the way down to the lobby, she wondered why she'd said "thank you." Those were probably the words most people would say to the doctor when the appointment was over.

You have cancer.

Thank you.

How ironic.

§

What would she tell Bobby? *How* would she tell Bobby? And her parents? She would not tell now. She must wait until *we know for certain what we are dealing with.*

She raised her face toward heaven, and silently asked God, *Why?*

She saw Wedgwood blue lilac blossoms hanging above her head. Some petals had turned brown. Their time was over. On a nearby bush, new white flowers were just beginning to bloom. These, too, would soon turn brown on their stems. Lilac blossoms were short-lived, and that was what made them so exceptional — each blossom's unique beauty and lovely fragrance was so fleeting.

IN THE DOORYARD BLOOM'D

Chapter 56

ADAM PAYNE SELDOM thought of Mary Chapman or Bobby Coyle. Mary was dead, and he hoped that Bobby was, too. If it weren't for the periodic phone calls from detectives David Long of the Massachusetts State Police and Jack McTeague of the Army National Guard Military Police Investigations Unit, he'd never give a second thought to either one.

Killing Mary Chapman was just something unpleasant that had to be done, like paying taxes or taking out the trash. Adam wasn't proud of it, but neither was he ashamed. It just had to be done.

Payne always took the detectives' calls, though. One of them might be calling with news of Bobby Coyle, or his remains. Long had skipped a year a few times, but not McTeague. That struck Payne as odd: the detective handling the assault and desertion charges against Bobby Coyle was more tenacious than the one handling the murder investigation. *My tax dollars at work*, he thought.

Still, McTeague bothered him in the way that Charles Dugway, the old history department chair, had. Payne always had the feeling that Dugway could see right through him. *I know what you are,* Dugway's eyes seemed to say.

Jack McTeague had looked at him that same way, and it had made him feel... vulnerable. Payne hadn't seen McTeague in twenty years, but his periodic phone calls always had the same effect on Payne: *He knows what I am.*

Chapter 57

THE SPECIALIST HAD called Lilas to make an appointment to discuss the results of her bone marrow tests.

Bobby sat in stunned silence on the living room sofa. Lilas sat beside him, tearfully recounting what the doctor had told her, so far. He studied her face closely, and felt ashamed that he had not noticed until now how frail and frightened she looked. Afterward, they held each other tightly. He stroked her hair as she wept.

Bobby assured her that everything would be fine, but all the while his mind was racing. He was trying to figure out what he could do to fix it. *Surgery? Radiation? Drugs? Transplant? Health food? What?* He knew nothing about leukemia, but he would learn all there was to know, and together they would fix it.

He would judge the specialist and make sure of his qualifications. He would study everything he could find on the subject. Wherever the best doctors in the world were, that's where he would take her.

§

The appointment was at ten in the morning at the Montreal General Hospital. By 10:15 Bobby was angry. *How could a doctor schedule a patient for an appointment to tell her what kind of cancer she has and then have the gall to be late? Shouldn't the patient be called as soon as the tests are complete, even if it's the middle of the night? Don't they know what it's like to be waiting?*

IN THE DOORYARD BLOOM'D

Feeling helpless, Bobby kept these thoughts to himself. He acted calm and assured for Lilas's sake. He smiled and held her hand, when what he really wanted to do was find the doctor, grab him by the collar, and force him to focus exclusively on curing Lilas.

At 10:20 they were shown from the waiting room to an examination room, where they sat for another ten minutes before the doctor arrived.

"Bonjour," the doctor said distractedly. His eyes were on the contents of the manila folder he held. Reading it must have reminded him of Lilas's diagnosis. His expression changed from dispassion to sympathy.

He looked at them for the first time since entering the room. "Lilas, Monsieur Nolan. Well, we have the results of the bone marrow tests. You have what we call acute myelogenous leukemia, AML..."

"What does that mean?" Bobby asked.

The doctor looked annoyed at the interruption. "It means that Madame has a cancer of the cells produced in her bone marrow. These leukemia cells are not allowing her healthy blood cells to form as they should. The abnormal cells are growing and taking up more room, so there is less room available for the healthy cells."

"So how do you fix it?" asked Bobby.

"It is not so easy, Monsieur, but the recommended treatment is chemotherapy, where we give very strong drugs orally and intravenously to try and kill the bad cells."

"How long until she's better?"

"Madame, Monsieur, I must tell you that the patient does not always get better. We always have hope, but fewer than fifteen percent go into remission for five years or more."

The specialist paused to allow time for the Nolans to understand. Then he continued. "Madame is young and otherwise healthy, which is in our favor, but the chemotherapy treatments are harsh. Unfortunately, the drugs must be so strong that they kill some healthy cells as well as the cancerous ones, so you may expect to have, besides your pain, some nausea and vomiting, diarrhea, fatigue. The chemicals also kill the hair cells, so you will probably suffer temporary loss of that beautiful hair." He ended with an empathetic smile.

For the next forty-five minutes, the doctor answered all of their questions fully and patiently. The appointment ended with the scheduling of more tests to determine if the cancer had spread. Lilas's first round of chemotherapy would begin immediately. Bobby decided that, bedside manner aside, the doctor apparently knew his specialty inside and out.

Bobby and Lilas left the hospital the same way they had entered, holding hands and talking optimistically. But now, deep down, they both knew that each was saying what the other wanted to hear.

Chapter 58

IN LILAS'S ROOM at Montreal General Hospital, the vigil had begun. The chemicals had not done their job. Neither had the hospital been able to find a matching marrow donor. Some of the bad cells had migrated to other organs, and with her inability to repel the disease, infection triumphed throughout her frail body.

Except for the time it had taken him to collect Aimée, Bobby had been at Lilas's bedside for the last seventeen hours. Four hours ago, in early morning, the specialist had declared that the last battle, and thus the war, was lost. It could be any time now,–from hours to days,–the doctor had said. "I'm sorry, nothing more can be done."

"There has to be something... Try more drugs! Try..." Bobby had pleaded before Lilas grasped his hand to interrupt.

"Thank you, Doctor," she said, a signal to the physician that she wanted to be alone with her husband.

They watched the wide hospital room door close silently behind the doctor. Lilas clutched Bobby's hand with as much strength as she could summon. Bobby looked deep into her eyes.

"No, mon Coeur, no more." Her feeble smile somehow showed bravery and resignation at the same time.

"No," Bobby said, shaking his head.

"I am tired, and God is calling me."

"No, don't give up."

"It is time, Bobby."

"No." His lips trembled. "Please, don't. I can't live without you. I don't want to live without you."

"Yes, you can. You must… for Aimée."

He put his forehead to hers. His tears fell on her face, mixing with her own. "I can't… I love you so much. Please stay with me."

For a long time they stayed forehead to forehead, whispering all of the things that were vital to say while there was still time to say them.

§

She cupped his face in her hands. "I need you to bring Aimée to me. I want to hold her and kiss her and tell her how much I love her."

Bobby nodded.

"And I need you to tell Moman and Popa and Giselle to come."

"I'm afraid to leave you."

"Don't be. I will be here."

§

Bobby concentrated on his mission now. Lilas had asked for something, and he would accomplish it as quickly as possible. He hurried to Willy and Justine's apartment to pick up his four-year-old daughter. He tearfully explained the urgency to the Mazes.

Justine suggested that she and Willy accompany them to the hospital so that they could bring Aimée back home with them. Bobby wouldn't have to leave the hospital again. Justine did not mention that Bobby could have just telephoned them and they would have brought Aimée right away. She suspected that Lilas had given Bobby a task to occupy him.

Willy and Justine waited outside the hospital room so that the Nolan family would have privacy. After half an hour, when Bobby brought Aimée out from her mother's room, Willy and Justine went in to say their goodbyes.

Not long after the Mazes left with Aimée, the Bellefontaines arrived at the hospital. Gil must have broken every speeding law in Canada to have driven from the farm in such a short time.

Gil made a few small concessions to Bobby: He did not mumble his usual *Rosbif* moniker, and when he looked at Bobby, his expression was impassive rather than dismissive.

By the time Gil turned to Lilas, Elaine and Giselle had already flanked her bed from both sides. Each held one of Lilas's frail hands. Each talked through her tears. Gil approached the foot of the hospital bed.

Lilas smiled weakly. "Popa."

"Ma Pêche." Gil choked out the two words, and then looked to Elaine with watery eyes.

"Popa, don't be sad," Lilas said.

Bobby slipped quietly from the room to give the Bellefontaines the privacy they deserved, and paced the corridor.

After a long while, Gil emerged from the room. His eyes locked with Bobby's for a moment. He gave a sheepish look, and then walked the corridor in the opposite direction. Alarmed by the farmer's expression, Bobby raced to his wife, bursting into the room.

The three Bellefontaine women were startled. Bobby blushed. "I'm sorry. I saw your father come out... I didn't know... I'm sorry."

Still, something in the women's expressions was not right. "What is it?" he asked.

Lilas shook her head. "Nothing, mon Coeur."

"It *is* something," Giselle said.

Elaine was silent, her eyes trained on the floor.

"What?" Bobby insisted.

Giselle sighed heavily. "Lilas asked Popa to do something for her."

"What? What do you need, mon Coeur? I can do it," Bobby said.

Giselle hesitated for a moment before answering for her sister. "Lilas told Popa that she would like for the two men she loves most in the world to take her to her garden."

Bobby, taken aback, followed with a foolish question. "Now?"

Bobby took a deep breath and rose to his full height. He turned and marched through the doorway into the hall. He spotted his father-in-law leaning against the corridor wall, hands in his pockets.

Gil caught Bobby's approach in his peripheral vision and turned to look at him. The older farmer saw something different in his son-in-law's eyes— madness perhaps, or fire. Someone must have told him. In a show of bravado, a wide-eyed Gil said, "Rosbif?"

IN THE DOORYARD BLOOM'D

Bobby put his forearm to Gil's chest and pushed him hard against the wall. Gil made an attempt to struggle free, but Bobby pushed again, harder this time, and held him fast.

Bobby spoke through clenched teeth. "I know you don't think I'm good enough for your daughter."

Gil rolled his eyes.

"Well, here's a newsflash for you: I know I'm not. I've *always* known. Lilas is so… good, and so… pure, I think she could teach the pope how to be a better person.

"But she chose *me*. I don't know why, but she chose me. And every day, I try to be… worthy."

Bobby's eyes welled, and his voice cracked. "If what Lilas wants is you and me, together, in her garden, then, so help me God, if I have to tie you up and carry you on my back, that's what she's gonna have! Comprenez-vous, you goddam frog?!"

Gil Bellefontaine stood transfixed, and slowly nodded his head.

Chapter 59

BOBBY TOOK SEVERAL deep breaths outside Lilas's room. Though still red-faced, he entered the room with an almost casual air and smiled at his wife.

"We're ready now," he said to her.

He lowered the side bar on her bed and lifted his frail wife, with top sheet and blanket still covering her. Her weight seemed no more than a doll's. Afraid of hurting her, he left his grip as slack as he dared.

The family encountered two orderlies in the hall, whose first inclination was to stop them. The two young men weren't sure what was happening, but they knew it didn't look right, and they moved as if to block Bobby's path. Gil Bellefontaine stepped in front of the orderlies, puffed out his chest, and challenged them with his eyes. "Elle est ma fille," the farmer said. *She is my daughter*. The orderlies looked at each other, and then stepped aside.

"Merci," Gil added as his family regained their stride.

Gil drove to Jardin Botanique. Elaine and Giselle sat in front with him, while Lilas lay across the backseat with her head resting on Bobby's lap. Gil parked in the lot closest to the lilac grove. Bobby slid out of the car and cradled Lilas in his arms once again. When the family paraded through the gate, a young ticket seller looked ready to protest. Then she recognized Bobby. And then she looked at what he carried.

"Lilas," the young girl mouthed.

Bobby led the way, crossing in front of the large building where Lilas had her office, past the Peace Garden, through the Courtyard of the Senses, past the exhibition greenhouses and the ornamental vegetable patch, until they reached the Collection des Lilas.

"Which part would you like to go to?" Bobby asked Lilas.

"Just walk slowly."

"Of course." He slowed his pace, and the Bellefontaines slowed behind him.

"Are you too tired to carry me, Bobby?"

"No," he said. "Never."

"Popa," she called.

"Oui, ma Pêche." Gil ran around to the front. Lilas held out her hand to her father. He took it in his.

"The sun is so warm on my face," she said. Then her brow furrowed.

"What is it, mon Coeur?" Bobby asked.

"You must tell Guillaume that this bush needs attention. The graft is not taking as it should."

§

As they passed through the various sections of the Lilac Collection, Lilas had clear visions, vignettes projected by memory. She saw herself as a toddler holding hands with her moman and popa as they first explored her garden; Guillaume Lefevre patiently sharing his vast knowledge with his young protégé; Bobby making love to her for the first time; Bobby on bended knee, proposing. Toi et moi toujours. *You and me forever.*

§

"Put me down here. I want to feel the warm grass."

Bobby lowered her to the ground and rested her on a slight, sunny incline. Her family knelt around her.

Lilas closed her eyes, smiled, and inhaled deeply. "This is wonderful — the sun, the lilacs, the scent. I think this must be what heaven will smell like," she said as she exhaled.

It was her last breath.

§

"No!" Bobby cried, cradling her, holding her face next to his. "Please, mon Coeur, don't leave me. I need you. I don't want to be here without you. Please don't go." He pulled his face away from hers and looked at her.

He let out a low moan that grew in intensity and filled with such sorrow and anguish, it made Gil turn to his wife as if seeking guidance. On his knees, Bobby hovered over Lilas and retched with sobs of grief.

From behind, Gil reached out with his large, rough hand, brought it close to Bobby's shoulder, and then retracted it. This he did twice more, until finally he placed his hand on Bobby's shoulder and drew him to his farmer's iron breast.

Chapter 60

When lilacs last in the door-yard bloom'd,
And the great star early droop'd in the western sky in the
*   night,*
I mourn'd — and yet shall mourn with ever-returning
*   spring.   —*

                                        Walt Whitman

UNTIL LILAS BECAME ill, Bobby hadn't cried since he'd broken down and confessed everything to her in her garden, eleven years before. Now he cried often. He couldn't control it. Late at night, unable to sleep, he would stand over his sleeping daughter, heave, and sob.

One night, the sounds of her father's grief awakened Aimée.

"I'm sorry, ma Pêche. Popa didn't mean to wake you."

"It's all right, Popa." Aimée rose to her knees and put her arms around his neck. "Does your heart still hurt?"

"What?"

"Moman said your heart is hurt and I can help you fix it."

Aimée's words unleashed more tears. He sat on the edge of her bed and held her, sobbing into her shoulder.

"I'm sorry. Popa's so sorry," he said over and over while the uncontrollable flood continued.

"It's okay, Popa. You can cry in my room anytime."

He felt ashamed that his four-year-old daughter seemed to cope with Lilas's death better than he. He hadn't heard what Lilas had whispered to their daughter that last day in her hospital room, but he remembered seeing Aimée nod her head as her moman spoke, as if the little girl was receiving instructions.

Bobby had followed Lilas's wishes precisely. Her body was cremated. There had been a funeral Mass said at the small Catholic church of her hometown by Father Benoit, the priest of her childhood, the one who had married them.

During the Mass, the old priest lost his composure when he tried to say what everyone in attendance knew. "There walked an angel among us."

Half of Lilas's ashes were buried in the Bellefontaine cemetery plot. She wished some of her ashes to be spread at the farm, and some to be spread in her garden. She had told Bobby that he didn't have to keep any. She wanted Bobby and Aimée to be happy, and if having part of her close would be a sad reminder, then she would understand.

Bobby didn't want to listen and tried to change the subject, tried to quiet her when she came back to it. But Lilas was persistent.

"We must talk about these things, mon Coeur."

"There's no need to. You're going to be fine," Bobby had said.

IN THE DOORYARD BLOOM'D

After the funeral service, the family had gone to Bellefontaine Farm, where Bobby, Gil, Elaine, and Giselle had spread some of the remaining ashes.

A few days later, Bobby secreted a small container of ashes in his jacket pocket and went to the Jardin Botanique. Lilas had not specified where her ashes should be placed in the Lilac Collection. Bobby found the grafted lilac bush she had been so concerned about on her last day. He knelt and scraped a shallow hole at the base of the plant with his fingers. He poured the contents of the container into the hole, covered it with earth, and patted it gently.

Later, he went to the shop where he had bought Lilas's engagement ring. He bought a petite gold vial-locket and chain.

Once home, he put a small amount of Lilas's ashes into the vial-locket, strung her engagement ring and wedding ring so that one hung on either side of the locket, and placed the chain about his neck.

Toi et moi toujours.

Chapter 61

CHANCELLOR ADAM PAYNE often hosted catered cocktail parties for alumni with a history of generosity to the university endowment. He knew from experience that glad-handing and ego-stroking over expensive finger food and top-shelf liquor was the surest route to their bank accounts. The tipsier the golden geese became, the larger the checks they scrawled in their drunken script.

Judy had become an invaluable asset at these affairs. A gracious hostess, she possessed an intelligence and genuineness that guests admired. Not only could she greet them all by name, but she knew their children's names. Her classical education and family upbringing had prepared her to speak intelligently on just about any subject and to feel at ease in any social setting.

People liked Judy. And because her appearance was so plain, Adam knew, female guests—many of whom were trophy wives—never felt threatened by her.

One of the wives caught Adam's eye this evening. Marnie Marshall was a trophy wife if ever he'd seen one. Why else would a thirty-something, sweet piece of ass like Marnie be married to such a slovenly, paunchy gasbag as Christopher Marshall, MD, FACS? The doctor had to be at least twenty years older than his bride. Payne guessed that she was his second wife, maybe even his third.

The bare-legged Marnie wore a short, V-neck cocktail dress that hinted at taut, tan thighs and gravity-defying cleavage. Her black dress stood in marked contrast to her husband's expensive but ill-fitting, gravy-stained light grey suit.

Marnie Marshall reminded Adam of the steady stream of professional wives his health club membership had supplied. But when he became chancellor, in keeping with his stature, he'd had a private exercise room, complete with sauna and steam, constructed in a room adjoining his office.

Marnie had been exchanging knowing glances with Payne all evening long, at one point even sucking suggestively on the stemmed cherry of her cocktail. He would have liked nothing better than to drag her to an adjacent room and fuck her brains out. But he would have to wait.

Payne would play it smart, bide his time. For now he'd keep his distance from her. At the right moment, he'd discreetly pass his business card to her. He had two sets of business cards — one for the general public that listed his assistant's phone number, and one that listed his private line.

He'd be having Marnie before the week's end; he had no doubt of that. Finally, the opportunity he'd been waiting for arrived. The sweet piece of ass and her husband had just broken from a circle of other guests. Dr. Fat-Ass had gone to get fresh drinks and, of course, couldn't pass by the food table on his way.

The chancellor excused himself from his group and held Marnie's gaze as he crossed the room toward her. When he approached, he held out his hand to shake hers.

"Mrs. Marshall, how nice to see you." He pressed his card into her hand, squeezing it gently as he leaned in to kiss her cheek. "Call me tomorrow," he whispered. Then he headed off to greet another group.

§

Only three people in the crowded room had paid attention to the brief exchange, one of whom was Judy. Her heart sank. A familiar choking feeling came to her throat as she observed their hands slip apart, with Marnie clutching whatever Adam had slipped to her.

Two women standing against the wall, sipping their cocktails, had also noticed. One murmured, "The wife is always the last to know."

The other replied, "No, the wife is always the last to *admit* she knows, and the husband is always the last to know the wife knows."

§

During the drive home, Adam showered his wife with praise about how popular she'd become with the alumni and how indispensable she was to him in his work. But while complimenting Judy, he imagined himself entering a buns-up-and-kneeling Marnie Marshall from behind, and felt a partial erection straining at his boxer shorts.

He didn't notice that, all the way home and for the rest of the evening, Judy was silent.

Chapter 62

JACK MCTEAGUE'S SECOND visit to Montreal had thus far proved as fruitless as the first a few years before.

This time he'd done more prep work, which included studying firsthand accounts and autobiographies by American war resisters and deserters who'd fled to Montreal in the sixties and seventies. Most of the hangouts they referred to in their memoirs were gone now, and the few that remained had changed over the years and turned into dead ends for Jack.

He revisited the Yellow Door coffeehouse. The same waitress who McTeague determined had recognized Bobby's picture still worked there, but after the last "Fuck off, pig!" reception he got from her, he didn't want to push his luck.

He was feeling down. Forty-five minutes, three Marlboros, and two more cups of black coffee later, he was struck by a revelation, and smacked his forehead with the palm of his hand. He hurried back to his room at the Holiday Inn, dug out the local phone book, and started calling.

"Why didn't I think of this before?" he muttered.

After several calls, he thought he'd found the person he sought—Michel Levesque, a private detective who'd been a Montreal cop in a previous life. It also helped that Michel spoke English and hadn't told Jack to *fuck off*. McTeague took a taxi to Levesque's office. It was one room on the second floor of a shitty building on Rue Sainte-Catherine Ouest.

Levesque was short and thin, with black curly hair. He was about fifteen years younger than Jack. Levesque offered coffee that tasted as if it had been brewed several days before, and then got straight to business. He told Jack, in no uncertain terms, that he wanted to know everything, and that if Jack lied or left anything out, he'd know it, and that would be the end of their conversation.

McTeague believed him.

Although he took a chance and omitted the part about Bobby being wanted for murder, he told Levesque everything else. He made it clear that he had no intention of making trouble for Bobby, that he wasn't acting in any official capacity whatsoever, and that Bobby's family just wanted to know if their son was alive and well. He told Levesque that his job would be to find Bobby Coyle and report back to McTeague, nothing more. There would be no contact of any kind with the subject. He finished up with the lead about the waitress named Linda at the Yellow Door. Levesque had listened intently, watching McTeague's eyes the whole time.

When Jack finished, the French detective sat in silence, considering all he'd been told. Finally, he spoke, his eyes still locked on Jack's. "Monsieur McTeague, I sense that you have omitted something."

McTeague shifted in his chair. "You know, you remind me of me. You're right, there is something I can't tell you, but everything I did tell you is true. I'm only here to try to help him, not hurt him."

Levesque took a few more moments to consider. "Okay. I'll need five hundred U.S. dollars to start, and a picture."

"Agreed. I have nothing recent, just this high school class picture, which is about twenty years old now."

Levesque studied the photo while McTeague studied Levesque. "You ever seen him?"

After a long pause, the French detective looked up and answered. "Perhaps. I'm not sure. It was many years ago when I was a uniformed officer. There was a young man who resembles this picture. I used to see him with a big black man, a drug addict. They lived on the streets. But it was a long time ago, and I can't be sure."

Levesque shrugged. "Maybe something, maybe not. Give me a few days. How can I reach you?"

Jack gave the French private dick his hotel and Boston home phone information, shook his hand, and left.

Michel Levesque watched from his office window as Jack McTeague walked on Rue Sainte-Catherine in search of a taxi. He had a few things to check out before he searched for Bobby Coyle. Some things didn't add up. With his contacts and the Yellow Door lead McTeague had given him, he knew it wouldn't take him long to track Bobby down.

A few days later, Levesque stood on the flat roof of a nearby apartment building in the Little Italy

B. ROBERT SHARRY

section of Montreal, held his 35mm camera with telephoto lens, and took pictures of Philip Nolan and his daughter, Aimée, on their backyard terrace.

The French detective would require some truthful face-to-face answers from McTeague, however, before he'd release what he had discovered.

Chapter 63

DAN LEWIS AND GENE Coyle were in their sixties now. The beginnings of eye cataracts had made driving at night uncomfortable for Gene. His eyes were sensitive to the glare of lights, particularly headlights. So Dan called and offered to pick Gene up on his way to the VFW meeting.

When he pulled up in front of the Coyle house, he could see Gene watching for him from the front bay window. Gene opened the door and put on a show of hustling to the car. A moment later Mickey Coyle appeared in the doorway, smiled, and waved.

"How are ya, Dan?" Mickey called.

"Just hunky-dory, Mickey. And you?"

"Right as rain. My love to Miriam."

"You bet. I won't keep him out too late." Dan nodded toward Gene.

Mickey waved, turned back into the house, and closed the front door behind her. Gene settled into the passenger seat with a grunt.

"Hey, pal o'mine, glad you could make it," Dan said cheerily.

"How ya hittin' 'em, Dan?"

"Sliced and into the woods. Say, here we have a boys' night out, but we're too old to do anything with it."

"Or can't remember how," Gene chuckled. He adjusted his glasses on the bridge of his nose and asked about Dan's new Ford Taurus.

"It's new, but a leftover '89, so I got a good deal on it. Seems they're already introducing the '90s.

Gets earlier every year. Wouldn't be my first choice of color, but what the heck."

"She's a beaut. I like this shade of green," Gene said.

Dan hesitated before speaking again. "Miriam told me about Mickey's mammogram. How's she doing?"

"Oh, you know Mickey. It'll take more than a little lump to keep her down." Gene continued to face forward.

"What's next?"

"More tests, I guess. She doesn't talk much about it."

"I'm sorry. I hope everything works out okay. You know our prayers are with you both."

"Thanks."

As they drove to the meeting, Gene sat in silence and thought about the VFW group. The local Mount Plain membership consisted of many of the same men who constituted the Rotary roster. He disliked the idea of being in the same room with men who had treated him as persona non grata after Bobby's desertion. He'd never know for certain who had made the stinging anonymous calls to his home, but he remembered the ones who had made a conspicuous show of the Pledge of Allegiance at the time, tossing it in his face.

He'd decided back then that, as much as he despised these fair-weather friends, he would not allow them to ostracize him or to foreclose his right to honor the flag. When the time came for the Pledge, Gene Coyle became the first to stand at every meeting, the first to face the banner, the first to speak, and the loudest.

"I PLEDGE ALLEGIANCE TO THE FLAG..."

The others would join in and follow his lead. Over time the strategy had worked, and the men now treated him as if nothing had ever happened. Gene sometimes even deluded himself into thinking that maybe they'd forgotten, even if he couldn't.

Now there existed a growing movement to protect the flag from those who would tread on it, burn it, or otherwise desecrate it. When the business portion of the meeting came to order, the commander of the Mount Plain VFW Post, Karl Schmidt, long the president of the Mount Plain Savings Bank, made his report and asked if there was any other business.

Gene Coyle stood and cleared his throat. "Commander, our Congress did their job back in '68 when they passed the Flag Protection Act, but now it seems our illustrious Supreme Court has decided that our flag is not worthy of protection. In *Texas v. Johnson* the Supreme Court said that protecting Old Glory is unconstitutional. The Court says it's just free speech when some scumbags decide to desecrate the flag so they can get some free publicity.

"The flag's been there for us. Now it's time for us to be there for the flag. It seems the only way to do that is to beat the Court at their game—change the Constitution. There's a proposal to amend the Constitution so that Congress will be able to protect the flag. We want to urge all members to contact our

U.S. congressman congressmen and senators and urge them to support the amendment."

"Any discussion?" asked Commander Schmidt. "Anything else?"

Dan Lewis stood up. "Gentleman, although I certainly respect my good friend Gene's opinion and share his and your love for our flag, I can't help but think that perhaps the Court has a point on this one."

There were low murmurs throughout the hall. Gene looked up with an expression of disbelief, but Dan didn't look back at his friend.

"Our flag is a great symbol, to be sure, but I can't ignore the idea that it doesn't always represent the same things to all of our people, and when citizens are dissatisfied with their government, they need ways to express it. As distasteful as it is to us, I think that one of the ways they should be able to express that dissatisfaction is by desecrating a symbol.

"When we wrap ourselves in the flag, we need to take care that we don't cover our eyes and ears with it."

Gene still stared at Dan when a red-faced Schmidt broke the silence that had come over the room.

"Refresh my memory, Lewis. Just where, exactly, were you in combat during the war?" asked Schmidt.

"You know I wasn't in combat, Karl."

"Oh, that's right—you're a lawyer."

"The army needed lawyers, too, Karl."

"Right. Somebody's gotta do the paperwork. Anything else?" Schmidt added while glaring at Dan. When he sat down, Schmidt whispered to the veteran next to him, "We save their asses from the Nazis, and this is how they repay us. Fucking Jew-bag."

For the rest of the meeting, Gene ignored Dan's attempts to talk to him, refusing to answer him or even look at him. As soon as the meeting ended, Gene stormed out of the post. Dan followed and caught up with him in the parking lot.

"I'm sorry, Gene, but I just couldn't be silent about it."

"What is it with you? You always gotta stick your two cents in, don't you? You just gotta stir up trouble wherever you go. Well, I'm sick of it."

Dan sighed heavily. "Come on, Gene, I'll take you home."

"You will not. I can make my own way home."

"All right, Gene, if that's the way you want it."

Dan straightened his shoulders and marched toward his car.

§

That same night the anonymous phone calls began. And the messengers had a new weapon in their arsenal: the facsimile machine. They couldn't leave a swastika on a Jew's answering machine, but they could now fax one to his office. Or they could paint one on his front door in the middle of the night.

Chapter 64

PRIVATE DETECTIVE MICHEL Levesque called Jack McTeague a week after their first meeting. He said he had information about Bobby Coyle, but insisted on a face-to-face meeting. McTeague asked why they had to meet in person but didn't get a straight answer.

McTeague arrived in Montreal the following Friday night, checked in to the same Holiday Inn, and had dinner in Chinatown. The next morning, he met Levesque in his office at 10:00 a.m. McTeague brought his own coffee this time.

"So, why is it that we had to meet in person, Michel?"

"You waste no time, Monsieur."

"Forgive me, but my time is limited. It's a thirteen-hour round trip for me."

"Of course." Levesque took some time before he spoke again. "Monsieur, before I tell you the results of my investigation on your behalf, I wish to satisfy my own curiosity.

"I know you told me that there was something you could not divulge, but I felt compelled to make my own inquiries. As a police detective yourself, surely you can understand this."

"Come to the point, Michel."

"Of course. It is only natural for me to want to know about my clients and the subjects of my investigations, so I took the liberty of finding out about you, Jack. It seems you are an experienced detective, a distinguished career, commendations, only recently retired…"

"Monsieur Levesque…"

"Please, Jack, allow me to finish."

McTeague blew out his cheeks in exasperation.

"Then I inquire about Robert Coyle and find that he is a suspect in a murder investigation from long ago. Is this not what you wished to conceal from me?"

McTeague gave a sheepish nod.

"I further discover that this crime was not within your jurisdiction."

"So?"

"So I ask myself, Monsieur: Why does an experienced homicide detective not wish to apprehend a murderer?"

"*Alleged* murderer."

Levesque trained his eyes on McTeague's. "Exactly, Jack. This is the same conclusion that I arrive at. The reason you take interest in a case outside of your jurisdiction, for a man that you do not wish apprehended, is that you have decided that he is innocent, no?"

Jack hesitated. "Yes, that's correct."

The French detective sat silent for a long moment. "Thank you, Jack." Levesque seized a large manila envelope from his desk. "Here is my report," he said, handing the envelope to McTeague.

Jack turned the envelope over in his hands without opening it. "You're one helluva good detective, Michel," he said, with eyes targeting the package he held. Then he lifted his eyes to Levesque. "I'm sorry I deceived you."

"But you did not, Jack. As you said, everything of what you did tell me was the truth. Otherwise, we would not be having this meeting."

Jack nodded his head and turned for the door.

"There is something I must tell you, Jack. You'll see it in my report, but... Robert Coyle has recently suffered a terrible tragedy. He lost his young wife to cancer less than a year ago. Now it remains for him to care for his young daughter. She is just five years old."

"Thank you, Michel. Okay if I call you with any questions I have?"

"Mais oui. In fact, if you ever wish to share more of this story with another pair of ears and eyes..."

McTeague thought for a moment, and then smiled. "Let's get a cuppa coffee. I'll tell ya all about it."

Levesque gestured toward his office coffee pot. McTeague winced. "Not here, my friend. I've been a cop for almost forty years, and I've drunk some really shitty coffee, but yours, by far, is the shittiest I've ever had."

The two detectives walked to a café on Rue Sainte-Catherine. Three hours later, with the help of Michel Levesque, Jack McTeague emerged from the café armed with a plan.

Chapter 65

ADAM PAYNE WAS SURPRISED to get two calls from Jack McTeague in the same year. The first had been the annual documenting-the-file bullshit. This second call was different, though.

He was intrigued when McTeague told him he needed to speak with him in person, and that he preferred they meet somewhere other than Payne's office. Try as he might, Payne could get no clues as to what McTeague wanted to discuss. Sounding as nonchalant as possible, Payne asked if Detective Long of the state police would be joining them.

"No," was all Jack said. Then he suggested they meet at the Miss Florence Diner, a landmark old-fashioned eatery not far from the university.

Payne felt the hairs on the back of his neck rise. He sensed… something. He didn't see how this meeting could be good for him, but his curiosity got the better of him. He agreed to meet for lunch.

This put a crimp in plans he'd already made. He had scheduled a nooner with Marnie Marshall. Marnie would be on her way to the Sheraton Tara hotel by now, and he had no way of reaching her. He could rush down to Springfield, explain to Marnie that an emergency had come up, then speed back to the Miss Florence Diner. That would be the considerate thing to do.

Let her wait. Maybe, if I have time after lunch…

§

Jack McTeague sat at a window booth with a half-empty cup of coffee in front of him. He studied

Adam Payne as Payne approached the diner. They hadn't seen each other in almost twenty years. McTeague had done his homework, researching Payne through university records and newspaper archives that documented the chancellor's public life. Even without his research, Jack felt certain he would have recognized Payne. The professor's appearance had changed remarkably little in the last two decades.

Payne was no sooner through the front door of the diner than Jack half stood up from his seat, smiled, and waved him over. Payne forced the same disarming smile he used with donor-alumni and extended his hand to be shaken a good three paces before he reached the table.

"Jack! I can't tell you how surprised and pleased I was to hear from you twice in one year."

McTeague shook hands with Payne. "Glad you could make it, Doctor."

Payne glanced around the diner. "Great choice, Jack. I haven't been here in years. Takes me back. By the way, drop the 'Doctor' and call me Adam, won't you?"

This was another psychological ploy that Payne often used with midlevel alumni. Nothing made little people feel as important as being on a first-name basis with someone *more* important.

McTeague blushed and nodded. "Cigarette, Adam?" He held out a pack of Marlboros in the crushproof box.

"Don't mind if I do."

McTeague held his Zippo out to light the cigarette.

"Might as well enjoy it while we can," Payne said. "You know, the antismoking crowd is pushing for a twenty-five-cent tax increase on every pack."

"Twenty-five cents on every pack?" McTeague let out a *holy shit* whistle. "It'll never pass."

"Don't be too sure. They're pretty well organized."

A brief but awkward silence followed. As casually as he could, Payne asked, "So what'd you want to see me about, Jack?"

At that moment, a seventy-something waitress whose nametag read *Fern* arrived at the booth, carrying a coffee pot.

"First things first, Adam—I'm starving." He looked up and smiled at the waitress. "I'll have the blue plate, darlin'."

"You want a warm-up, hon?" Fern asked.

"Please. And a vanilla Coke, when you get a chance."

"You got it, hon." Fern turned to Payne. "And for you, sir?"

Payne hastily scanned the menu. "Just bring me a cup of the soup and a cheeseburg special, medium rare."

"Coffee, hon?"

"Yes, please, and a glass of water."

"You got it. I'll put the order right in and be back with your drinks in a jiff."

The next few minutes spent waiting for their appetizers could have been awkward were it not for

Jack's jovial small talk. The retired detective spoke as if he were having a beer with a close friend. He talked of UMass sports, leered at a younger waitress, and leaned in to Payne as he derided the influx of immigrants to Boston and the increase in crime that followed.

Payne, half-listening, smiled and nodded politely. Then it dawned on him, and he raised his head abruptly: McTeague was using the same tactic on him that he had used on McTeague, acting friendly so as lull the other to lower his guard.

You son of a bitch, McTeague – what are you playing at?

They were interrupted by Fern's lollygagging shuffle as she delivered McTeague's salad and Payne's soup.

"Here you go, boys. Let me getcha a clean ashtray."

"You're a doll, Fern," said McTeague. "And if I were a few years younger…"

Fern tittered like a school girl. "Keep dreamin'," she laughed. "No offense, but I like mine with a full head o' hair." Fern ran her weathered fingers through Payne's thick, curly hair. "Now, this is my kinda guy, hon."

Payne blushed. "Behave yourself, young lady. People will talk." *Get your goddamned wrinkled, bony fingers off me, you ugly old bitch. I should be eating Marnie Marshall right now instead of this reheated Campbell's soup.*

When Fern was out of earshot, McTeague snickered and leaned in, whispering, "Geez, Adam, you always get the pretty ones. I'll bet she's got hemorrhoids that are older than you."

"You think so?"

"Uh-huh." Jack began to dissect his salad.

So, Lieutenant Columbo, just what are you up to?

"So, Jack, why are we here?"

"Well, Adam, I'd like to get your input on something, if you don't mind."

"Happy to, Jack."

McTeague took a large mouthful of salad. "Mmm, I like this house dressing. You wanna try?"

"No thanks."

"How's the soup?"

"It's fine, Jack—the soup's just fine. You were saying?"

"Hmm? Oh, yeah. I wanted to run something by you. You gonna eat those crackers?"

"Help yourself."

"Thanks."

McTeague fiddled with the cellophane wrapper on the saltines, then popped one into his mouth and spoke while he chewed. "It's about Mary Chapman."

"Mary Chapman?"

"Uh-huh." McTeague brushed cracker crumbs from his tie.

"But..." Adam started to say just as Fern reappeared with a cheeseburg and a meat loaf dinner.

Jack rubbed his hands together. "Ooh, this looks good, darlin'. Smells good, too."

"Good." Fern smiled, and then turned to Payne. "You boys want ketchup?"

"Yes, please."

"Mmm, you wanna taste this meat loaf, Adam? It's really good."

"It looks good, but no, thanks."

Jack looked thoughtful for a moment, and nodded his head. "'It looks good' reminds me of something my mother used to say."

Oh, Christ, here we go.

"'It looks good from the street,' Mom used to say. She told me that when she was a little girl growing up in a mill town, there was a local rich girl, about her age, who was the daughter of the mill owner. Anyway, the way my mother tells it, she was impressed by all the trappings of wealth— the rich girl's clothing, her father's shiny automobile, the way the mother dressed and carried herself. You get the idea.

"Anyway, the way my mother tells it, she was just gushing on and on about this rich family and the big new house they'd built on a hill overlooking the town. But *her* mother- —my grandmother— knew that there was trouble in paradise. She knew that the mill owner wasn't such a nice fella, especially when he'd been drinking, and that his nattily attired wife and daughter had the bruises to prove it.

"So when my mother remarked about how beautiful the new Victorian on the hill was and how lucky the mill owner's family was, her mother simply said, 'Yes, it looks good from the street.'"

Payne's annoyance began to show. "Is there a point to this, Jack?"

"Well, yes. The point has to do with appearances, Adam. Here was my mother, young and impressionable, thinking that wealth equaled happiness. The point is, a beautiful home doesn't mean a happy home. It looks good from the street, but might be completely different inside."

"I got the point of your story, Jack. What I mean is: Does it have any relevance to Mary Chapman?"

"Oh." Jack shook his head. "No."

"Correct me if I'm wrong, Jack, but as I remember, Mary Chapman was the state police's jurisdiction, and you were concerned only with young Coyle's desertion, even though the two were connected."

"That's the thing, Adam: See, I don't think they were... connected." McTeague's eyes locked on Payne's. "I don't think Bobby Coyle had anything to do with Mary Chapman's death."

Payne was silent for only half a beat. His eyes blinked. "You think it was suicide, Jack?"

"No, I don't, Adam."

"What... proof do you have, Jack?"

"Nothing, yet."

"And how can I help?"

"Well, remember it turned out that Mary Chapman was pregnant when she died?"

"Yes, now that you mention it, I do seem to recall something about that."

"I know this was a long time ago, Adam, but do you remember anyone else that she might have been seeing at the time?"

Payne took his time and shook his head from side to side. *What do you know, Jack?*

"No," he said. "Sorry. Like I said at the time, I barely knew the girl. She was in one of my classes, but that's it. I'd have no way of knowing anything about her personal life. And, as you say, it was so long ago."

Fern reappeared. "You boys save room for pie?"

"No, just the check, please, darlin'," said Jack.

Fern turned to Payne. "Uh-oh, handsome, you got some o' that cheeseburg in your pearly whites." She took a cellophane-wrapped toothpick from her apron pocket and handed it to Payne. "Be back in a jiff," she said.

"Let me get the check, Jack."

"No, no, no. I invited you."

"Well, I wish I could have been more help to you."

"Oh, you've been a big help, Adam."

"I don't see how."

"Hey, most people of your status wouldn't even be taking my calls after all these years. In fact, in my experience, people-—especially wealthy, influential people—go out of their way to avoid cops. And yet, here you are all these years later, always took my calls, never tried to avoid me... That's highly unusual, Adam."

"Really? Guess I just have a good sense of civic duty."

Fern returned with the check.

Payne thanked McTeague and rose from the booth.

Jack turned to Fern. "You know somethin', darlin'? I think I will take you up on that pie. Adam, change your mind?"

"No, thanks—gotta run. Thanks again for lunch."

McTeague watched Payne walk to his car, and then pull away from the curb.

"How'd I do, hon?"

"You did just great, Fern."

"Here's your baggies back, hon. This one's got his cigarette butt; this one's got the soupspoon he used; this one's got his hair."

Jack took the sealed baggies from her and placed them in his pocket. He pulled more new baggies from his coat pocket and retrieved Payne's toothpick, water glass, and coffee cup, and a second cigarette butt.

"Here's another twenty, darlin'. Remember, just you, me, and the lamppost."

"My lips are sealed, hon." Fern palmed the twenty-dollar bill.

Chapter 66

ON FRIDAY, MAY 11, 1990, two days before Mother's Day, Mickey Coyle kept an appointment with a young man she thought of as *Baby-Face*.

"Stage IV means that the cancer cells have spread beyond your breast, in this case to your lymph nodes and lungs. If we had caught it at stage II, or stage III, even...," the baby-faced specialist explained. "The treatments just haven't worked. I'm sorry," he said with sincerity.

She liked the young doctor. He was about the same age as her Bobby and one of the most empathetic physicians she'd ever come across. He even resembled Bobby, physically.

From the doctor's office, she went directly to Miriam Lewis. They cried together for a long time that day. She said a lot of things to her old friend that she wished she could say to her husband.

"I don't know why we couldn't help each other, Miriam. There was a time when we could, you know. You remember, don't you, Miriam? We weren't always this way, were we?"

Miriam didn't speak, but gave a sympathetic smile and shook her head.

"We were fine until..." Mickey finished the sentence in her mind. Then, audible again, she continued: "God knows he's stubborn, but he's a good man, Miriam. He's not going to do well on his own, though. I know it's a lot to ask, but I hope you and Dan will keep in contact with him."

Miriam's expression must have given something away.

"What's happened?" Mickey asked.

Miriam debated whether or not to tell Mickey about Gene and Dan's falling-out. Deciding it was no time to keep things from her best friend, she told Mickey the VFW story the way Dan had related it to her.

Mickey sighed. "That's Gene all over, the stubborn old fool."

"I've upset you, Mickey. I shouldn't have said anything."

"No, no, Miriam. I'm glad you did. Today has opened my eyes to some things that need to be set right, not just with Gene but with me. Gene's not the only one who's been stubborn, Miriam. I've let him down, too."

Miriam watched from her front window as her dear friend navigated the front walk to her car. Though thin and frail and wearing a cheap, grey wig, Mickey strode with a dignity and erectness that made Miriam choke with admiration.

Chapter 67

"GENE, I NEED TO speak with you," Mickey said in a soft, calm voice from her seat on the couch.

Gene sat on his La-Z-Boy with the clicker clutched in his right hand. He looked up from the TV as James Earl Jones announced, "This... is CNN."

"Do you suppose we could turn the TV off, Gene?"

He gave an exasperated sigh. Then he extended his right arm its full length and pointed the remote at the television set. He pressed the *power* button, and then returned his clicker-clutching hand to his cardigan-covered lap. He stared now at the blank screen.

"Gene, I saw the doctor again today."

Gene's head turned as he sat up, and his eyes shot from the darkened tube to his wife.

"Nothing's worked... and it's spread."

"Oh, Mickey... what does it mean?"

She smiled and shook her head. "It means I'm dying, Gene."

Gene slumped back in his chair, and then suddenly sat up again. "What can I do?"

"You can talk to me."

"Yes, but what can I *do*?"

"You can't fix it, Gene. You always had a hard time understanding that there are some things you just can't fix."

He looked lost, like a little boy.

"You can't fix it, but you can help."

Gene looked hopeful. "How can I help?"

"You can *talk* to me. There're so many things we need to talk about-—things we've left buried for so long, so many things we need to say to each other... at least I need to. We've wasted so much time, darling."

She hadn't called him *darling* for twenty years. He hadn't realized how much that simple word had meant to him. Just hearing her say it, after so, so long, softened him.

"What do you want me to say, Mickey? Tell me what to say, and I'll say it."

"It's not a test or a trick, Gene. I can't tell you what to say. You... we need to say what's in our minds and in our hearts. I need to tell you I love you. I've loved you since I was a young girl. But we lost our way when Bobby left."

Gene stared at her.

"And, yes, I need to talk about Bobby, too. I need to talk about our baby." She brought her hand to her mouth. "Before it's too late. I need to talk about what a beautiful boy he was, how bright and loving and joyful. Do you remember?"

Gene's eyes were watery now. "Yes, darling, I remember. I loved him so much, you know."

Mickey held her arms out to him. "Yes, I know you did. I know you *do*."

Gene hurried to the couch and embraced his wife of over forty years, kissed her lips, and held her. "I love you, too, Mickey. You know I've always loved you, from the first time I saw you."

As daylight turned to twilight, and twilight to nightfall, they sat on the couch and reminisced — first about their courtship and old friends, then about Bobby. Each had memories the other had forgotten about or perhaps never even known; some stories brought laughter, some tears.

In the darkness, Gene said, "Shall I get out the photo albums, darling?"

He'd used *darling* countless times since Mickey had first uttered it. It felt as if he had a million *darlings* stemmed by a dam. Mickey had breached the barrier, and now they could all flow out.

"No," she said. "I know them all by heart, and I'm tired now."

"All right — maybe tomorrow. Let me get the light, and I'll help you to bed."

Gene reached for the switch on a three-way lamp and turned it to the first position. He could see Mickey's eyes, swollen and red from the hours of tears.

"There's one more thing, darling." She had all but decided to leave it till morning, but fear of lack of time made her want to get it out. "You have to make things right with Dan Lewis."

"Aw."

"Before you say anything: Dan never said a word about it. He never would. Miriam told me what happened."

"Mickey, he's a big boy."

"This isn't for him, Gene. This is for you."

"What do you mean?"

"I know what they did to you. I should have helped you, and I didn't."

"Who?"

"You know who: The so-called *men* in town. Do you have any idea what they're doing to Dan and Miriam?"

Gene's dumbfounded expression told her that he did not.

"They're calling them all hours of the night, saying the vilest things, just like they did to us. And swastikas, Gene—those hateful ninnies have been sending them swastikas on the facsimile machine. Someone snuck in the dead of night and painted one on their front door, too.

"And they call themselves men. Dan Lewis is more of a man than they could ever hope to be. There aren't half a dozen real men in the whole lot. Most of them are decent, but they're just sheep, and they're following a few loudmouthed bigots.

"Dan has been your friend for over thirty years. He was the one who stood by you when Bobby...

"Don't you let them do the same thing to him that they did to you. Don't you let them make you turn your back on him. He's always been there for you. *Always.* Now he needs you, and if you don't stand by him, you'll never forgive yourself. You have to *do* something."

"Me? What can I do?"

"You can speak up."

"They won't listen to me. Who am I?"

"Who are you?" Mickey stood more erect than her health should have allowed. "Who are *you*?"

Then, the woman whom Gene Coyle had never heard utter an expletive in her entire life looked straight at him and, with tears welling, said, "Don't you know who you are? Don't you remember? You're Gene *Fucking* Coyle, that's who."

Mickey made a fist and shook it. "I want you to fight 'em! You fight 'em like you fought those Nazi bastards. You gave them what-for and you licked 'em good! And these weasels are no different. They call a man's house in the middle of the night and frighten his wife half to death, and then they run and hide.

"You're Gene *Fucking* Coyle. You're my hero, and you're Bobby's hero, too. *That's* who you are. You forgot for a while, but you remember now, don't you, darling?"

Mickey's expression changed. She stared into space for a moment. Then she clutched her chest. Her eyes rolled back, and she collapsed.

"Mickey! Darling!"

Chapter 68

MICHELINE PIDGEON COYLE
1924–1990

MOUNT PLAIN – Micheline Pidgeon Coyle,
65, of 110 Jericho Drive, Mount Plain, died
Sunday, May 13, 1990, at Mercy Hospital.

Born Nov. 17, 1924, daughter of Jean P. Pidgeon
and Nicole Filtault Pidgeon, in Saint- Nicolas,
Quebec, Canada, she attended local schools
in Palmer and Wilbraham and graduated
from Palmer High School and Westfield State
College (formerly Westfield State Teachers College).

She leaves her husband, Eugene M. Coyle,
whom she married on June 18, 1949.

Besides her husband, she leaves one son,
Robert M. Coyle.

FUNERAL NOTICE: A Liturgy of Christian
Burial will be performed on Wednesday, May 16,
at 10 a.m. at Our Lady of Lourdes Roman
Catholic Church in Mount Plain. Burial will
follow at St. Ann's Cemetery.

Calling hours are Tuesday from 4 to 7 p.m. at
Laughlin Funeral Home, 10 Main St., Mount Plain.

§

Mickey Coyle died at the hospital two hours
after the ambulance brought her there. It seemed
everyone who worked at the hospital added the
same *blessing in disguise* phrase to their condolences
to Gene. They said Mickey's heart failure spared her
incredible suffering from the cancer which would

have ravaged her in its turn. Some would start by saying, "This is small consolation, but…"

Though Gene listened politely, he knew it was more than small consolation. He knew that people rarely died of cancer. They died from the complications that cancer caused. The death certificate had said that Gene's own mother died of colon cancer, but he knew she had died of starvation. He knew because he had watched her starve to death, unable to take nourishment because the alien cells would not allow it.

As much as his own heart ached with grief, it was, indeed, a large consolation to Gene that his wife's heart had ended her suffering. The pack of vicious wolves that was cancer had surrounded her at the edge of a cliff and would slowly tear her apart, piece by piece. Her heart had said, *Take my hand; let's jump, and not give them the satisfaction.*

He left the hospital and walked. He walked around his small town for hours until he found himself in front of the stately old Victorian on Elm Street. He started up the front walk he'd first traversed some thirty-seven years before, bearing a housewarming gift. A new coat of primer on the front door did not prevent the apparition of a swastika from showing through.

The front door flew open. Dan Lewis hurried down the steps, embraced his old friend, and brought him into his home.

Chapter 69

ON THE MORNING OF Monday, May 14, 1990, Detective Lieutenant David Long of the Massachusetts State Police sat with crossed ankles propped on the edge of his desk and perused that morning's edition of the *Springfield Republican*.

He dropped his feet and sat up straight when he saw Mickey Coyle's obituary. He read it carefully, then turned to a colleague and remarked, "Geez, will ya look at that? I've had this murder case for twenty years now. The perp disappeared in 1970, and now his mother has died. We always assumed that he headed for Canada. It turns out his mother was born up there, somewhere in Quebec."

"Cheer up," Long's colleague said as he walked by to get a refill for his coffee mug. "Maybe your perp will show up for the funeral."

Long chuckled. "Wouldn't that be nice?"

The detective pushed back in his chair and repropped his feet on his desk, then pondered his own words. "Wouldn't that be nice?" he repeated in a low murmur. "What have I got to lose?"

Within a few hours, he had contacted the major daily newspapers in Montreal, Quebec City, and Toronto, spoken to their obituary departments, and secured the necessary fax numbers to which he would send a copy of Mickey Coyle's obituary.

With luck, Bobby Coyle just might see it and feel guilt-ridden enough to make an appearance. *Wouldn't that be nice?*

Chapter 70

JACK MCTEAGUE CALLED Dan Lewis late on Tuesday morning and asked if Dan had time to meet with him that afternoon.

"For you, I'll make time," Dan said.

"I think you'll be glad you did. Let's see... it's almost noon now. Take me a couple hours to get there. Sometime between two and three okay?"

"Sure—take your time. Anything you can tell me over the phone?"

"I could, but I don't want to. I wanna see the look on your face. Besides, it's much more dramatic this way. I'm retired now, remember? This is the only excitement I have."

Dan turned solemn. "Jack, Mickey Coyle passed away on Sunday."

"That's too bad," said Jack. "She would have wanted to hear this."

McTeague flew so fast down the Massachusetts Turnpike that he got pulled over by an unmarked statie. He discovered that being a retired cop carried about as much weight in Massachusetts as being a Republican. The traffic cop held him up a good half hour before handing him the ticket. Just after 3:00 p.m. he arrived at Lewis's office.

"Sorry it took me so long. Got stopped on the Pike by a statie. What an asshole. The guy never even changed expression. He looked like RoboCop."

Tantalized by McTeague's call, Dan had been watching for him. "Don't keep me in suspense."

"Okay, you've suffered enough. First, I found him."

"Bobby Coyle?"

"Almost two weeks ago. I'm wishing now I'd told you sooner, especially what with his mom dying and all. I had no way of knowing that would happen, Dan. I was hoping to give you a nice, neat package, all wrapped up. I'm sorry."

"Me too. Nothing we can do about that now."

"He lives in Montreal, like everybody's more or less assumed, under the name..." Jack referred to Michel Levesque's report. "Philip Nolan."

"The Man Without a Country," Dan said.

"Huh?"

"It's a story. Philip Nolan was the name of the main character. He was 'The Man Without a Country.' What else?"

"He had a normal life working as a carpenter until about a year ago, when his wife" — again he referred to the French detective's report — "Lilas, died of cancer. Now it's just him and his daughter, a five-year-old named Aimée." McTeague handed Dan one of the photos Levesque had taken of Bobby and Aimée on their terrace.

Dan studied the photo for a long time.

"There's more," McTeague said, forcing Dan out of his trance. "Some background first. This DNA shit is getting more sophisticated by the day. Used to be you had to have a blood sample to do a paternity test. The latest stuff doesn't require blood. It's called *poly-something chain reaction*, or PCR. Turns out that DNA cells are the same throughout the body; doesn't matter if it's blood, skin, hair, saliva, whatever. You with me?"

"Think so," said Dan.

"Okay. So they take sixteen DNA fragments from a kid. They match half to the mother, and the other half belongs to the father. Okay so far?"

"Uh-huh."

"Bobby Coyle was *not* the father of Mary Chapman's unborn baby."

"Well, that's good news!" said Dan.

"It gets better."

"Wait a minute, wait a minute, back up," Dan said. "How'd you get Bobby's DNA?"

"I didn't. I got the father's."

"The fa… you know who the father is?"

Jack grinned and nodded his head. "You better sit down, Dan."

"Thanks, I think I will."

Dan sat, and Jack handed him a piece of paper. He read it and shot back to his feet.

"Payne? The chancellor of UMass, Payne? Adam Payne, the radio guy? How? When?"

"Just a gut feeling I had, Dan. He didn't seem right to me from the start, but I couldn't say anything. I learned early on, as a young cop, you can't go around casting aspersions on the high and mighty without proof-positive 'cause it will come back to bite you on the ass every time—guaranteed. And until now, with all this new DNA crap, I didn't have anything but an old-fashioned gut feeling, so I couldn't say anything."

"Holy shit!" Dan said as he sat back down.

"Yeah, how 'bout it?" Jack laughed.

"Is this admissible?"

"I don't have the slightest idea. Tomorrow, I'm just gonna turn it over to that dickweed, Long, over at the staties and let them figure it out. If I could get his DNA, they sure as hell oughtta be able to figure a way."

"How did you get the DNA of Mary Chapman and the fetus?"

"I didn't. I took Payne's DNA to the state police crime lab, where they already had Mary's and the fetus's. I've known those people for years. They must not know I'm retired, must've assumed I was there on official Boston PD business."

Dan checked his watch. "Listen, I've gotta go. Mickey's wake starts at four o'clock. I've gotta get home, pick up my wife, and get over there to the funeral home."

Dan started for the door. "Say, Jack, why don't you come? You could join me and Miriam for dinner later."

"I don't know. I've gotta find a motel, prepare to meet with Detective Dickweed tomorrow."

"If you change your mind, it's at Laughlin's on Main Street till seven."

"Okay."

"And, Jack, thank you. Thank you very much."

Jack McTeague smiled and nodded his head.

Dan took the file with him and drove home to pick up Miriam. On the short drive to Laughlin's Funeral Home, he told Miriam what Jack McTeague had revealed.

"I've been debating with myself about how and when to tell Gene," he said. "I don't know if it's better to wait until after the funeral or not."

"No." Miriam was emphatic. "He has to be told as soon as possible. He has to know."

"I can't just walk into the wake and blurt it out, Miriam."

"No, of course not. We'll stay until it's over and convince Gene to come back to the house for coffee."

Gene declined the offer at first, but Miriam cajoled him by saying that it was important to her that he come.

As she made coffee in the kitchen, Dan began recounting what McTeague had discovered. Gene listened intently as his old friend revealed fact after fact about Bobby's innocence and his life over the past twenty years. He told Gene that he had a granddaughter named Aimée.

Tears streamed from Gene's eyes to his chin. "I failed him. I failed Mickey. I failed us all. It was my job to protect the family, and I failed."

"Don't do this to yourself, Gene," Miriam said.

"Miriam's right, Gene. You can't beat yourself up over it. I just wish I'd gotten this information before, so that Mickey could have known, too."

"Mickey?" said Gene. "Mickey knew all along. She never doubted for a moment. I was the one too stubborn and proud to have faith in Bobby. I thought he had shamed me, but it was the other way around, wasn't it? I turned my back on my own son when he needed me most. I spent my whole life trying to protect him, and then I hurt him worse than anybody else ever could."

Dan slid the file up and down through his left hand with his right. "His phone number is in here, Gene. It's never too late. You could call him."

"He called me. Twenty years ago, he called me. I never said anything, even to Mickey, because I told him never to contact us again. Later, I was ashamed of myself, and I could never bring myself to tell Mickey. How could he ever forgive me now? God, what have I done?"

Chapter 71

ON TUESDAY MORNING, May 15, 1990, Bobby Coyle dropped off his daughter, Aimée, at Willy and Justine Maze's home for day care. The Mazes had continued to be the most loyal friends that Bobby could ever have asked for. He had no idea how he could ever repay them for their countless kindnesses and support over the years.

Bobby walked through the back door of their apartment, holding Aimée's hand and carrying a bag filled with toys and extra clothing. He was surprised to see a face that was familiar but looked out of place in Willy and Justine's home. Sitting at the kitchen table was Freddy from the long-defunct Montreal Council to Aid War Resisters. Bobby couldn't remember if he had ever known Freddy's last name.

"Freddy! Good to see you, man."

"Good to see you, Bobby," Freddy said, and then shot a look to Willy, who stood at the kitchen counter pouring coffee.

Bobby caught the exchange and looked to Willy. "What's up?"

Willy averted his eyes for a moment. Addressing Aimée, he said, "Sweet potata, why don't you go play with Roberta? She's in her room."

Bobby watched as Aimée left the kitchen. He turned his gaze back to his old friend.

"Sit down, man," said Willy. "We got some bad news. Sit down, my friend."

"Okay," Bobby said as he pulled out a kitchen chair and slumped into it. "What is it?"

Willy handed Bobby the morning newspaper, which he had folded to make the reading of Mickey Coyle's obituary easier.

Bobby read the notice of his mother's death without the slightest change in expression. After a while he looked up to see that Justine had entered the room and that the three of them were now looking at him with sadness and compassion in their eyes.

"I'm sorry," all three seemed to say at about the same time.

"Thanks," Bobby said, and nodded his head.

"Freddy saw it first thing this mornin' and come right over to ask me if you would see it."

"Thanks, Freddy — I appreciate it."

Freddy nodded his head. "Bobby, I'm sorry about your mom, and I feel kind of funny even being here at a time like this, but..."

"But?"

"I don't know how to say it, so I'm just gonna say it. You know this showing up in the local paper is no accident."

Bobby's face had reddened, and his eyes had clouded over a little. "I know," he said.

"I just wanted to make sure you understood that whoever published this is trying to trap you."

"I know."

"Is there anything I can do for you, man?" Willy asked. Bobby seemed in a trance. "Bobby?"

"Hmm? No, no, man, nothing."

Silently, the three watched Bobby as he sat deep in thought. He finally rose from the table. "You mind if I keep this?" he said, holding up the newspaper.

"'Course not," Willy said.

"Justine, would you get Aimée for me? I think I'm gonna take her to see her Mémé and Pépé."

"She's welcome to stay here," Justine said.

"I know. You've both been great. Thank you, but please get Aimée for me?"

"Mais oui," Justine said.

Bobby scooped his daughter into his arms and smiled broadly at her. "We're gonna go see Mémé and Pépé!"

Holding Aimée on his hip, he shook Freddy's hand, then hugged Justine. Then he put his arm around Willy.

Willy touched his forehead to Bobby's. "You sure 'bout this, Bobby?"

Bobby nodded his head, causing Willy's head to nod as well.

"I love you, man," Willy whispered.

Bobby nodded again, patting Willy on the pack.

After Bobby left, Justine turned to Willy. "Why wouldn't he just leave Aimée here with us? It would be so much easier."

Willy stared absently at the door through which his old friend had just gone. "'Cause he knows he ain't comin' back."

IN THE DOORYARD BLOOM'D

Chapter 72

JACK MCTEAGUE HAD had trouble getting to sleep the night before. The last he remembered, the clock on the motel nightstand had read 3:14 a.m.

He awoke at 8:00. After a shower and shave, he drank coffee until he began to feel human. At 9:00 a.m. he called Detective Lieutenant Dickweed of the Massachusetts State Police.

"Detective Lieutenant Long," the dickweed had answered.

"Jack McTeague here."

"If you're hoping to share the credit, you're a little premature. We don't even know if it's gonna work. He didn't show at the wake."

"What?"

"How did you find out, anyway?"

"Find out what?" McTeague asked.

"What, did you talk to Dr. Payne?"

Jack sighed in exasperation. "Can we start over? Because I have no idea what you're talkin' about."

"Oh. Then why are you calling me?"

"I have some info for you on Mary Chapman. Can I come over?"

"Now? Are you kidding? The funeral starts in an hour."

"Detective, I'm really not being coy. Can you please tell me what you're talking about?"

Detective Long took his turn sighing in exasperation now. "Coyle's old lady kicked the bucket the other day. I faxed the obit to some Canadian newspapers and got them to run it. If he's up there, and still alive, maybe he saw it, and the little bastard'll come down to say bye-bye to Mommy."

"Did you run it in Montreal?"

"Of course."

"You mentioned Payne. Did you tell Payne?"

"Why?"

"Did you tell Payne?" Jack shouted.

"Hey, who do you think you're talking to?"

"Bobby Coyle did not kill Mary Chapman. Adam Payne did."

"What? Have you been drinking, McTeague?"

"Payne was the father of Mary Chapman's unborn child. I've got DNA tests to prove it. That's why I'm calling you. Now, one more time: Did you tell Adam Payne?"

"Well, yeah. I had no reason not to. I just wanted somebody who'd help identify him if he showed."

"What did Payne say?"

"He said he wouldn't feel comfortable hanging around at the wake or the funeral, but that he'd be available to identify him if we picked him up."

"You have to find Payne, pick him up, and hold him."

"For what?"

"Because if Coyle does show up, Payne may try to kill him! As far as Payne knows, Bobby Coyle is the only person who could dispute his version of events that day."

"Listen, cowboy, I don't know how they do it in Boston, but out here we don't just go and arrest our most prominent citizens without real proof. So

IN THE DOORYARD BLOOM'D

here's what we'll do: I should be back in the office by one or two o'clock at the latest. You come over at two, and I'll take a look at what you got. Okay, sport?"

The only response Detective Dickweed got was a dial tone. Jack McTeague couldn't waste any more time.

Chapter 73

BOBBY COYLE BROUGHT Aimée to the Bellefontaine farm on Tuesday night. He showed his mother's obituary to Gil and Elaine and told them that he planned to attend his mother's funeral.

Of course, they said, they would be happy to care for Aimée for as long as necessary.

Later, Bobby took Gil aside and handed him a sheaf of legal papers. Then Bobby removed from his neck a gold chain, on which hung a vial-locket, a diamond-and-sapphire engagement ring, and a gold wedding band. Next, he opened his wallet and carefully removed the tattered and soiled parchment. He looked at the miniature watercolor of a lilac blossom, signed *Lilas*.

"For Aimée," he said as he handed the keepsakes to his father-in-law. Then he explained to Gil that he needed his help.

Early the next morning, Bobby set out to retrace the original steps that had brought him to the Bellefontaine Farm more than twenty years before. He crossed the apple orchards to the brook where Gil had found him unconscious and rescued him. He crossed the brook and took to the woods and fields beyond.

He walked until he came to the railroad tracks in North Troy, Vermont. For the first time in more than twenty years, Bobby Coyle stood on his native soil. He crossed the tracks and walked toward the center of town.

IN THE DOORYARD BLOOM'D

Gil drove his car to the nearest U.S. border crossing and entered the United States. He drove to the center of North Troy, picked up Bobby, and drove back toward the railroad tracks. Both men got out of the car. When they broke their embrace, Bobby got behind the wheel of Gil's car, and Gil Bellefontaine crossed the tracks on foot and walked north to his farm.

Bobby calculated that it would take him about four hours to reach St. Ann's Cemetery in his hometown of Mount Plain, Massachusetts. His change of clothes hung in the back of the car. He would change at a rest stop on Route 91 into his only suit, the one he'd bought for Lilas's funeral.

Driving east from North Troy, it didn't take him long to reach Route 91 and enter the southbound lane of the highway. With luck, he'd be in Mount Plain by noon.

Chapter 74

FOR THE FIRST TIME in his adult life, Dr. Adam Payne felt panic. Detective Long of the Massachusetts State Police had confided his long-shot plan to draw Bobby Coyle into the open and asked if Payne would help identify him.

Payne told his wife he was heading to the driving range to work on his swing.

"Don't forget: Shayna's driving in later this afternoon," Judy said.

"I won't."

He walked to the carriage house where he garaged his car. For the second time in as many days, he climbed the steps to the second-floor attic and retrieved the long, canvas-wrapped package he'd secreted in the rafters on the day his daughter was born.

He removed the canvas wrapping to reveal the .30 caliber Springfield M10903 sniper rifle with telescopic sight he'd bought at a flea market from a World War II vet years before. *Just in case*. He had gone through the ritual of cleaning and oiling the rifle many times throughout the years.

But yesterday and today were different. There existed the possibility, however remote, that he would look through the telescopic sight and see Bobby Coyle. Last night he had watched from a safe distance as friends and family came to pay their respects at Mickey Coyle's wake. Today he would stand watch at her funeral. Today could be the day.

IN THE DOORYARD BLOOM'D

Payne was not about to allow the one man who could ruin him tell his version of what happened the day Mary Chapman died. He knew the risk he was taking, but Payne also knew that the risk was just as great if he brought in a third party to take care of Bobby Coyle. He should never have trusted that junkie, Chuck Barber. If Payne had handled it himself in 1970, Bobby Coyle would be long dead.

Payne rewrapped the rifle and placed it on the backseat floor of his 1990 midnight blue Cadillac.

Chapter 75

JACK MCTEAGUE DONNED his shoulder holster, checked his Glock 17 semiautomatic pistol, and inserted a clip of seventeen hollow-point bullets. He liked the velocity of hollow-points and their ability to mushroom, especially when striking a soft target like human flesh. He also liked hollow-points because whatever he shot at was stopped in its tracks.

He holstered the Glock, put on his sport coat to conceal the weapon, and got in his car. He reached Our Lady of Lourdes Church just after 10:00 a.m. and parked where he could observe inconspicuously. He looked for anything out of the ordinary in general, and for Bobby Coyle or Adam Payne in particular. On the passenger seat beside him, he kept a picture of Bobby that Michel Levesque had taken with a telephoto lens. The photo was of good quality, and McTeague felt confident he'd know Bobby on sight.

Within a few minutes, the procession arrived from the Laughlin Funeral Home. He recognized two of the pallbearers—Dan Lewis and a young man who looked like Dan did when McTeague first met him as a young prosecutor in Boston. The younger man had to be Dan's son.

A standard-issue, unmarked Massachusetts State Police vehicle trailed the procession. Long sat in the passenger seat. A younger, steroid-riddled RoboCop occupied the driver's seat.

IN THE DOORYARD BLOOM'D

McTeague did what he had done for a large part of his life: he sat, he watched, and he waited.

Chapter 76

BY 11:30 A.M. THE funeral Mass had ended. Mickey Coyle had often lamented the demise of the Mass said in lingua Latina, so Gene had located a priest of the old school and convinced him to come out of retirement long enough to say one last Latin Mass.

Mourners began to stream from the front door of the church and head for their cars. Most of them left immediately. A few sat with motors running, waiting for the procession to go on to St. Ann's Cemetery.

Gene and Dan were standing on the sidewalk in front of the church when Karl Schmidt approached with his protégé, Chip Wilson, in tow. Karl took Gene's right hand in both of his. "Gene, I can't tell you how sorry I am. Mickey was a fine lady, and she'll be greatly missed. My thoughts and prayers are with you. If there's anything I can do, anything at all, you just let me know."

Gene nodded and turned away. He stared at his right hand for a moment, and then he turned back. "There is something you can do, Karl."

Karl looked surprised. "Name it, old friend."

"You can crawl back under your rock."

"Gene," said Dan Lewis.

"It's all right," Karl said. "I know it's the grief talking, Gene. We haven't always seen eye to eye."

"You'll never be eye to eye with me, Karl, because you're a small man. You think you're a big fish in this pond, but you're just a minnow in your own pool of spit, and you're not fit to be near Mickey. Now, get out of my sight." Gene turned and boarded the waiting limousine.

The black hearse, two black limousines, and a few civilian vehicles formed the slow-moving convoy. The procession entered the cemetery and stopped close to the *Coyle Angel*, a winged statue that watched over the remains of two, soon to be three, generations of Coyles in America.

McTeague noticed the state police vehicle park just inside the gate. Then he watched as RoboCop and Detective Dickweed walked up the hill and stopped a hundred yards from the gravesite.

Jack parked on the street in front of the graveyard and stayed in his car.

He sat, he watched, and he waited.

Chapter 77

BOBBY COYLE PEERED from behind a tall pine at the wooded edge of St. Ann's Cemetery. The back of his neck tingled as he watched the graveside ceremony taking place two hundred yards from his hiding place. Only vaguely aware of the earthy aroma surrounding him- —a mixture of soft soil, pine needles, and bark- —he had trouble concentrating. He thought of his mother, remembering her as she had looked when he last saw her. Narrow streams of tears raced down his cheeks.

Anxiously, he tapped his finger against sticky pinesap, and watched the gaping earth receive his mother's casket. Bobby saw his father. From a distance, the white-haired and stooped Gene Coyle resembled an animated question mark as he made the sign of the cross.

Bobby continued to watch from his hiding place until the ceremony ended. Mourners trickled to their cars and drove away. Gene Coyle stood alone at the graveside now, his back to Bobby. A black limousine, its driver's head reclined as if napping, waited.

The time had come. Bobby Coyle stepped from behind the large pine and crossed a carpet of spongy pine needles. He stopped at the edge of the lawn, breathed deeply, and steeled himself.

Chapter 78

THE SERVICE CONCLUDED, Jack McTeague watched as the mourners got into their vehicles and exited the cemetery. He noticed that RoboCop and Dick-weed had been the first to leave the cemetery grounds.

"Smooth move, Dickweed. You wouldn't wanna get made," McTeague muttered to himself.

He watched Dan Lewis and his son enter a limo with four other pallbearers. Once that car left, only two people remained: Gene Coyle, who stood graveside with head hung low, and his limousine driver, who sat in the car.

Ah, well, better safe than sorry, Jack thought. He pulled away from the curb and headed toward his motel. He'd pack up, grab a quick bite, and then drop off his evidence to Detective Dickweed at two o'clock. With any luck he'd be back in Beantown just in time for the first pitch of the Red Sox game.

As he drove past the side street that bordered St. Ann's Cemetery on the south, he happened to glance up the street. He hit his brakes hard and backed up. Far up the street, on the right-hand side, he saw a familiar vehicle parked. After their luncheon at the Miss Florence Diner, Jack had watched Adam Payne walk to his car. He was certain it had been a new, dark blue Caddie.

McTeague's car rolled slowly up the street while his eyes darted in every direction. He pulled over behind the Caddie. It had a UMass parking sticker on it. He got out and silently swung his car door to just shy of closing.

Jack crouched low and approached the Caddie.

He checked the interior. Empty.

A little farther up the street sat an older, light green Chevy. As he got closer, McTeague saw that it had a Quebec license plate.

"Shit. Call for backup, Jack. You can't call for backup, Jack. Let's review: You're not a real cop anymore, and you don't even have a radio, dumbass," he muttered.

He crept up behind the Chevy. There were clothes piled in the back seat—jeans, blue work shirt, work boots, and a John Deere baseball cap.

He headed into the thin woods that separated the street from the cemetery. Keeping to the tree line, he moved slowly, scanning in every direction.

In the distance, he caught sight of Gene Coyle, standing graveside. The limo driver waited behind the wheel. McTeague thought the driver had his head back and eyes closed but couldn't tell for sure.

Jack looked to his left.

There! Someone was walking downhill from a stand of pine trees, approaching Gene Coyle from behind. *Bobby Coyle!*

"Come on, Payne, where are you?" Jack whispered to himself. "Where would I be if I were you?"

Chapter 79

BOBBY COYLE STOPPED two yards behind his father. Gene was sobbing quietly, his slumped shoulders heaving.

Suddenly, Gene's head lifted, and his back straightened. He turned around slowly and came face-to-face with his son.

Neither spoke at first. Gene stared for a moment through tear-filled, bloodshot eyes. "Bobby."

Bobby took a step forward. "I'm here, Dad. I'm home."

Like his outstretched, beckoning arms, Gene's voice quivered. "Forgive me."

A sharp *crack* split the serenity of St. Ann's Cemetery.

Bobby stood still for a moment, stunned by the tiny missile that had pierced his chest. Then he fell into the arms of his father.

In that instant, Gene Coyle journeyed back to a bloody battlefield in France.

"Medic!" he cried.

Chapter 80

JACK MCTEAGUE RACED toward the copse of poplars from which he knew the shot had come. In seconds he was there.

Adam Payne peered out at the gravesite, trying to judge the effectiveness of his sniping. McTeague stole up behind him, gripping his Glock with both hands. "Drop it, Payne!"

Payne stiffened, but did not turn around.

"Drop the rifle!"

"You know I can't do that, Jack," Payne said, still facing away.

McTeague spoke softly. "It's over, Adam. There's nowhere to go."

There is if I get you first, Jack.

Payne let his shoulders droop in a show of resignation and defeat. McTeague relaxed slightly. In one swift movement Payne pivoted, brought his rifle up, and fired from his hip. McTeague dove to his right and fired twice before he hit the ground.

Payne dropped the rifle, screamed, and fell.

McTeague got up quickly. He kept his Glock trained on Payne as he cautiously approached. Jack kicked the rifle away, and then assessed the chancellor's wounds.

The first hollow-point bullet had entered Payne's left shoulder, mushrooming on impact and forcing him to drop the rifle. The second had struck his groin. It, too, had exploded and mushroomed on impact.

IN THE DOORYARD BLOOM'D

McTeague winced when he saw the damage. He let out a low whistle. "You'll live. You might not *want* to, but you'll live."

Payne, wide-eyed with terror, stared at his mangled genitals. "No, Jack. Finish it," he begged.

McTeague shook his head. He handcuffed Payne to a poplar tree. Payne writhed in agony and continued to plead with him. Jack didn't respond. He turned and ran downhill toward the gravesite.

"Please, Jack, please!" Payne screamed after him.

B. ROBERT SHARRY

Chapter 81

GENE COYLE CAME BACK from the battlefield in France. He looked to the driver for help, but the chauffeur had slid down in his seat and hid when he heard the shot and saw Bobby fall.

Gene heard a second *crack*. He covered Bobby's body with his own. Then two more shots followed in rapid succession. These were pistol shots, he knew— semiautomatic.

He hunched over his boy for a long time, waiting to be sure the gunfire had ended. Finally, he lifted his head to look around. He held his son in his lap, as a pietà. Bobby tried to tell his father something in rasping whispers.

Gene brought his ear to Bobby's lips. But instead of speaking, Bobby moved his head slightly and kissed his father's cheek. A serene countenance flooded Bobby's face. Just as Eddy had done on the battlefield, Bobby stared at the sky.

"No! Bobby, stay with me." Gene Coyle went to work at a pace that belied his years. He removed his suit coat, tie, shirt, and undershirt. "Not this time, Eddy! This is my boy. I'm sorry I couldn't save you, Eddy, but this is my boy. I'm not letting him go again."

A tranquil smile came to Bobby's lips. "Lilas."

"Bobby? Bobby! Don't leave me, son! Stay with me! Stay with me!"

He ripped Bobby's shirt open and surveyed the wound. He folded his undershirt in half three times, and then pressed it hard against the hole in Bobby's chest.

Gene looked up. A man was running toward him. The man had a gun! Gene stood and ran toward the gunman.

McTeague froze the moment he realized what was happening. An old man—his naked torso scarred by three ancient bullet wounds- —was racing to engage, barehanded, a gunman who threatened his son. Gene, red-faced and breathing hard, held his fists out in front of him.

Jack raised his hands in the air. "Mr. Coyle, I'm Jack McTeague. I'm a friend of Dan Lewis's. The man who shot your son is handcuffed to a tree up there. He can't hurt him anymore. We need to get help for Bobby now."

Jack lowered his hands slowly, and holstered his pistol. "Mr. Coyle, your driver probably has a radio in the limo. I'm going to have him call for an ambulance."

Gene Coyle lowered his fists. He turned and hurried back to his son.

Chapter 82

IT TOOK MORE THAN a year for the charges against Adam Payne to be brought to trial.

F. Xavier Bascom, the preeminent defense attorney in Massachusetts, had surprising difficulty finding people to act as character witnesses for his client. Ed Stein halfheartedly agreed, but Bascom found Stein so lacking in enthusiasm that he decided not to use him. In the end, the renowned attorney had only two witnesses willing to attest to the moral fiber of Adam Payne. Judy and Shayna Payne spoke lovingly of their devoted husband and father.

Payne testified that he and Mary had gone to the rooftop for privacy to discuss her pregnancy. Payne said that Mary had threatened to reveal all to Judy Rosen, the woman he loved, and bring an end to their engagement.

He said that Mary had become irrational and gotten physical, "like a crazy woman," and that when he attempted to defend himself, a tragic accident occurred. With the prosecution unable to prove premeditation or malice aforethought, the jury found Adam Payne guilty of involuntary manslaughter.

As to Bobby Coyle, Payne said he remembered fearing that his innocent wife and daughter would be forever stigmatized by his youthful mistakes. Beyond that, he remembered nothing. "I'm so sorry and ashamed. I must have just snapped under the pressure."

IN THE DOORYARD BLOOM'D

F. Xavier Bascom spoke passionately of Adam Payne's "exemplary life" following a "tragedy" and a regrettable "grave indiscretion of youth." Payne was so guilt-ridden, said his attorney, he couldn't remember anything about shooting Bobby Coyle or even where the rifle he used had come from. Attorney Bascom suggested that no one could punish Adam Payne more than he already punished himself, and that his loving family needed him home as soon as possible.

At sentencing, Dr. Adam Payne appeared sincere in his remorse. "Your Honor, I'd like to apologize to the Chapman and Coyle families for the suffering caused by my panic and my irrationality, and to my own family, whom I've disappointed and dishonored.

"My most fervent wish is that I could somehow turn back time and spare all of these good people their incredible grief. I hope that the court will realize that I am not a monster, and be able to show some compassion for a man who has tremendous remorse and wants only to be with his family and spend the rest of his life atoning for his sins."

Judge Maxine LaBott listened patiently but was unmoved. "Adam Payne, the court sentences you to ten years for the manslaughter of Mary Chapman and, in the case of Robert M. Coyle..."

Adam Payne looked around the courtroom for Shayna.

"...sentences to be served consecutively."

When Judge LaBott finished, she rose from the bench. Adam watched her walk to the door that led to her chambers, and disappear through it. Only a mortified F. Xavier Bascom heard Adam Payne's muttered "Cunt."

IN THE DOORYARD BLOOM'D

Chapter 83

Lilac and star and bird twined with the chant of my soul,
There in the fragrant pines and the cedars dusk and dim.
— Walt Whitman
Mansonville, Quebec, Canada, June 9, 1991

THREE GENERATIONS OF Coyles emerged hand in hand from a dirt path between rows of apple trees. With his free hand, Bobby Coyle fingered the vial that hung from a gold chain about his neck.

It's your thirty-seventh birthday today. I hope you can see how beautiful Aimée is. I miss you. It still hurts so much. But I'm home, mon Coeur, I'm home. Toi et moi toujours.

Aimée tugged from the middle, bidding her father and grandfather to move faster. "Come on! Mémé and Pépé are waiting."

Bobby looked to his father. Gene's face beamed the smile that Bobby remembered from his youth.

"Come on, Popa. Come on, Grampa." Aimée pulled their hands as she pleaded.

"Ma Pêche, Grampa can't go that fast," said Bobby.

"Speak for yourself, young fella," Gene said. Aimée giggled as Grampa Coyle scooped her up and began to run. "Last one there's a rotten egg!"

Gil and Elaine Bellefontaine stood arm in arm and waved from the top of the hill by the farmhouse. Nearby, a long table, set for a family meal, sat in the shade of a blossoming lilac.

Acknowledgements

Many family and friends have given encouragement for which I will be eternally grateful.

A special thanks to my longtime friend, Paul G. O'Connor, a gifted and award-winning writer, for countless hours of inspiration, invaluable suggestions, and great advice.

Lilac Illustration courtesy of www.albion-prints.com

Editing by Katherine Duke

UQTT

Lilas.